## "What are you doing here?"

Coy swallowed. "I work here. What are you doing here?"

Becky's dark eyebrows furrowed. "Since when?"

"Since last fall." He shoved his hands in his front pocket to stop them from shaking.

"You've been here that long?" A flicker of concern crossed her face. Her gaze scanned over him. "Are you still injured? You haven't ridden since you got hurt in Fort Worth."

The worry on her face almost made him smile. Hope bubbled in his chest. "You kept tabs on me."

"No." Her face turned red and her words began to tumble out. "Yes. Your bull riding news still comes to my email. You haven't been on the roster of any events. Are you training to make a comeback?"

"If you ever answered my phone calls, you would know."

"I couldn't." She closed her eyes and rubbed her temples. "I didn't have anything else to say. But I came back to Arizona for the summer to find you. I have something for you."

Dear Reader,

I love second chance romances, and I knew from the moment Coy and Becky appeared in *His Hometown Redemption* that they were the ones who needed it. Dolly Parton once said, "If you don't like the road you're walking, start paving another one." That's exactly what my characters in this story had to do to find each other again.

I hope you enjoy Coy and Becky's story as much as I enjoyed writing it. I love hearing from readers. You can connect with me at leannebristow.com, Facebook.com/authorleannebristow and Instagram.com/authorleannebristow or email me at leanne@leannebristow.com.

Blessings,

*LeAnne*

# HER HOMETOWN BULL RIDER

## LeANNE BRISTOW

**Harlequin**

**HEARTWARMING**

If you purchased this book without a cover you should be aware that this book is stolen property. It was reported as "unsold and destroyed" to the publisher, and neither the author nor the publisher has received any payment for this "stripped book."

**Harlequin®**
**HEARTWARMING™**

ISBN-13: 978-1-335-05160-8

Her Hometown Bull Rider

Copyright © 2025 by LeAnne Bristow

All rights reserved. No part of this book may be used or reproduced in any manner whatsoever without written permission.

Without limiting the author's and publisher's exclusive rights, any unauthorized use of this publication to train generative artificial intelligence (AI) technologies is expressly prohibited.

This is a work of fiction. Names, characters, places and incidents are either the product of the author's imagination or are used fictitiously. Any resemblance to actual persons, living or dead, businesses, companies, events or locales is entirely coincidental.

For questions and comments about the quality of this book, please contact us at CustomerService@Harlequin.com.

TM and ® are trademarks of Harlequin Enterprises ULC.

Harlequin Enterprises ULC
22 Adelaide St. West, 41st Floor
Toronto, Ontario M5H 4E3, Canada
www.Harlequin.com

Recycling programs for this product may not exist in your area.

**Printed in U.S.A.**

**LeAnne Bristow** writes sweet and inspirational romance set in small towns. When she isn't arguing with characters in her head, she enjoys hunting, camping and fishing with her family. Her day job is reading specialist, but her most important job is teaching her grandkids how to catch lizards and love the Arizona desert as much as she does.

### Books by LeAnne Bristow

### Harlequin Heartwarming

#### *Coronado, Arizona*

*His Hometown Redemption*
*Her Hometown Cowboy*
*Her Hometown Secret*
*Her Hometown Soldier's Return*

*Her Texas Rebel*

Visit the Author Profile page
at Harlequin.com for more titles.

A special thank-you to Patty and Doris for their valiant efforts to keep me on track, encourage me and for never letting me forget why I do this. I couldn't do this without your help. B&H!!!!

# *CHAPTER ONE*

Coy Tedford leaned against the side of the barn and scanned the land that stretched out behind the corrals of Whispering Pines Campground. Tall grass waved in the slight breeze. Yellow, white and red flowers decorated the meadow. He sucked in a deep breath of pine-scented air. There was nothing like the White Mountains of Arizona in the summer.

Behind him, the soft whinny of horses indicated they were restless and wanted their breakfast. He placed the cowboy hat back on his head and went inside the barn. Four horses poked their heads over the stalls and watched him. As he walked toward the tack room, a palomino mare tossed her head and nickered.

Coy stopped to rub the horse's nose. "Good morning, Maze."

Maze pushed his chest with her head.

"I'm going, I'm going." Coy laughed. "I thought Stacy taught you better manners."

"I blame it on her trainer," a voice laughed from behind him.

He turned to see his cousin standing at the entrance and his stomach dropped. It was the third time this week she'd made an unexpected visit. She had something on her mind, but he wasn't going to press her. She would tell him when she was ready. For now, he wouldn't let on that he was suspicious.

"Let me guess." He nodded toward the office. "You need coffee."

She pinched her lips together. "I hate being predictable."

He followed her into the small room situated off the main entrance of the barn. "Why don't you just get a new coffeepot? Or better yet, get some from the market. You have an entire store at your disposal."

"Because this is the only place I can get some peace and quiet." She rested a hand on her swollen stomach. "Besides, I'm out of decaf at the market and my next order doesn't come in until Thursday."

"Well, don't stress. It's already Tuesday." Coy laughed and grabbed a coffee mug from the top shelf of the cabinet and set it down for her.

"Thanks." She poured a cup of coffee for herself and topped off his cup. "Yours tastes much better than mine."

"It's the same brand!" he laughed. "Enjoy your coffee. I better serve breakfast before Maze starts a coup."

As he tossed flakes of hay into the feed troughs, he debated asking Stacy why she was really here. The only time she'd watched over him like this was right after he came back to Coronado. He told everyone he was fine without Becky, but Stacy didn't believe it. She'd hovered around him like a mother hen, dragging him out of the cabin, volunteering him for projects and putting him to work at the campground. She didn't give him a moment of peace. Someday, he'd have to thank her.

It had been over a year and a half since he and Becky had separated. Surely, Stacy wasn't still concerned about him? He'd done everything he could to prove he was surviving. Something was definitely up, though.

When he walked back into the office, she was staring at the pictures that covered the wall. His gaze followed hers to the photo of a young woman with twinkling eyes and a huge smile. Guilt hit him in the chest. Becky was right. He was a selfish jerk. This wasn't about him at all.

He took a deep breath. "You really miss her, don't you?"

"Yeah." Her voice was little more than a whisper.

"And with the baby coming, you're missing her even more."

Even though she was surrounded by family, it was almost a whole new family. He was one of the few links she had to the family she grew up with.

That was the reason she'd been clinging to him a little more tightly.

"Missy would've been a fantastic grandmother." He stared at the picture of the once vibrant woman. Huntington's disease had taken her life far too young.

Stacy didn't answer. Her gaze had drifted back to the frames on the wall. This time she was staring at a photo of both their parents. The two couples posed in front of a pickup truck.

She nodded. "My mom never talked about grandchildren. Not once. Aunt Rachel, on the other hand, talks about it all the time."

Coy flinched. His mother had no idea how close she'd come to getting her heart's greatest desire. Now he was glad he'd listened to Becky when she cautioned him against making any premature announcements.

"Missy knew the chances of living long enough to see grandchildren were slim and she didn't want to put any pressure on you," he said. "My mom has no such qualms."

Stacy laughed. "I guess I should be grateful for that. I've seen Aunt Rachel in action."

His parents' divorce had been hard for him to accept, but at least he still had both of them. He couldn't imagine losing either one. "How long has Missy been gone?"

"Three years next month."

"That's all?" Coy's brow furrowed. "Seems like longer."

Stacy nodded. "Probably because so much has happened since then. I met Caden just a few months before she passed. Now we're married with two beautiful girls and a little boy on the way."

"Speaking of little girls…" Coy adjusted his cowboy hat. "Are Khatia and Marina coming for their riding lesson?"

She nodded. "They're at Vacation Bible School all morning, but Caden will bring them after lunch."

"Is he going to stay and help?"

For the last three years, Caden had managed the campground and the horses. When Coy arrived in Coronado last fall, he needed something to do, so he went to work with Caden at the campground. Now Caden only showed up when Coy asked him to.

"No," she said. "He has some things to do."

He took a drink from his coffee, contemplating the question that had been bothering him for the last few weeks. "Is Caden upset I'm still here?"

Her dark green eyes widened in alarm. "No! Of course not. Why would you say that?"

He shrugged. "I know you only gave me this job to get me out of my funk. He's probably ready for me to leave so he can have his job back."

"Actually—" Stacy tucked a strand of hair behind her ear "—we've been wanting to talk to you about that."

Coy took a deep breath. He'd never stayed in one place long enough to wear out his welcome. He didn't like the feeling.

"Caden's been juggling electrical jobs on the side, along with the market, the girls and the campground for a while now. Luke has been doing HVAC jobs on the side, too." She pulled up a picture on her phone and handed it to him. "They want to make it official."

Coy looked at the logo on the screen. *Coronado Home Services. HVAC, Electrical and Plumbing Installation and Repair.*

"Does Luke have time to open a business right now?"

Luke Sterling had been his best friend since they were in kindergarten. He'd moved to Nashville to pursue a music career a few years ago. He found out he was better at writing songs than singing them, so he moved back to Coronado last winter to be closer to his son. Shortly after that, he married Emily, his son's mother, and they moved to a large house on the outskirts of Coronado. They had converted one of the rooms into a recording studio and it wasn't unusual to find Matt Spencer, one of country and western's biggest stars, at their house working on a new song.

Stacy laughed. "Luke says that in order to write songs about life, he needs to have a life."

Coy swirled his coffee around inside his mug. It seemed like everyone he knew had a life, but him. Stacy's family was growing and she was happier than ever. Luke had a songwriting career and a family. Even Luke's brother, Noah, who'd always been kind of a hermit, was married and making his ranch profitable again.

What did he have? Nothing. No family. No career. Nothing to look forward to.

"So…?" Stacy's voice trailed off.

He pulled himself out of his thoughts. "What?"

She gave him a look that said she was clearly frustrated with him. "Are you ready to stay in Coronado and take the campground over?"

Whatever he thought she was going to say, that wasn't it. "You want me to commit to staying here permanently?"

"Don't you think it's time?"

"I don't know." Other than trying to recover from the injury that ended his career, he hadn't given much thought to his future. The only thing he did know was that he wanted Becky in his future. "I need to find out what Becky's plans are."

She arched one eyebrow. "How long has it been since you talked to her?"

Two hundred and ten days. He didn't count a random text here and there, or the three-minute phone conversation they had last fall. "A while."

"I talked to her when she graduated from veterinary school." Stacy's voice was soft. "She seemed happy."

Was she happier without him? It was no secret that he'd been holding her back for the last several years. It took her six years to finish her undergraduate courses because she was juggling school and his rodeo schedule, but without him, she finished veterinary school in record time.

He clenched his jaw. Like everyone else, his cousin didn't think Becky was coming back. He refused to believe he'd messed things up that much. He and Becky were still tied to each other and that gave him an ace in the hole.

"You've been here for nine months. You haven't stayed in one place this long since you were eighteen. The only time you leave your cabin is when Luke's playing at the Watering Hole. It's like you're…lost."

Coy swallowed hard. Of course he was lost. Becky had been his compass since they were twelve years old. Without her, he didn't know what to do.

He tossed the last of the coffee into the sink. "Maze's foot has an abscess again. I'm going to call Dr. Evans to come take a look."

"For what it's worth—" she touched his arm as he walked past her "—I think she's just as lost as you are. She just hides it better."

He swallowed. "I'll think about what you said."

Her face grew serious. "If you figure out who

you are without Becky, you can be the man you need to be *for* Becky."

Without looking at her, he walked out of the office and toward the back of the barn. He heard Stacy slide the entrance door to the barn open, but he still didn't look up.

"You know," she said, "the only person who can find you, is you."

He dared not breathe until he heard her vehicle start and drive away from the barn.

BECKY MAXWELL LET go of the steering wheel of her Ford F-150 truck just long enough to extend her fingers, stretching out the cramped tendons. Behind her, the sun was starting to peek over the horizon, illuminating the vast expanse of the New Mexico desert. Not that she needed the light to know there was nothing to see. Nothing but sparse grass, brown rocks and sky. Kind of like her life.

She rolled her shoulders, but she knew it wouldn't relieve the tension. The closer she got to home, the tighter her nerves became. For the first time since she graduated high school, she was coming home alone.

Why hadn't she told her parents that she and Coy had broken up when they came to her graduation last month? A part of her hoped he would show up and surprise her. She imagined him waiting for her as she exited the stage with her diploma in hand. He would tip his hat and then gather her in his arms and promise her everything was going to be all right.

But he hadn't. When her parents asked where he was, she'd told them Coy was busy and couldn't get away. Thank goodness they didn't ask her what he was busy doing, because she had no idea.

Her gaze drifted to the manila envelope on the passenger seat of the truck. As soon as the document was delivered and signed, she'd be free to start a new life. This time, her world wouldn't revolve around a man who was more worried about his next accomplishment than he was her. If she ever fell in love again, it would be with someone who put her first. Someone who wanted to be with her as much as she wanted to be with him.

First, she had to face Coy. His name hadn't appeared on a bull riding roster in over a year. His official social media channels had been silent for longer than that. Not surprising since she had always been the one to update his accounts. There was one article about him in *Bulls-N-Broncs Magazine* that said he was taking some time off to recuperate. When the interviewer pushed for an answer to when Coy planned to return to competition, Coy said he didn't know when or even if he was going to return.

While the rodeo world speculated on where he was and what he was doing, she knew there was only one place he could be. Coronado. That's where he always went to recover from an injury. Or to train. Or both. She wished she knew which one it was. Not that it would change her decision. She still cared about him and even thinking about the last injury he'd suffered caused the familiar feeling of fear to squeeze her heart. She'd lived with it for nine years and she would never stop worrying, whether they were together or not.

Up ahead, the large entrance to the Maxwell Ranch stretched across the dirt road leading to the main house. Cattle dotted the flat, grassy landscape. Even though the ranch had been in her family for four generations, she'd spent most of her childhood in a small two-bedroom house in Coronado.

She glanced at the clock. It was almost 6 a.m. Her father would be enjoying one last cup of coffee before heading to the bunkhouse to meet with the foreman. She lifted her foot from the gas. With any luck, her father would already be gone by the time she got there. Not that she didn't want to see her dad, but if she was going to get bombarded with questions for showing up alone, she'd much rather it be her mom doing the questioning.

Her mom would be surprised to see her without Coy, but she wouldn't push her too much for answers. Actually, her mom might be a little relieved. She'd never been a fan of Coy's rodeo lifestyle. Her father, on the other hand, loved everything about Coy. Her dad would probably pick Coy over her.

Relief filled her chest as she pulled up to the

ranch house and saw that her father's truck was missing from its usual spot. Her mother would be able to help her come up with a game plan to break the news to her dad.

She parked in front of the closed garage and shut off the truck. The front door was probably locked. Only guests used the front door, and those were few and far between. Everyone else used the back.

Becky opened the screen door of the mudroom. She slipped her boots off and set them against the wall. Her mother was in the house alone. She knew because no one would dare enter the house with their shoes on and her boots were the only ones on the porch.

She knocked on the wooden door three times in quick succession before opening the door. She wanted to surprise her mother, not give her a heart attack.

"Hi, Mom," she greeted the woman washing dishes at the sink.

Autumn Maxwell's face broke out in a huge smile. "Becky! You're home!"

She wiped her hands on a towel and rushed across the room to hug her daughter. "We weren't expecting you until the end of the summer."

Becky hugged her mother, breathing in the scent of dish soap and lavender. "I passed my national licensing exam, and after a lot of thought, I decided not to do the internship after all."

Autumn frowned. "It's not a requirement?"

"Only if I want to specialize in equine." She opened one of the cabinets and picked out her favorite coffee cup.

"I thought that's what you wanted to do." Autumn filled Becky's cup.

It had been…when she was with Coy. As an equine veterinarian on the rodeo circuit, she would never be without clients. She swallowed. "I want to keep my options open. Why limit my choices?"

"I imagine you have a lot of new choices to make, now that you and Coy broke up."

She almost choked on her drink. She set the cup on the counter and wiped her face. "You know about that?"

Her mother raised one eyebrow. "We've known about it for over a year. The question is, why haven't you told us yourself?"

"I…" Her heart raced.

"You didn't think it would be a permanent separation," Autumn said.

She nodded. When Coy left, she never imagined that weeks would turn into months and months into a year apart. "Up until graduation, I still wasn't sure."

Her mother reached out and stroked Becky's hair. "And when he didn't show up, you were forced to come to terms with it."

The sympathy in her mother's voice was almost her undoing. Becky fought the lump that formed in her throat. "Something like that."

"Well, maybe it's for the best," Autumn said. "Coy's not the type that can stay in one place for very long. He's always after the next big thing. That's why he was so suited for the rodeo life. You're not like that. You need roots."

"You both knew when you came to Texas for my graduation?" She clutched her coffee mug in front of her chest. "Why didn't you say anything?"

"We were letting you start the conversation," she said. "You've been pining after Coy since you were twelve years old. It has to be hard."

Becky took a sip of her coffee and didn't answer.

"Is that why you want to stay in Texas?" Her mother gave her a pointed look. "To avoid him?"

"Partly." She shrugged. "And partly because..."

She stopped. She loved her parents and didn't want to hurt them, so how could she tell them she was avoiding them, too? As soon as she started showing an interest in animals, her dad started making plans for her to take over the ranch. Or, maybe he was hoping that Coy would take over the ranch. She wanted to take care of animals. She wanted to live in the country. She didn't want to run a ranch.

"You don't want your father pressuring you."

Becky swallowed. "You know that, too."

"I think you'll find out I know a lot more than you think I do." Autumn opened the refrigerator and removed a basket of eggs. "You must have driven all night. I'll make you breakfast, then you can get some sleep."

She had been so nervous about facing her parents, she hadn't thought about how tired she was. Suddenly, she felt as if she'd been hit by a truck. "Forget breakfast, Mom. I'd probably fall asleep before you finish cooking."

Autumn looked skeptical, but put the eggs back in the refrigerator.

"I'm going to take a nap." Becky poured the remainder of her coffee down the sink. "I need to go to Springerville and see Dr. Evans this afternoon. Do you want to go with me? We can have lunch at Doris's Diner."

"You just got home." Her mother frowned. "I'm sure Dr. Evans would understand if you waited until later in the week to go see him."

Becky yawned. "I would love to, but he's leaving for Florida tomorrow. Part of the reason I drove all night was to get here before he leaves. He's asked me to cover for him while he's gone."

"That means you're staying for a while!" Her mother beamed. "I'd love to go with you. I need to pick up a few things in town anyway."

Becky trudged up the stairs to her room. She couldn't believe her parents had known about her and Coy breaking up and hadn't said anything. A twinge of guilt gnawed at her. What would they say if they knew the truth?

# *CHAPTER TWO*

It was almost two o'clock when Becky finally opened her eyes. She probably would've slept longer if her stomach hadn't woken her up. She swung her feet out of the bed and stood up to stretch.

Her suitcases were sitting against the wall next to her bedroom door. Who'd brought them to her room? Alarm bells rang in her head. Whoever it was, had they seen the manila envelope on her passenger seat? She didn't think either of her parents would open it, but it wouldn't stop them from asking why she had documents from a legal firm for Coy. She took a deep breath. Her suitcases were in the bed of her truck, so they wouldn't have had a reason to look inside the truck.

She felt the front pocket of her jeans and sighed. Her keys were still there. Locking the doors to her vehicle was a habit from living in a college town for the last few years, so her secret was safe.

She picked up the smaller suitcase and laid it on her bed. Opening it, she pulled out the small bag that held her toiletries. She needed a quick shower and to brush her teeth before she did anything.

By the time she emerged from the bathroom adjoining her room, she felt like a new woman. Her stomach was growling as she jogged down the stairs to the kitchen.

"Good afternoon, Pumpkin," Levi Maxwell called to her from the small room situated next to the kitchen.

She halted from her path and veered into his office. "Hi, Dad. I didn't mean to sleep so long."

Most of her life, she'd been up by five in the morning. If she dared sleep until six, she was reprimanded for sleeping the day away when there was work to be done.

He stood up and met her halfway across the room. "You're allowed a few hours' rest after driving all night." He pressed a kiss to her forehead. "Tomorrow, though, I expect you in the barn by six."

"Yes, sir." His tone was joking, but they both knew she would be there. "Thanks for bringing in my suitcases."

"Felipe did it," he said. "He didn't want all your beauty items to melt in the heat."

She laughed. Even though Felipe was younger than she was, he'd always seemed wise beyond his years. He'd grown up on the ranch and probably knew more about the operation than anyone, other than her father. "Tell him I said thank you."

Levi nodded. "Your mom tells me y'all are heading to Springerville this afternoon."

"Yes." She nodded. "Dr. Evans asked me to cover his calls while he's in Florida. I need to meet with him and go over the schedule."

Levi nodded. "He's anxious to see you. He always said you were the best veterinary assistant he ever had. I think he may be even prouder of you than we are."

Dr. Evans and his wife were expecting their first grandchild at the end of June, so they were planning an extended vacation to visit their daughter. Becky was 99 percent sure that Dr. Evans was going to ask her to join his practice. Covering for him while he was in Florida was just a formality.

"Do you need anything while we're in town?"

"No." Levi shook his head. "Don't eat too much at Doris's. I've got a brisket on the smoker for dinner."

Her mouth watered. "I could eat an elephant and still make room for your brisket."

His laughter followed her all the way to the kitchen. There was no sign of her mother, so she opened the refrigerator and searched through the leftovers. She was making herself a ham sandwich when her mom appeared with a laundry basket of clothes.

Autumn's gaze went to the stack of food in front of her. "I thought you wanted to eat at Doris's?"

"I'm starving." Becky took a bite. "Besides, Dad's cooking, so this will tide me over until then."

Her mother shook her head. "Why do I have the feeling we're still going to Doris's?"

"You can't go to Springerville and not stop for pie." Becky grinned. "That's just wrong."

"In that case, make me a sandwich while I hang these clothes on the line."

"Okay." She took another bite of her sandwich and searched the pantry for potato chips.

Twenty minutes later, Becky got into the passenger seat of her mother's Cadillac for the hour drive into Springerville. It was a relief when they crossed the state line from New Mexico into Arizona and started the steady climb into the mountains.

"I never feel like I'm home until I get to the pine trees," Becky said.

"I imagine Coronado feels more like your home than the ranch," Autumn said.

For most of her life, she only saw her father on the weekends and during the summers because she and her mother lived in Coronado during the week. "Why didn't you send me to a school closer to the ranch?"

If she hadn't gone to school in Coronado, she never would have met Coy. How different would her life be right now? Her heart twisted in pain at the thought of never knowing him. She still loved him. She just couldn't be with him.

"I switched schools a lot growing up," Autumn

said. "When I married your father, I told him I would follow him all over the world, but when we had children, we were done. We were living in Coronado when you started school, so that's where we stayed."

Becky glanced at her mother. Autumn's face was tight. "Why do I have the feeling there's more to it than that?"

"There is," her mother said.

Becky had a pretty good idea of what had driven a wedge between her parents and caused them to separate for a brief period of time. She desperately wanted her mother to be able to confide in her about those reasons.

She waited, but her mother didn't elaborate. "Well?"

"One of these days, we'll talk about it." Autumn shot her a sideways glance. "But not today."

"What's wrong with now?" Becky's stomach clenched.

"One, I don't like having serious conversations in the car." Autumn turned off the main road onto a side street. "Two, what happens between a married couple is no one else's business."

Becky bit her bottom lip. "I'm your only child," she said. "I'm pretty sure it's my business. Especially if I was the one keeping you apart."

Autumn pulled into the parking lot of the Springerville Animal Clinic and stopped the vehicle. She turned in her seat to face Becky and gave her a sad smile. "Sometimes you were the only thing that kept us together."

"I don't understand."

"A story for another time," her mother said. "You better get in there. I know Dr. Evans wants to leave work early today."

"Aren't you coming in?"

"No. I've got some errands to run," Autumn answered. "I'll meet you at Dr. Evans's house when you're done."

Autumn and Dr. Evans's wife, Kay, had become friends when Becky was in high school and working at the clinic. Autumn would often visit Kay while waiting for Becky to finish work. The women could talk for hours. Becky hoped that the impending arrival of Kay's grandchild would dominate the conversation and keep them from talking about her and Coy.

She pushed open the glass door and entered the facility. Except for an older man holding a Yorkie on his lap, the waiting room was empty.

"Hi, Mr. Harper," she greeted him. "How's Lady?"

The dog lifted her head at the sound of her name.

The old man grinned at her. "Well, look what the cat dragged in! How are you, Rebecca?"

"Doing well. How about you?"

"I'm as right as rain." He patted the dog's head. "Lady, on the other hand, needs to stop eating everything she finds. She has a heck of a tummy ache."

"Becky!" A lady dressed in scrubs stepped from behind the counter. "It's so good to see you."

She gave the veterinary assistant a hug. "Hi, Shawna."

"Dr. Evans is in his office, go on back." Then she turned her attention to the elderly man and handed him a small paper bag. "Here you are, Mr. Harper."

While Shawna explained the medications to him, Becky made her way past the counter and down the hall. She knocked on the door to the veterinarian's office, even though it was already open.

Dr. Evans looked up from his computer and smiled. "Becky! Or should I say, Dr. Maxwell?"

He waved her in.

"Becky will suit just fine," she said, laughing, as she sat down in the chair across from his desk.

"Have you decided what you want to do, now that you've graduated?"

"I'm not sure yet," she said. "I've been offered a job with a clinic in San Marcos, but it's mostly small animals. I had an interview yesterday afternoon with a clinic in Abilene. I should hear from them next week."

He nodded. "You're more interested in large animals?"

"I'm a rancher's daughter," she said. "Livestock is all I've ever known."

"I was hoping you would say that." He removed

his glasses and folded his hands on top of his desk. "That's why I asked you to meet with me today."

She tried to suppress her grin. "I thought you just wanted to give me the schedule before you left to visit your daughter."

He gave her a slight smile. "That, too, but I do have something to discuss with you."

Her pulse quickened as she leaned back in her chair. Working for him for a few weeks would be just what she needed to keep her mind off Coy, but she wasn't sure if she wanted to stay permanently.

She glanced around the roomy office. It was then that she noticed a pair of crutches leaning against the wall. She nodded toward them. "Yours?"

"Yes," he said. "That's what I need to talk to you about."

"What happened?"

"I had a little run-in with one of Noah Sterling's wild horses." He turned his chair sideways to reveal the leg brace on his left leg. "I have a comminuted patella fracture."

"A shattered kneecap," Becky breathed. "How are you?"

"I'll be fine. Or at least I will be after one more surgery and a few months of physical therapy." He tapped his thumbs together. "Dr. Klein is going to cover the office while I'm visiting my daughter, but that's to free you up for the livestock side of the practice, not because I don't think you can handle both."

Pride surged through her. She'd started working for Dr. Evans when she was just sixteen. All through high school and much of college, she followed him around, learning as much as she could about caring for animals. Knowing that he had enough faith in her to allow her to be part of his practice, even for a few weeks, was an honor.

"I'm never going to be able to keep up with the large animal portion of my practice," he said. "I don't want you to just help out for a while. I want you to stay on permanently. As a partner."

She gasped. "Partner? I don't know what to say."

"Don't say anything yet." Dr. Evans pulled a file from his desk and slid it across to her. "Cover for me while I'm gone. That should give you plenty of time to see what you're getting yourself into. I'm sure you'll want to discuss it with Coy as well."

Heat flooded her neck, and she picked up the folder. The first pages were scheduled appointments for the next few weeks. It was the pages after that caused her to pause.

"This is a partnership agreement." Her fingers turned another page. "And copies of all your financial information. Should you be letting me see this?"

"I want you to have all the information you would need to make a decision," he told her. "No pressure. You can give me your decision when I return."

She glanced at the first appointment on the

schedule. *Whispering Pines Campground and Stables. Horse with possible abscess hoof.*

Her heart jumped in her chest. Whispering Pines belonged to Coy's family. His cousin Stacy managed both the campground and the market. Stacy would know exactly where Coy was.

Coy was shoveling horse apples into the wheelbarrow when a shaggy dog walked into the corral and sat on his haunches.

"Good morning, Max." Coy patted the shepherd mix on his head. He looked around for Caden.

A man with dark red hair peered over the corral fence.

"Hey!" Coy stopped and wiped the sweat from his brow. "What's up?"

"I tried calling, but you didn't answer your phone."

Coy felt the back pocket of his jeans. Where was his phone? "I must have left it in the office."

It wasn't like he needed it anyway. He rarely heard from his friends on the rodeo circuit anymore. They were all too busy with their own world. A world he was no longer a part of. And having his phone with him all the time made it too tempting to text Becky.

"Someone from Dr. Evans's office will be here this morning to take a look at Maze."

"Dr. Evans isn't coming?"

Caden shook his head. "No. He's going on vacation to see his daughter and when he comes back, he won't be doing the large animals anymore."

"Is it because of the accident?" Coy picked up the handles to the wheelbarrow. He had been at Noah's ranch when the horse kicked Dr. Evans. He still felt guilty for not getting to him sooner.

"I think so." Caden opened the gate for him. "I hear that if it wasn't for you, Dr. Evans might not have made it out of there at all."

Coy pushed the wheelbarrow through the gate. "All I did was distract the horse so they could get him to safety."

Caden gave him a lopsided grin. "Using some of the same moves that saved you more than once."

"It gave me a whole new respect for bullfighters, that's for sure." Coy set the wheelbarrow down. "I already let the horses into the pasture. I better bring Maze back in."

"Want some help?"

He shook his head. "I can handle it."

"I know you can," Caden said. "Did Stacy talk to you about taking over the campground?"

"She mentioned it. Said you want to go into business with Luke." Coy picked up a lead rope from a hook hanging on the wall.

"Does that mean you're going to do it?"

Coy shrugged. "I said I'd think about it. There's no rush, is there?"

"I'd like to give Luke an answer by next week."

Next week? That meant he was going to have

to call Becky again. She would probably let it go straight to voicemail. If she didn't respond to his calls or texts, he'd drive to Texas and settle this, one way or another.

"I'll be right back," he murmured, gripping the lead rope like it was a lifeline.

"I'm going, anyway. I just wanted to give you the message about the vet." Caden patted his leg and Max jumped up and ran to his side. He was almost to the entrance when he whirled around. "I almost forgot. Stacy wants you to come to dinner this evening."

"What time?"

"Five thirty," Caden said.

"Sounds good."

"Hey," Coy called to him.

"Yeah?" Caden turned around.

"What will you do if I say no?"

Caden frowned. "I guess things will go back to the way they were before you got here. I'll manage the campground and Stacy will manage the market."

"What about Luke?"

"I'll tell him it's not the right time."

"So if I say no, you can't do what you really want to do?" Guilt washed over him. "Have you thought about selling the place?"

Caden laughed. "Have you met your cousin? This place means too much to her. Besides, you can't sell something that's not yours."

Coy frowned. The campground and the market had both been owned by their grandfather. After his death, Stacy's parents took over the market, while Coy and Stacy inherited the campground. When her mother went into a nursing home due to her illness, Stacy returned home from college to help run the store and discovered that her father was on the verge of losing the store and she needed money fast.

By this time, Coy had already started traveling the rodeo circuit and none of the horses at the campground were being used, so he agreed to let Stacy sell them, and in exchange, she signed her part of the campground over to Coy.

Traveling the circuit was expensive and Coy refused to let Becky pay for everything, so he borrowed money from his father and signed the campground over to his father, with a stipulation that both he and Stacy had to agree if Frank wanted to sell. Coy had since repaid his dad the money, but he'd never taken the campground back. He wasn't around to run it, so there was really no point. He was sure his dad had told him that Stacy and Caden wanted to buy it. His dad had even given him some papers to sign.

As soon as Caden left, Coy exited the barn and went to the pasture behind the corrals. He didn't want to be responsible for Caden not being able to follow his dreams. But he also didn't want to make a promise that he couldn't keep. He'd never intended to stay in Coronado this long. He'd already stayed here longer than he intended. He should've returned to Texas months ago and begged Becky to take him back.

Even if he went to Texas, what were the chances he could convince Becky to take him back now? He was a washed-up cowboy with nothing to offer. No money—all his savings had been spent on hospital bills and physical therapy. Returning to the rodeo circuit wasn't an option.

It seemed the only thing going for him was that his cousin had enough faith in him to ask him to take over the campground. His gaze swept the countryside as he leaned against the fence. The light scent of hay and grass swirled together. He loved this place as much as Stacy did. The trouble was, he needed more than just a place to belong.

He chuckled to himself. Yep. Stacy nailed it when she said he was lost. *If you figure out who you are without Becky, you can be the man you need to be for Becky.* Stacy's words replayed in his head. If only he knew where to start.

The horses in the pasture lifted their heads when he opened the gate and entered. Most of them regarded him for a moment before returning to graze. The palomino mare closest to the gate didn't. She looked at Coy with sad brown eyes. Coy could almost feel the pain radiating from the horse.

"It's okay." He stroked her velvet-soft nose. "The

vet will be here soon and we'll get you all taken care of."

He latched the lead rope to her halter and started walking toward the barn. It was slow going and he let Maze set the pace. They were almost back to the barn when a brand-new Ford F-150 pickup pulled up to the barn. His pulse quickened at the sight of the vehicle. Would he ever be able to see a truck like Becky's and not have his heart try to jump out of his chest?

The driver of the vehicle made it to the barn before he did, but he didn't see anyone when he led Maze through the back entrance. He tied the rope to the grooming stall and walked into the office.

"Hello?"

A few seconds later, he heard the toilet flush in the office bathroom.

The bathroom door swung open. "Sorry," a feminine voice said. "It's a long drive from Springerville."

Coy's heart stuck in his throat. The door shut with a bang and a pair of brown eyes peered into his. "Becky." His voice was barely more than a whisper.

Her eyes widened in surprise. "I…uh… What are you doing here?"

For a brief moment, he'd let himself imagine that she was there for him, but the shock on her face made it obvious that he was the last person she'd expected to see.

He swallowed. "I work here. What are you doing here?"

Her dark eyebrows furrowed. "Since when?"

"Since last fall." He shoved his hands in the front pockets of his jeans to stop them from shaking. "I told you. I asked you to come to the Harvest Festival so we could talk. Remember?"

He'd been so sure she would show up that he told everyone he had a surprise date.

"You've been here that long?" A flicker of concern crossed her face. Her gaze scanned over him. "Are you still injured? You haven't ridden since you got hurt in Fort Worth."

The worry on her face almost made him smile. Hope bubbled in his chest. "You kept tabs on me."

"No." Her face turned red. Her words began to tumble out. "Yes. Your bull riding magazine and news still come to my email. You haven't been on the roster of any events. Are you training to make a comeback?"

"If you ever answered my phone calls you would know."

"I couldn't." She closed her eyes and rubbed her temples. "I didn't have anything else to say. But I came back to Arizona to find you. I have something for you."

He felt like he could float away. "We have a lot to talk about."

She shook her head and looked over his shoulder. "Later. Is Maze the one with the abscess?"

Coy rubbed the back of his neck with one hand. She was good at changing the subject when she wanted to avoid conflict. "Yeah. Are you working for Dr. Evans now?"

"Just for a few weeks." She picked up a black case sitting on the desk and brushed by him. Coy followed her into the breezeway and waited for her to examine the horse.

"I see you've given her a poultice wrap. What else have you been doing for her?" She set the bag on the ground and removed the dressing he'd put on the hoof.

Coy stood close enough to see what she was doing, but far enough back to give her room to work. "I drain it every day, but it doesn't seem to be getting any better."

"Have you tried soaking it in Epsom salt?" She nodded at the bag. "Hand me the hoof knife."

He opened her medical kit and handed her the instrument. He'd used the same thing a million times, but never as deftly as Becky did.

"No," he told her. "I was hoping that by draining it, it would go away, but it hasn't helped."

"Uh-huh." She was concentrating on her work now and Coy knew it would be useless to say anything until she was done.

A half hour later, she set Maze's foot down and stood up. "Has her stall been cleaned?"

"Yes. Scrubbed top to bottom."

"Put her in there." Becky put both hands on her

back and stretched. "I'll be right back. I'm going to fix a soak bag for her foot."

Coy's insides felt like Jell-O as he led Maze to her stall. She was back. More than that, she came back to find him. Was she ready to try again?

"Here." Becky handed him a large manila envelope.

"What's this?"

Becky didn't answer. She was busy sliding Maze's foot into a large bag filled with liquid. A few minutes later, the bag was securely taped to the horse's leg.

He opened the envelope and slid the papers out. His stomach dropped. "You can't be serious."

Becky put her hands in her back pockets. "It's been a year and a half. It's time."

"Only because you locked me out of your apartment and won't answer my phone calls." He shook his head and tried to hand the packet back to her. "It won't be time until we make an actual effort to make things work."

"Right." Sarcasm laced her voice and she crossed her arms, refusing to accept the envelope. "You were so anxious to work things out that you couldn't wait to run away."

"I was in danger of losing the points I needed to qualify for the finals," he pointed out. "That's not running away."

She pressed her lips together, causing the tiny

dimple on the left side of her mouth to stand out. "Admit it, you wanted to leave."

Coy clenched his jaw and inhaled through his nose. "Maybe. But only because you let me know that nothing I did was right. We both needed some space."

Pain flickered in her dark brown eyes. "I didn't need space. I needed you."

Frustration clawed his chest. "It would've been nice if you told me that. I'm not a mind reader. How am I supposed to know what you want, or how you're feeling, if you won't talk to me? Instead, you packed my bags and kicked me out."

"You're right." Becky's expression hardened. "I didn't handle things as well as I should have. I'm sorry."

Coy's heart raced and he stepped closer to her. It was the first time she'd admitted that their lack of communication wasn't all his fault. He reached out to touch her arm. "You're done with school. I'm done with the rodeo. There's nothing to come between us now. We can start again. Together."

She stepped backward. "Until something else goes wrong. When things get tough, all you know how to do is run away."

His stomach balled into a knot. "What have I ever run away from?"

She crossed her arms. "The only reason you joined the circuit to begin with was because you were running away from your parents' divorce."

He'd already planned on doing the circuit with Becky, but she was right in that it had provided him with a much-needed escape from the drama at home. She knew this, so why was she trying to hold it over his head now? "You were the one riding the circuit first. I joined to be with you."

"Only because I was your safety net." Becky gave him a sad look.

Coy cocked his head. "What's that supposed to mean?"

"I kept you grounded when you didn't know what was going to happen to your family." Her voice was low. "But when I needed you to be the steady one, you didn't know how." Becky's face remained stoic. "Why are you fighting me on this? You're the one who never wanted to get married."

"That's not true." Frustration rose in his chest. "I was just waiting for the right time."

She raised one eyebrow. "Did you tell anyone we got married?"

"Did you?"

"Why would I?" She pressed her lips together. "I knew you were going to leave as soon as you could. And I was right."

Coy took his hat off and ran his hand through his hair. "You told me to leave."

She stifled a laugh. "And you ran like a jackrabbit."

He thought he was giving her the space she

needed. He never imagined that she would turn things around.

She turned and walked toward the entrance. "Sign the papers."

Coy didn't move until he heard her truck pulling away. He stared at the papers in his hand. *Petition for Divorce.*

# *CHAPTER THREE*

BECKY'S HANDS WERE shaking as she got back into her truck. She started the vehicle and drove from Whispering Pines faster than she usually drove on dirt roads. When she got to the main road, she pulled over on the side and put her truck in Park. With both hands clutching the steering wheel, she rested her head on her forearms and tried to gather her composure.

Why hadn't Stacy warned her that Coy was at the campground? She'd called Stacy this morning to tell her she was heading over to check on Maze, but Stacy hadn't said a word.

She inhaled deeply, held it for a moment and let it out slowly. Why was she so upset? This was what she wanted, wasn't it? Her plan was to take care of the horse, then go visit Stacy and find out where Coy was. This was the entire reason she'd chosen to come home to Arizona for the summer instead of staying in Texas.

No one knew they had gotten married. That's why she wanted to give him the papers herself rather than have them served publicly. Never in a million years had she imagined he'd refuse to sign them. Now what was she supposed to do?

She sat up straight. He was in shock, that was what it was. As soon as he had some time to process things, he'd see it was for the best. Tomorrow, they would be able to have a civilized conversation and he would see that this was best for both of them.

Stacy still should have warned her. She put her truck in gear and pulled back onto the dirt road. Her next appointment wasn't for two hours, which gave her plenty of time to stop at the Coronado Market for a cup of coffee, a few snacks and a long conversation with Stacy.

The market was busy, which wasn't unusual for the summer, but not so busy that she couldn't find a parking spot. Coronado was a haven for people to escape the heat of the Arizona desert. She glanced at the clock on her dashboard. It was nine thirty. Perfect timing. She'd missed the early morning crowd and was ahead of the lunch rush.

She got out of her truck and headed for the entrance. As she opened the door to go inside, a tiny boy darted out, running into her legs. "Hold on there, buddy!" She scooped the toddler up. "Where's your mama?"

"Thank you!" A woman hurried over to her. "Becky! I didn't know you were in town."

Becky immediately recognized the blonde woman. "Hi, Emily. This must be your little one."

"That's my monster. He's determined to give me a heart attack." Emily's blue eyes twinkled as she reached for her son. "Congratulations on finishing school. Are you back permanently?"

"Thank you. And no, I'm just here for the summer," she said.

Emily bounced the little boy on her hip as he struggled to get down. "I better go. Maybe we can catch up later."

"Sure." A stab of envy hit her.

She was the one who had been in a steady relationship since she was in high school. Well, before, really. When people thought of Coy, they thought of her. They were a pair. They were supposed to be together forever. She was the one who was supposed to be married and raising a family.

Only, she wasn't. And everyone else was.

Envy turned into guilt.

She was happy that Stacy and Emily were finally getting their happily-ever-afters.

Stacy, especially, had a rough time for a while. Her mother's illness and her father's drinking had torn Stacy's family apart. At one time, she was on the verge of losing the market and was struggling to make ends meet. Then Caden came to town, determined to fix everything in an effort to redeem himself.

Several months later, her mother died, her

father reappeared in her life, and she and Caden were married. It was hard to believe that Stacy and Caden had gone from newlyweds to parents in just a few short months. The couple had traveled to the country of Georgia for their honeymoon and fallen in love with two little girls while visiting an orphanage there.

As for Emily, her father had been killed in action when she was eight. Later, her mother remarried another military man. When he was stationed overseas, they shipped Emily to Coronado to live with her grandparents. She'd gone through several years of teenage rebellion and when her grandmother died from cancer, her grandfather kicked her out, too.

Now both Emily and Stacy were happy and had the family they deserved. The family Becky had always wanted. She couldn't help but be a little envious of her friends. She could be happy and jealous at the same time, right?

"Hi, Donna," Becky greeted the lady standing behind the counter. "Is Stacy around?"

The middle-aged woman nodded toward the back. "She's helping Caden with the inventory."

"Thanks."

Becky walked through the breezeway that separated the main part of the store from the storage area.

Caden and Stacy were standing close to each

other, their heads almost touching as they looked over a clipboard.

"Hey," Becky said. "Sorry to interrupt."

They glanced up and saw her. "Hi, Becky." Caden grinned at her.

"Hi." Stacy avoided looking right at her. At least she had the decency to look guilty. "How's Maze?"

A horrified look crossed Caden's face. He leaned closer to his wife. "You sent her to the campground?" he tried to whisper, unsuccessfully.

"Yes." Becky gave Stacy a pointed look. "She threw me to the wolves without a hint of warning."

"Well, look at that." Caden glanced at his watch. "It's almost time to pick the girls up from Vacation Bible School."

He handed the clipboard to his wife and disappeared into the main part of the store.

"Chicken," Stacy called after him.

Becky crossed her arms and waited to hear her excuse. Stacy set the clipboard on the counter next to her. Until that moment, Becky hadn't realized the clipboard had been covering up something very important.

"You're pregnant," Becky gasped.

Stacy's smile beamed as she rubbed her tummy. "Seven months."

"How am I supposed to yell at a pregnant woman?" She wrapped her arms around Stacy and gave her a hug. "Congratulations! But you're still in trouble."

"Let's go somewhere we can talk. Are you hungry?" Stacy linked her arm through Becky's and led her toward the door that connected the store to an apartment. "I need a snack."

Once inside the apartment, Stacy rummaged through the refrigerator. "How does it feel to be a full-fledged vet?"

She shrugged. "I'm not sure yet. I keep waiting for Dr. Evans to call me and tell me to stop messing with his patients."

Stacy set a basket of fruit on the counter and offered Becky a cheese stick.

"Thanks." She took the snack. "Has Coy really been here since October?"

"I'm as shocked as you are." Stacy waved for Becky to follow her to the sofa.

Becky pushed a bright pink cushion aside so she could sit down. She glanced around the tiny apartment. "How on earth is a family of five going to fit in here?"

Stacy laughed. "Hopefully, not for long. We're building a house in between here and the campground. It's supposed to be ready by the time the baby gets here."

"That's wonderful! What are your plans for the apartment?" She couldn't remember a time when Stacy hadn't lived at the store.

"We offered it to my dad—" Stacy popped a grape in her mouth "—but he had a different idea."

"Your dad?" That was the last thing she expected to hear. She knew that Vince had come back to town to make amends with Stacy just before her mother died, but Stacy had no tolerance for his drinking.

"He's been sober for over seven years." Stacy sighed. "And he's such a good grandpa. He spoils the girls rotten."

"What was Vince's idea?"

"He thought it would be better to use it as a nursery-slash-playroom-slash-office."

Becky wrinkled her nose. "A what?"

Stacy giggled. "The small bedroom that the girls use right now will be a nursery for the baby while I'm working. The main bedroom will be a playroom for the girls, and we'll set up an office here, in the living area. The kitchen will be available for employees to use for their breaks."

Silence filled the room for a moment. Finally, Becky cleared her throat. "Why didn't you warn me?"

"Isn't it obvious? I didn't want to give you time to find an excuse to not come."

Becky pressed her lips together. "I wouldn't do that. Not when an animal needs me."

"You could've gotten someone else to do it." Stacy's voice was quiet. "How did it go?"

"How do you think it went?" She slumped against the back of the couch.

Stacy reached over and touched her arm. "Coy

may be my cousin, but you're my friend, too. What happened? Why did you break up?"

Becky pulled a throw pillow onto her lap and hugged it against her stomach. Stacy was more like a sister to Coy than a cousin, and she was surprised that Coy hadn't revealed their secret to her. "It's complicated. He became so obsessed with winning his next championship, that's all that mattered. And he didn't have to worry about anything else, because I did it all. I took care of the bills and the entry fees and the lodging and the food. I guess I got tired of being the only one doing all the giving."

Stacy gave her a sad look. "And when you decided to put yourself first for a change, he couldn't handle it."

She tried to mask the relief she felt. It was obvious Coy hadn't told her everything. "Something happened that made me realize I've been fooling myself. If he wanted to marry me because he loved me, he could've done that years ago."

"I get it," Stacy said. "I do. But I've never seen Coy like this. Is there any hope for the two of you?"

"I don't think so." Her breath hitched. "I want to be someone's partner. Not their secretary, or their mother. Until he has to do something for himself, he'll never appreciate anyone else."

The corner of Stacy's mouth lifted slightly. "I seem to recall telling him something along those same lines."

Becky's watch vibrated and she looked at the screen. "I've got to go. I have another call."

Stacy stood up and walked her to the door. "I'm not giving up. Coy's a little lost, but he'll find himself. You'll see."

Becky just nodded and headed out the door before Stacy could see the lump in her throat.

As soon as the sound of Becky's truck faded, Coy wadded the papers into a tight ball and threw them into the trash can. He put his hands behind his head and linked his fingers together. Invisible bands around his chest were strung so tight he could barely breathe.

What just happened? He dropped his arms and stormed out of the office. He paced back and forth in the breezeway of the barn, his anger building with every step. By the time he reached the back of the barn for the third time, he was so full of pent-up energy that his vision was blurry and his pulse pounded in his ears.

As he turned on his heel, his shoulder brushed against the hay bales stacked against the wall. Something inside him exploded and he clenched his fists and punched the hay bale that had been unfortunate enough to be in his way. A satisfying crunching sound echoed through the barn and he hit the hay again. And again. And again.

Sweat ran down his back and his chest heaved as his vision began to clear. He turned and leaned against the hay, wiping sweat from his brow with his forearm. He slid to the floor and rested his elbows on his knees. What was he going to do? Was this what she really wanted?

He pulled his phone out of his back pocket and swiped to unlock the screen. Becky's face smiled at him. He'd snapped the picture of her at the last rodeo they attended together. He always rode better when she was there, which was why he hated it when she couldn't be on the road with him.

He stared at the picture. Her brown eyes sparkled and her smile was contagious. He opened the folder with his pictures and scrolled through them until he found the photos of their wedding day. The justice of the peace had married them and his wife had taken a few photographs.

His brow furrowed as he studied the picture. Her smile wasn't the same. Sure, the corners turned up, just like on his home screen, but her eyes weren't the same. He enlarged the picture with his thumb and forefinger and his heart thumped loudly in his chest.

She wasn't smiling, not really. Her eyes looked almost sad. His gaze drifted to himself. His smile was huge and there was no denying the joy in his expression. He'd been so happy, he'd completely missed the fact that she was miserable. But why? All she ever talked about was getting married. And all he'd ever done was avoid the conversation. She was getting what she wanted, so why did she look so sad?

His breath hitched in his chest. When had she changed her mind about wanting to be with him? His mind raced over the last several years. They hadn't seen each other as often as they wanted. Or at least as often as he wanted. It was easier when she'd been working on her bachelor's degree. Most of her classes were online, so as long as they had internet, she could keep up. It was when she started her graduate classes to become a veterinarian that they ran into a problem.

Their long days together on the road became weekends here and there. There were times she was so busy that she couldn't even talk when he called. He let out a long, slow sigh. They'd started drifting apart even before they got married.

He lifted his phone up again and flipped through more pictures. His finger paused over a fuzzy black-and-white image. His throat tightened and he sank onto a bench next to the wall. He smiled as he let his finger trace the lines on the screen. It had taken him four days to see the details that Becky pointed out to him. Now, he didn't need anyone to point out the features of his baby.

His baby. He swallowed. Last month their child would have turned one year old. Would it have been a boy or a girl? Ten weeks. That's how far along Becky was when the bleeding started. The next few weeks had been a blur. Between the tears and the anger, they barely spoke.

When he had to leave to go to a rodeo a couple of weeks later, he'd been almost relieved. It seemed nothing he did was right. A few days apart would be good for both of them. But when he got back, his bags were packed and sitting on the porch with a note saying she needed more time.

A week turned into a month. One month turned into several. At first, he called her every day, but she rarely answered. When she did, she always said the same thing. More time. The last time she answered his phone call was in October. He asked her to come to Coronado's annual Harvest Festival so they could talk. She agreed. Then she didn't show up. His daily calls became weekly calls. But he hadn't given up. Apparently, she had.

Coy stood up and shoved the phone into his back pocket. He needed to clear his head and come up with a plan. There was only one way he knew to do that. He walked out of the barn toward the pasture. As he approached the fence, he lifted one hand to his mouth and used his thumb and middle finger to let out a shrill whistle. One horse at the back of the pasture lifted his head and began trotting toward him. The closer the horse got to the fence, the faster his gait became. The gelding came to a stop just in front of him.

"Hey, Shucks." Coy reached over the fence and

scratched between the horse's ears. "Want to go for a ride?"

He opened the gate and the large black horse stepped through and came to a stop in front of him. Coy signaled for him to bow. Shucks moved one front leg behind him, keeping the other one straight, and leaned into the bent leg, lowering the front of his body.

Coy latched the gate back, held on to the base of his mane, and swung his leg over the horse. Shucks immediately stood up straight, waiting for Coy's command. He turned Shucks toward the riding trail that led out of the campground and toward the Black River.

Shucks was as eager to escape the confines of the campground as he was and seemed to sense Coy's restlessness. With little urging, he broke into a run. Coy leaned low over the horse's neck and held on.

As they approached the end of the meadow, Coy signaled for Shucks to slow down. By the time they stepped onto the path that would wind down the canyon and into the river bottom, the horse was walking.

The trail wasn't as worn as it had been when he was a kid, but it wasn't overgrown, either. When his grandfather had been alive, the campground had been more than just a campground. It offered boarding for horses, trail rides and riding lessons. All that changed after Coy joined the rodeo circuit.

Becky accused him of running away. Maybe she was right, but when his parents announced they were getting a divorce after more than twenty years of marriage, he needed to get away. Stacy had already left for college, but her parents managed the market. Pap, his grandfather, assured him he could handle things for a while and encouraged him to go with Becky, who had just qualified for the national finals in barrel racing.

He borrowed some money from his father and left Coronado to hit the rodeo circuit, too. After a while, he discovered he was better at bull riding than the average cowboy and it wasn't long until he'd won enough money to pay back his dad.

He had no idea that his grandfather was struggling to manage everything until he came home to visit and discovered that Pap had sold most of the horses. Without horses at the campground, there was no reason for him to stick around, so he went back to rodeoing.

Up ahead, the trail widened and the ground began to flatten out. He let go of Shucks's mane and let the horse pick his own path beside the river. He placed his hands behind him on the horse's loins, closed his eyes and leaned his head back, enjoying the feel of the sun on his face.

Downstream, he heard the sound of gravel crunching and voices. He sat up straight and used his knees to guide Shucks off the main path to give the group of approaching riders room to go by.

The group consisted of four young riders and one older man, all watching him with interest. The only girl in the group leaned close to the boy beside her and whispered, "That horse doesn't have a saddle or anything."

"That's 'cause he's a real cowboy," the boy whispered back. He nodded at Coy. "Hey, mister. How do you do that?"

"Do what?"

"Get your horse to go where you want without any reins."

Coy patted Shucks's neck. "I use my knees to guide him."

The first boy was clearly impressed. "You can do that?"

"If the horse is trained to."

"Who trained him?" The man at the back of the group spoke up.

"I did."

"You from around here?" the man asked.

"Born and raised," he said.

The man nodded. "Who do you work for?"

Coy wasn't sure how to answer that. What was he supposed to say? That he was a charity case for his cousin? "Whispering Pines Campground."

"I've heard of it. When they shut down their trail rides, it sent us a lot of business."

He ignored the stab of guilt that hit him. "We still have stables if campers want to bring their own horses."

"Most people don't have their own," the man said. "Are you interested in getting out of this small town and doing something with your talent?"

Coy almost laughed, but he could tell by the man's face that he was serious. He kept his face blank. "What did you have in mind?"

The man sent the kids ahead and moved his horse closer to Coy. He reached into his front shirt pocket and pulled out a business card. "I run a riding camp in Eagar and I can always use a good wrangler, especially one that can train horses themselves."

Coy scanned the man's card. "I appreciate it, Mr. Montgomery, but I'm not really looking for another job right now."

"I understand." He nodded. "But if you ever decide you'd rather work with horses than campers, give me a call."

"Thanks." He tucked the man's card into his pocket.

He waited for the man to catch up with the group of kids and disappear around the bend before sliding off Shucks's back. The horse followed him to the edge of the river and Coy sat down in a grassy spot.

He leaned against a tree and scooped up a handful of pebbles. He tossed one into the water and watched the ripples travel from the bank toward the center of the stream.

How many times had he sat under this same tree

with Stacy and talked about their future? While most kids in Coronado dreamed of growing up and moving someplace bigger, he and his cousin dreamed of staying there. They'd had so many ideas and dreams for their future...and all of them revolved around Whispering Pines.

He sat up straight. That was it. She wanted him to be the steady one. What could be more steady than owning and running a business? Not just any business. Whispering Pines.

# *CHAPTER FOUR*

THE AFTERNOON SUN was high in the sky when Coy made his way back to the campground. He looked around the property with fresh eyes. At the far end of the property were the cabins, a common area and hiking trails. The barn and corrals were located closer to the entrance from the main highway.

The campground was clean, well maintained, large enough for families and secluded enough for those who wanted privacy. Still, it didn't receive as much business as it once had. Other campgrounds attracted a lot more campers, despite Stacy's aggressive social media campaigns. Was it because Whispering Pines was located at the end of a five-mile stretch of dirt road that didn't seem to go anywhere? The campground was in a perfect location for people interested in trail rides and riding lessons, but some people might think it a little too far off the beaten path.

Coy opened the gate to the pasture and Shucks ambled inside. He leaned against the fence and watched the horses graze. Maze was in her stall, so there were only three horses in the field. He remembered a time when there were as many as twenty horses in the pastures. Twelve of them belonged to the campground, leaving plenty of room for campers to bring their own horses.

Adrenaline rushed through his system. When his parents divorced, all he'd wanted to do was get out of Coronado. All the ideas for the campground and the plans he had disappeared. Is that why he was lost? Because he had never replaced the dreams he had for Whispering Pines with something else?

Could he rebuild the dreams he gave up and his marriage at the same time? Feeling lighter than he had in months, he went to the barn to check on Maze.

The horse was comfortable, so Coy went to the office and dug through the desk until he found a package of unopened Post-it notes. The wall above his desk held a bulletin board, a calendar and a few pictures. He lifted the board from the nail holding it on the wall then took down the calendar and the pictures. Digging through the desk again, he found a roll of masking tape.

He pulled a long strip of tape off the roll and taped it to the wall. He continued pulling off strips until he'd created three columns and three rows. It wasn't the fanciest kanban board he'd ever seen, but it would work.

On the Post-it notes, he jotted down ideas to

improve the campground's appeal. Then he jotted down things that would need to be done in order to transition Whispering Pines from a campground to a guest ranch.

After sticking the notes into the correct columns on the kanban board, he stepped back to review his makeshift workflow chart. There was just one thing wrong. He was trying to make plans to build a business that legally wasn't his. The campground belonged to his father. Yes, it was originally supposed to be his, but he'd turned it over to his dad when he joined the rodeo. At one point, he knew that Stacy and Caden had discussed buying it, but they never followed through with it.

Tonight, when he went to Stacy's for dinner, he would talk to her and Caden about the idea of him not just managing the campground, but taking it over completely.

On the opposite wall of the desk was a large whiteboard that contained his list of things to do around the campground. Cabin Three had a leaky shower. The toilet in Cabin Five was backed up. There were a few other minor things but plenty of time to finish them all before he had to be at Stacy's for dinner. On his way out the door, he gave the trash can holding Becky's document a good kick. He had a plan now.

A few hours later, he was holding a box of cupcakes and knocking on the door to the two-bedroom apartment behind the market where Stacy and her growing family lived.

Caden opened the door. He had a shocked look on his face. "You're here."

He frowned. "Am I not supposed to be? You said five thirty, right?"

"Yeah." Caden stood back and held the door open. "But you usually call and cancel."

"I do not."

"Yes, you do," Stacy called from the kitchen.

He gave his cousin a hurt look. "In that case, I'll take my cupcakes and leave."

"Quick," Stacy told her husband, "bolt the door so he can't escape!"

Coy laughed and came inside. The large dining table in the corner of the apartment was set and ready for everyone to sit. He glanced at Stacy. "The last time I was here, there were so many newspapers and magazines that you couldn't sit down."

Stacy set a large plate in the middle of the table with rolls stacked on it. "I got rid of all those when I found Abbie. If you showed up for dinner more often, you would know that."

"Is that why you kept them?" He put the box of cupcakes on the countertop bar that separated the kitchen from the living area. Once he'd picked up a magazine off the table, but abandoned it when he realized it was printed in another language.

She nodded. "It's funny. I searched through every magazine and newspaper published in Georgia looking for my sister, and she was in New York the entire time."

Stacy had been eight years old when his aunt and uncle adopted her from the country of Georgia. Her infant sister had been adopted by another couple, and Stacy spent a lot of time and effort searching for her. In the end, it was Abbie who found her.

"Something smells good," he said.

"Irish stew." Caden stood in front of the stove, stirring the food in the large dish. "It's my grandmother's recipe."

Stacy gave Coy a pointed look. "He wants the girls to know about their dad's Irish heritage, to go with their Georgian roots."

"I brought cupcakes for dessert." Coy grinned. "Plain ol' American sugar."

"You're in a good mood," Stacy said. "Does that mean things went well with Becky this morning?"

"Why doesn't it surprise me that you knew she was the one coming?"

"Don't look at me." Caden set his spoon on the counter and turned to his wife. "I didn't know until after the fact."

Coy frowned. "She examined Maze and is coming back tomorrow to check her again."

"And?" Becky's face was hopeful.

"And nothing."

She pinched her lips together. "I swear you two are the most stubborn people I've ever met."

"It's none of our business," Caden said. "Let Coy handle this."

"Thank you."

"Unca Coy!" A pint-size tornado flew across the room and wrapped around his legs.

Coy tossed the four-year-old into the air. "Hello, Goldfish."

The little girl sucked in her cheeks and made a fish face before breaking into giggles.

Coy copied her, causing her to giggle even more.

"Come to my room!" Marina wiggled out of his arms to the floor. She tugged his hand. "Come see what I made at Vacation Bible School."

He let her lead him to the tiny bedroom she shared with her older sister.

For the next fifteen minutes, she explained in detail how she drew her picture, including why she colored her lamb pink.

He turned around to exit the room to see Stacy leaning against the door frame. Her eyes were wide and she looked at him with an incredulous expression. "What?" he said.

"I've never heard her talk to anyone that much, besides me and Caden," Stacy whispered.

That didn't surprise him. Marina was very shy. The first few days she'd been home had been rough. All she'd wanted to do was hide behind her sister. It didn't take her long to warm up to him, though. He shrugged. "Probably because of riding lessons. She loves the horses, so she had to learn to trust me."

"Or maybe it's you." Stacy stepped away from the door to let him go through. "Come on, Marina. It's time to eat."

Marina frowned at her mother. "My name is Goldfish."

"Why Goldfish?"

Coy laughed. "When she gets nervous, she sucks in her cheeks, so I told her she looked like the goldfish we used to keep in the water trough."

Stacy and Caden stared at each other. Caden's brow furrowed. "She does?"

"How did we not notice?" Stacy shook her head.

Coy didn't miss the flash of guilt that crossed his cousin's face. "Maybe she's just more nervous around me. Where's Khatia?"

"She's at her first sleepover." Stacy sighed.

"Meaning, we will probably be going to pick her up at midnight." Caden pulled a chair out for Marina, then for his wife.

Coy sat in the empty chair at the end of the table.

"Can I say grace?" Marina asked.

He bowed his head as the little girl rattled off everything she was grateful for. He was startled to hear his name in her prayers.

"That was lovely," Stacy told her before passing Coy the plate of rolls. "So, why are you in a good mood?"

His mouth watered at the sight of the bread. "Did

Abbie make these?" Stacy's sister loved to bake and her rolls were the best.

"Yes. And don't try to change the subject."

He shrugged. "Maybe I'm not lost anymore."

"You're not?" His cousin leaned her elbows on the table and gave him a cockeyed smile. "Do tell."

"I have a few things I need to work out, first. But I need to know, why didn't you buy the campground from my dad? I know you talked to him about it."

Caden shook his head. "We talked about it, but we decided building a family home would be a better investment right now."

"Why do you ask?" Stacy gave him a puzzled look. "You don't want to try to sell it, do you? Because I—"

"I want to buy it back from my dad," he said.

"You do?" Stacy's green eyes lit up. "That means you're staying."

"I am."

Standing up, she moved over to stand behind him. Wrapping her arms around his neck, she hugged him tight. "You have no idea how happy that makes me."

The emotional lilt in her voice pulled at his heart. He stood up and turned to give her a proper hug. "I'm sorry I bailed on you."

"You're here now." She patted his chest. "But if you try to leave me again, I'll let the girls use you for roping practice."

His heart swelled a little. Stacy had always accepted him for who he was. When they were in school, everyone else expected him to be a star football player like his father, but Stacy encouraged him to make his own path. For his fourteenth birthday, she paid for him to go to a bull riding camp and even convinced his parents to sign the permission slip.

She would have accepted his decision, no matter what it was, but seeing how relieved she was that he was staying made him realize just how much pressure the campground had been on her.

He'd made the right decision. "After dinner, maybe we can make a list of all the things I have to learn before I take over."

Stacy blinked back the tears in her eyes and nodded. "Of course. But we'll take it slow. There's a lot to learn."

He waited for her to sit back down before he sat, too. Yes, this was definitely the right decision.

It was well after dark by the time Becky pulled up to the ranch house. There were no lights on inside, so she slipped in the back door as quietly as she could. Her mother always said that her dad went to bed with the chickens. Since she moved away, it looked like her mother did, too.

She left her boots in the mudroom and went to look for leftovers in the refrigerator. A large bowl, covered in aluminum foil, sat on the top shelf. Grinning, she removed the bowl and peeked under the foil. Her mouth watered at the sight of the pot roast swimming in gravy.

"Long day?" Her father's voice sounded behind her while she was heating the food in the microwave.

"Dad." She covered her heart with one hand. "You scared me."

"Sorry." He chuckled. "I forgot how jumpy you are. How was your first day on the job?"

"It was okay." She pulled the bowl from the microwave. "George Walker has a horse that's about to foal and he wasn't happy that I showed up instead of Dr. Evans. He's convinced I won't be able to handle it."

Levi nodded. "I'll give him a call tomorrow."

"Don't you dare," she gasped.

"Why not? I've known George for a lot of years. He probably didn't realize you were my daughter."

She set the food on the table and turned to him. "How am I ever going to be accepted as a professional if my dad has to call clients and assure them I know what I'm doing? I can handle it."

He held up his hands in surrender. "Okay, okay."

"Thank you." She slid out a chair from the kitchen table and sat down. "What are you doing up?"

"I just got back from checking on a calf and decided to wait up for you. I wanted to warn you—"

he sat down across from her "—Coy is in Coronado."

Her hand froze halfway to her mouth. "I know. I ran into him this morning."

"Are you okay?"

The tenderness in his voice touched her. She couldn't remember him ever being concerned about her feelings. He usually told her to suck it up and get over it. Then again, maybe he was secretly hoping she and Coy would get back together.

"I'm fine." She blew on the chunk of meat on her spoon.

"I knew you would be," he said. "You've always been the toughest Maxwell of all of us."

"Are you disappointed?" she couldn't help but say.

He gave her an odd look. "Why do you ask?"

She shrugged. "You like Coy. Sometimes I thought you liked him more than you liked me."

"Most of the time he liked me more than you did, but mostly, I liked that he made you happy." Levi gave her a sharp look. "Although, I won't deny that I also liked the idea of you marrying someone who would be willing to take over the ranch, since you don't seem to have any interest in it."

Her shoulders stiffened. The ranch was a touchy subject between them and she didn't want to argue with him. She took another bite of food to avoid having to say anything.

"I'm going to bed," Levi said, standing up and walking across the room. At the doorway, he paused. "Don't worry about George. He'll come around."

She nodded. "He'll have to. Dr. Evans is in Florida and Dr. Klein only takes care of small animals."

"Good night."

"Dad." Before he got out of the kitchen, she stopped him. "Most of my stops the next few weeks are closer to Alpine. Would it be all right if I just stayed at the house in town?"

He shook his head. "We sold that house when you started vet school."

Sold it? Her throat thickened. That house was the one she considered home. "Why? What happened to all my stuff?"

"No sense in paying for a house that sat empty," he said. "Your mother packed all your stuff and put it in storage. You want me to book you a room in town?"

"No." She swallowed. "I'll figure something out. Thanks."

She got up and poured herself a cup of milk. It was silly to feel a sense of loss over a house that she only lived part-time in. What was she going to do? She'd counted on staying in that house most of the summer while covering for Dr. Evans. The ranch was over an hour from Dr. Evans's office in Springerville and most of her calls were closer to Coronado than the office. She rinsed her bowl and put it in the dishwasher before trudging up the stairs to her bedroom. Two more days of this and she'd be a walking zombie. At least she could sleep in on Saturday.

Besides Maze's abscess hoof, she'd seen a chicken with bumblefoot, a bloated cow, a donkey who'd tangled with a coyote (the donkey won), and George Walker's pregnant mare. It had been a long day, but she hadn't done anything to justify the weariness she felt. At least not physically.

The deep ache in her chest had been with her for more than a year now. Stress had a way of wreaking havoc on a person's body. Maybe it would go away once things with Coy were settled. Then again, maybe it wouldn't.

It seemed like every time she thought things were getting better, she was struck with another reminder of all she'd lost. First, she lost her baby. Then she lost Coy. She had pushed herself at school, staying too busy to think about it. Last month, the loss hit her again, even harder. She should have been celebrating her graduation from vet school and her child's first birthday. Instead, she celebrated by filing for a divorce from a marriage that no one even knew had happened.

And tonight, the house she'd hoped to seek refuge in was lost, too. One more reason she needed to go back to Texas as soon as Dr. Evans returned.

She needed Coy's signature on the paperwork before that happened.

Before climbing into bed, she opened her cell phone to set an alarm for the next morning. A text message had come in earlier that she hadn't noticed. Her heart jumped when she saw it was from Coy. She slid her finger across the screen to open it.

I haven't given up on us.

She swallowed and closed the text without responding.

Alone in the dark, it was safe to cry. Only she couldn't. If she ever gave in and let the emotions take over, she wasn't sure if she could recover. She pushed down the lump in her throat and squeezed her eyes shut.

It seemed she'd barely closed her eyes when the alarm woke her up. With a groan, she rolled out of bed. Things would be better today. Coy had time to get over the shock of seeing her. Surely, once he read the terms of the settlement, he'd agree it was for the best.

By the time she got out of the shower, she felt better. After one cup of coffee, she'd feel like a whole new woman.

"Good morning." Autumn stood in front of the stove. "Breakfast will be ready in a few minutes."

"You don't have to make me breakfast, Mom."

Becky poured herself a cup of coffee. "I can grab something in town."

"Nonsense," her mother said. "I'm already making breakfast. It's not that difficult to make a little more."

She knew it would be useless to argue with her mother, so she nodded and turned to her dad, who was sitting at the table. "How's the calf?"

"What calf?" Autumn turned to look at her husband.

"The calf Dad was checking on when I got home last night."

"He's fine," Levi said, exchanging a quick glance with his wife.

Becky didn't miss the silent message that passed between them. She cleared her throat. "Need me to look at him this morning?"

Levi rolled his eyes. "You and I both know it was only an excuse for me to wait up for you."

"I know." Becky sat across from him. "I appreciate it, but I'm fine."

"Just because you're an adult doesn't mean we stop worrying." Autumn carried plates of food to the table. "Eat. I don't want you wasting your money on fast food."

Becky's stomach growled when she looked down at the plate of hash browns, sausage and scrambled eggs. "Yes, ma'am."

"What's on your agenda today?" Levi poured salsa over his eggs.

"First, I'm stopping at the office to check in with Shawna," she said. "Then I'll make my rounds."

"George's mare one of them?"

Becky didn't trust her father's tone. "Yes, but don't you dare call him."

"Didn't even cross my mind," he said.

Her phone rang before she was halfway done with her food. She glanced at the screen. It was the veterinary assistant from Dr. Evans's office. "Hi, Shawna. What's up?"

"Becky." Shawna's voice sounded panicked. "Are you coming to the office this morning?"

"I planned on stopping by before making my rounds. Why?"

"Dr. Klein has food poisoning and can't come in. Normally, I would cancel most of the appointments, but today is animal shelter day."

No wonder Shawna was frantic. Dr. Evans had a contract with the local animal shelter to spay and neuter all the animals that were being adopted. It was usually an all-day job and since people were eagerly waiting to take their new pets home, Becky didn't want Shawna to have to reschedule. "What time do we need to start?"

"Eight. But I can hold them off until nine."

"No." Becky stood up and walked over to the refrigerator. "I'll be there in plenty of time. Can you reschedule my appointments for this afternoon?"

"You're a saint," Shawna said. "I'll see you soon."

Becky disconnected the call and looked through the refrigerator. "Mom, do you have any flour tortillas?"

"On the bottom shelf. What's going on?"

She spied the package and removed one tortilla. "I've got to get to the office."

"Give me that." Her mother took the tortilla from her. She took a fork and mixed the food on Becky's plate together before scraping it onto the tortilla. "You never could roll burros tight enough to hold the food in."

"Thanks." Becky tossed the rest of her coffee in the sink and went upstairs to pack an overnight bag, just in case she decided to stay in Coronado.

She stopped at the mudroom to slip on her boots.

"Here." Autumn stood at the door to the mudroom and handed Becky the burrito, which was now wrapped in aluminum foil.

Becky waved to her parents and headed for her truck. She slid into the driver's seat and pulled up the text messages on her phone.

Something came up. Can't check on Maze until this afternoon. Can you change her soak bag?

Three seconds later, Coy responded.

Already did. Make this your last stop so we have time to talk.

She sighed. There wasn't anything left to say. He would apologize again for not handling things well when she miscarried, promise to do better, blah, blah, blah.

He didn't seem to understand that this wasn't about the miscarriage anymore. She'd had too much time to think about their relationship and had concluded that she wanted more than he could give her.

## *CHAPTER FIVE*

FOR SEVERAL SECONDS Coy stared at the message on his phone, waiting for her to respond.

After five minutes it was clear she wasn't going to. That was okay because he needed time to talk to his dad. Last night, after he left Stacy's, he'd called his dad and asked if they could meet for breakfast at the Bear's Den this morning.

He wanted to talk to his dad before Becky got to the barn, so he had arrived at the barn early to take care of the horses.

When he got to the restaurant, his dad was already seated. A dark-haired waitress stood next to his table talking to him. His chest tightened like it did every time he saw his friend Tommy's widow. Coy walked over to the table. "Hi, Maggie."

"Coy, it's so good to see you!" The tiny woman gave him a hug. "I heard you were still in town, but I didn't believe it. Shouldn't you be at a rodeo somewhere?"

"I'm retired now." Coy sat next to his dad.

Her dark eyebrows furrowed. "Sorry. I guess I don't keep up with the sport much anymore."

They both knew why. Tommy Littlebear loved the rodeo almost as much as he loved being a Hotshot. He was the one who took Coy to his first bull riding event and coached him through it.

"Then, welcome home," she said. "Do you need a menu, or do you know what you want?"

"I'd like a Big Bear omelet with hash browns," he said and glanced at his dad.

Frank nodded. "Sounds good. Make it two of them."

After she walked away, Coy leaned across the table. "I thought she was a teacher now. Why is she still working here?"

"June McNamara helped her out a lot after Tommy died, so Maggie works for her during the summers," Frank said.

Coy sipped his coffee. When Tommy died while fighting a forest fire, the entire town came together to help Maggie and their son. Coy had been at the top of the leaderboard at a rodeo in Oklahoma when he and Becky got word about Tommy. It was the first and only time he walked out in the middle of a competition. He and Becky took turns driving through the night so they could be in Coronado if Maggie, or Tommy's father, Harry, needed them.

Coy glanced across the table at his father. Frank had a somber expression and Coy guessed he was thinking about Tommy, too.

Several people stopped by the table to say hello and speak a few words with the sheriff. Coy used to hate going anywhere with his dad. It was hard to live in the shadow of a man like him. Frank Tedford had been a star football player, leading his team to two state championships. Then he was a decorated marine who served with distinction in Desert Storm. After the Gulf War, he left the military and worked a lot of odd jobs around town before finally becoming sheriff of the county. Everyone knew his dad and looked up to him.

When Coy was in high school all the coaches expected him to be as good at football as his dad was. It didn't matter that his father was almost six feet six inches tall and Coy was barely five foot ten. He knew he would never be as good at most sports as his dad was, so he gravitated to other things. After spending so much time around horses with his grandfather, rodeoing came naturally to him.

Frank set his coffee cup down and wiped his thick mustache with a napkin. "So what's on your mind?"

His dad never liked to beat around the bush. It was one of the few things he wished they had in common. "I'd like to talk to you about the campground. Stacy and Caden asked me to take over the management full-time. But I don't want to just manage it. I want to own it. I can't afford to buy it back from you right now, but I have some ideas to start making it more profitable. I was hoping we could come to some kind of agreement."

Frank leaned back and crossed his arms over his chest. "Are you going to stick around long enough to see it through?"

Coy swatted away the annoyance that flared up. Becky wasn't the only one who thought he liked to run away. "Where else am I going to go?"

"Tell me about your idea."

"Remember when Pap was alive and the campground was always full? It was because it wasn't just a place to sleep while visiting the White Mountains. It was its own destination. I want to go back to that. I want to turn Whispering Pines back into a dude ranch."

"The correct term nowadays is *guest ranch*," Frank said. "You want to add trail rides and riding lessons to the activities? That will be hard to do with only a few horses."

"I know," he said. "I'm exploring a few different options."

"Last time you explored your options, I didn't see you for two years."

Maggie appeared with their food, so the talking ceased for a few minutes while they both started eating.

Coy ignored his dad's comment. "I'm going to hit a couple of horse auctions to try to get some horses that are already broke, but what I'd like to do is buy some horses from Noah and train them myself."

Frank raised his eyebrows. "That's a good long-term plan. The adoption fee is ridiculously low and no one is a better trainer than you, but it takes a long time to get those horses to a point where they can be trusted to be around strangers all day."

"I have the time." He shrugged. "I'm not going anywhere."

Frank nodded. "Most of the wild horses I saw would just as soon buck you off a cliff as let you ride them."

"What did you say?" Coy dropped his fork. Excitement welled up in his chest.

"I'm just saying some of those wild horses have a mean streak. Not that you can't tell the difference between the ones with potential and the ones that don't. I've seen you train horses I never thought would be rideable."

"Dad, you're a genius!" He jumped up from the table and pulled his cell phone out of his back pocket. "I'll be right back."

The owner of the Bear's Den had a strict no cell phone policy. Not that he'd ever seen it enforced, but he wasn't about to be the first. As soon as he got outside, he pulled up Noah's number and hit Send.

"Hey, Coy. I was about to call you. I got your message about wanting to come look at some of my horses."

"Yes," he said. "But I have a question. Is there a limit on how many you can buy? And are there any restrictions on who you can sell to?"

"I'm authorized to sell as many as I want, whenever and wherever I want, as long as the buyer fills out the paperwork and proves that the horses are going to a good home and not a meat market."

"What about the rodeo? Could you sell them to a stock contractor for the rodeo?"

"I don't know why not," Noah said. "I never thought about it. Aren't those contractors pretty picky about the type of horses they want? I don't know enough about it to approach them."

Coy's pulse quickened. "The last time I was at your ranch, you complained about a few horses that didn't want to be broke, no matter what you did. I know a contractor that could use some good bucking horses and I thought we could come up with something that would be beneficial to all of us. Can I come out to the ranch this morning and look at what you have?"

"Sure. I'll be home all day."

He disconnected the call and went back inside the restaurant.

"Everything okay?" his dad asked.

"More than okay." Coy suddenly found his appetite had tripled and he waved Maggie over. "Can I get a side order of pancakes?"

"Coming right up." Maggie turned to walk away.

"And bacon!" he called after her.

He turned his attention back to his father. "Now let's talk about me buying the campground from you."

Frank laughed. "That's not possible."

"Why not?" He cracked his knuckles. Was his father going to hold his leaving against him?

"Didn't anyone ever tell you to read something before you sign it?"

"What are you talking about?"

Frank let out a sigh. "You already own the campground. You always have. I never transferred it out of your name. I knew sooner or later you would come back home."

"I thought I signed it over to you." His heart began to race. "If it's still in my name, what did I sign?"

"You gave me power of attorney to handle the insurance and taxes while you were gone."

"Why didn't you tell me?"

"I knew you weren't ready for the responsibility yet and I didn't want to pressure you."

Adrenaline flooded his body. The campground was already his? He couldn't believe it. "Does Stacy know?"

"No." Frank shook his head. "I didn't want her to pressure you, either."

Coy didn't want to believe that his cousin would have tried to talk him into leaving the rodeo circuit and returning to Coronado. But before Caden came along, Stacy was juggling her mother's illness and financial issues with the market. What would he have done if she'd asked him to come home and help her?

Thank goodness he never had to make that choice.

"You'll have to iron out a few details with Stacy." Frank used his toast to sop up the eggs left on his plate. "She's been running that place for a long time."

Coy nodded. "I had dinner with her last night and she gave me a crash course in campground management. For the last nine months, I thought I was managing the campgrounds for her. Turns out, I was just handling the maintenance. I don't know if I'll ever be able to repay her for everything she's done."

"She's the only thing that kept it afloat, that's for sure." Frank picked up a napkin and wiped his mustache. "Did you talk about compensation?"

"I told her I wanted to pay her for everything she's done, but she said that you already paid her a portion of all the profits for managing the place and I didn't owe her a thing."

Frank snorted. "I did, but it wasn't nearly enough."

"Agreed," Coy said. "That's why I intend to continue paying her the same portion of the profits from the cabin rentals in exchange for her running the website and social media for Whispering Pines. Goodness knows I can't do it."

"That's a nice gesture, but you've got to have enough money to operate on, and if you're planning to buy more horses, you'll have a lot more overhead."

"I've got some money saved up," he said. "But if the idea you gave me pans out, it'll provide some extra income."

Frank gave him a puzzled look. "What idea?"

"If some of Noah's horses buck as well as he says, I'm hoping to sell them to one of the stock contractors for the rodeo circuit. I might even be able to talk him into trading some of his saddle-trained horses for Noah's."

"Not a bad idea," Frank said. "Do you think the contractor will be interested?"

Coy shrugged. "I hope so, but we don't have the best history."

Frank laughed. "What did you do? Call him out on what he was doing wrong?"

"Something like that," Coy muttered. "I just hope he realizes it's more profitable for both of us to do business than to hold a grudge. I'm going to run out to Noah's ranch after breakfast and check out the horses before I give Scott a call."

Maggie appeared again and placed the rest of his food in front of them. "Want me to bring you a to-go box for whatever you don't finish?"

"I'll finish it." Coy picked up a strip of bacon.

Frank held his coffee cup out for a refill. As soon as she walked away, he gave Coy a serious look.

"Do any of these newfound plans have anything to do with Becky being back in town?"

"Yes and no." Coy could see the concern in his father's eyes. "The other day, Stacy told me I was lost and needed to find my purpose. I've been scared to do anything without Becky. But maybe if I take this step, it'll show Becky that I'm ready to grow up and settle down."

"You finally gonna ask that girl to marry you?" Frank smiled. "'Bout time."

Coy avoided looking his father right in the eye. "We'll see."

BECKY PULLED IN front of the barn at Whispering Pines. The sliding doors to the breezeway of the barn were closed and she couldn't see any light coming from under the door or around the crack. She glanced at the clock on the dashboard of her truck. She told him she would be here before eight and it was seven thirty. Where was he?

She got out and closed the door. With her medical bag in one hand, she approached the sliding door. Country music blared from within and she breathed a sigh of relief. She slid the door open and went inside. The familiar smell of hay, oats and dust swirled in the air and she followed the sound of the music to the office.

Coy was standing with his back to the door. The wall in front of him had been covered with white butcher paper and there were scribblings all over the paper. She leaned against the door frame and watched him as he tapped his foot to the beat of the music. He had a black marker in his hand and was making notes underneath large squares drawn on the paper. Arrows and lines stretched all over, connecting different boxes.

Becky had never seen him so entranced in anything before. Well, except for when he was getting ready to ride a bull. She wanted to get a closer look at what he was writing but she dared not disturb him.

A soft *click* echoed in the room when he snapped the lid onto the marker. He turned around and gave her a cockeyed grin. "I thought I heard your truck," he said. "Long day?"

"Yeah." She nodded. "The vet covering for Dr. Evans's office in Springerville got sick so I had to spend most of the day at the office before I could do my own rounds."

"Want some coffee?" He nodded toward the back counter where a fresh pot of coffee sat.

"I would love some, but I better not. If I drink coffee this late, I'll never get to sleep."

He grinned and poured a cup. He handed it to her. "It's decaf."

"Since when do you drink decaf?" He'd never been much of a coffee drinker to begin with. He never had more than one cup in the mornings, and even that wasn't very often.

"Stacy likes to come over in the mornings and

she can't have too much caffeine, so I started making decaf for her." He handed her two packets of sugar and two cream ones.

Becky opened the packets and stirred them into her coffee. Coy and Stacy had always been close when they were growing up. They were more like siblings than cousins. "I bet she enjoys having you back in town."

Coy poured himself a cup and leaned against the counter. "Mostly she enjoys having a quiet place to escape from the chaos that has become her life."

Becky chuckled and took a long drink. "Mmm. It's not too bad."

"You get used to it." He caught her gaze and held it.

The intensity of his stare sent heat waves down her spine. "I better go check on Maze."

He didn't follow her to the stall, which gave her a moment to collect herself. Being apart for so long was supposed to make it easier to ignore the way Coy always made her feel. Instead, it only seemed to intensify.

"How does it look?" he asked when she returned to the office.

"It's looking a lot better," she said. "Tomorrow morning we can take the soak bag off and wrap it."

"Will you be here in the morning to do it, or should I plan on doing it myself?"

She wasn't looking forward to the long drive back to the ranch. Maybe she could get a room at

Beaverhead Lodge. Normally, she would rent a cabin here, but that didn't seem like a good idea. "I'm not sure," she said, fighting a yawn. "Depends on what's on the agenda in the morning."

Coy's eyebrows raised slightly. "You don't have to drive all the way to the Springerville office before starting your calls, do you?"

She shrugged. "I'm driving in from the ranch, so it's on the way."

"That's over two hours away. Why don't you stay at your house?"

Becky poured herself some more coffee. "My parents sold the house here in Coronado, so for now I'm driving back and forth from the ranch."

His face softened with concern. "You can stay here. We have a couple of empty cabins. No strings attached."

She took a calming breath and prepared to address the elephant in the room. "Did you sign the papers?"

He ran his fingers through his hair. "I know I didn't handle things very well when…" He swallowed. "When you lost the baby. I'm sorry. But that doesn't mean you should give up on us."

"I didn't handle things very well, either." Becky crossed her arms over her chest. "But it's not about that anymore. I've had a lot of time to think since then and I've come to realize that it wasn't working. It hadn't been working for a long time."

He licked his lips. "That's because I was always

on the road and you were at school. But that's different now."

She closed her eyes and rubbed her temples. "I wish it was that simple, Coy. I do."

"It is." His voice was confident. "At least it can be."

The pounding of her heart had been replaced by a hollow feeling in the pit of her stomach. It was hard to swallow, but she cleared her throat and faced him.

"Maybe we became so comfortable with each other, we stopped trying. We've been together since we were kids, so I think we were going through the motions of being a couple, not because we loved each other, but because it was easy."

His blue eyes searched hers. "Loving someone should be easy. Maybe we did get too comfortable. I know I took you for granted, but I never stopped loving you."

Her heart ripped a little more, if that was even possible. "I've spent most of my adult life following you around and putting off my own dreams. I'm not doing that anymore. I have to start a new life." She looked up at him and whispered, "I love you, too, but I can't be with you anymore."

He lifted his chin, the muscles in his jaw tight. "I never asked you to do that. I never stopped you from going back to school. You chose to put it off."

"You're right," she acknowledged. "I stayed because I thought you needed me more than I needed school, not realizing that I was losing more and more of myself along the way."

He gave her a level gaze. "So it seems that you're just as lost as I am."

He stepped closer to her. His fingertips traced lightly up one arm. "Let's find each other together."

She sighed. "Did you look over the papers?"

"No," he said. "But I will make a deal with you."

A deal? Her heart wasn't up to negotiation. Curiosity got the best of her, however. "What kind of deal?"

"Noah Sterling has a contract with a company that manages wild horses. His contract is for off-range pastures. I'm applying for an off-range corral contract." Coy picked up a brochure off his desk and handed it to her.

She flipped through the brochure. "You want to be an adoption center for Noah's wild horses? Are you going to close the campground to do this?"

"Of course not," he said. "I'm hoping that it will actually attract more people to Whispering Pines. It'll also give me a large pool of horses to pick from to train for use at the campground and I'm hoping that if visitors see a horse they want to adopt, they'll be willing to pay me to train it for them."

She had to admit, it was a well-thought-out plan. "What does it have to do with an agreement between us?"

"I went to Noah's ranch today. He has a few horses he's been working with that are already saddle broke, but they need more training," he said. "I want to train them to use here, at Whispering Pines."

She frowned. "What kind of timeline are you thinking? I'm only in town until Dr. Evans returns."

He gave her a long look. "I want to do a reopening of sorts on the Fourth of July. It'll kick off with a trail ride, so I need them ready by then."

When Coy's grandfather was alive, almost every day started with a sunrise trail ride and every week ended with a picnic. But nothing compared to the Fourth of July. Coronado was packed for Independence Day, so the campground hosted trail rides all day, a barbecue and sometimes even a dance. When he died, the Fourth of July celebrations ended.

Stacy still held a trail ride and picnic on Labor Day weekend in September. Becky and Coy always came back to Coronado to help Stacy with that celebration. After Stacy sold most of the horses, they stopped offering trail rides at all. One family consistently spent a week at the campground every Labor Day weekend, but the Mitchells brought their own horses.

"That's a pretty tight deadline." She didn't doubt Coy's ability to work with horses that were ready to be trained. But horses that had grown up in the wild? It was risky since there was no way of knowing about their background.

He shrugged. "We can do it."

"I'll help, but my own job has to come first," she said.

"Agreed."

Her heart thumped inside her chest. Every year, when they returned to the campground to help with the trail ride for the Mitchell family, she secretly hoped Coy would be ready to stay. But by the time the weekend was over, he was going stir-crazy and couldn't wait to get back on the road.

Maybe he was finally ready to settle down. "It'll be nice to see trail rides happening again."

He grinned. "A trail ride, barbecue and even a dance thanks to the music of Luke Sterling."

She raised one eyebrow. "Luke is going to perform for you?"

He nodded. "And Abbie is going to cater it."

"Sounds like you have big plans."

"I do," he told her.

She pressed her lips together. "If I help you with the training, you'll sign the papers?"

His face tightened. Finally, he looked at her and nodded. "If you still want a divorce after Independence Day weekend, I'll sign the papers."

Relief flooded through her. She glanced at the clock on the wall. It was almost nine and she groaned. "I better head out. It's a long drive."

"You shouldn't drive down the mountain this late." Coy frowned. "Cabin Six is empty. It's the closest one to the barn."

"Where is your cabin?" She wanted to stay, but she needed to keep some distance between them.

"On the other side of the campground," he said. "I'm in Pap's cabin."

She scrunched her face, trying to decide what to do.

"Just stay," Coy said softly. "Once the horses get here, I'm going to need you close by, anyway."

"Okay, but this doesn't change anything."

# *CHAPTER SIX*

It was still dark when Coy stepped out of his cabin. He put on his cowboy hat and breathed in the crisp morning air. He'd slept better last night than he had in months. Just knowing Becky was in the vicinity helped him relax.

Instead of driving his truck on the loop that circled the edge of the campground, he took the road that cut through the center, passing by the cabins. Normally, he didn't drive through the middle that early in the morning because his pickup truck was loud and he didn't want to risk waking anyone up. While the campground had been full for the Memorial Day weekend a couple of weeks ago, it was now mostly empty, except for Becky and a group of fishermen who liked to be on the lake when the sun came up.

As he approached Becky's cabin, he noticed all the lights were still off, and his chest tightened. He knew she wanted to check Maze's foot, so his plan was to give her a ride to the barn, ply her with coffee and offer to take her out for breakfast. She rarely slept past 5 a.m., so if she was still asleep she was either sick or exhausted. Given her schedule yesterday, he picked the latter. Disappointment flooded him, but he drove past the cabin and headed for the barn.

After feeding the horses, he started mucking the stalls. He was on the last stall when he heard a noise in the entryway. It was either Becky or Stacy. His heart sped up like a jackrabbit. "Back here," he called.

There was no answer, but he heard someone go into the office. It must be Stacy, here for her morning cup. He finished the stall and went to join her.

When he got to the doorway, he stopped short. Becky was standing in the middle of the room, studying the wall above his desk.

She glanced at him and nodded at the Post-it notes covering the wall. "What's all this?"

"My kanban board."

She gave him an odd look, but turned her attention back to the columns that outlined his plans for Whispering Pines. "Marketing. Recreation. Expansion. I'm impressed."

Coy leaned against the door frame and crossed his arms. "You're the one who taught me how to use them."

"Not that." She shook her head. "Your plans. They're very detailed. You really do have a lot of great ideas for Whispering Pines."

He shrugged. "They aren't all mine. Some of

them are things Stacy and I talked about when we were kids. Some of them came from you."

"Me?" She looked at him in confusion.

"We stayed at a lot of campgrounds when we were on the road," he said. "You always had a lot to say about them. Some good. Some bad."

Her brown eyes widened and she looked at the list again. She touched one Post-it. "No dumpsters near the cooking area."

He nodded. "Remember those campgrounds in Salt Lake? We were going to cook hamburgers on the grill but the smell from the dumpsters ruined our appetite. That's all you talked about for days."

"You remembered that?"

"I remember lots of things," he said as he walked over to the coffeepot and poured them both a cup. "Like how you like your coffee." He handed her two packets each of cream and sugar.

"Thanks."

She averted her gaze from his, but he could see the conflict in her eyes and smiled. She didn't want to remember the good times because it would make it harder for her to walk away. Well, he wasn't going to make it easy for her. He was going to remind her about all the reasons they should stay together.

She set her mug on the desk to open the packets and pour their contents into her coffee. As she stirred the coffee, she picked up the brochure from the Wild Horse Management Program. "You're really going to train wild horses?"

He nodded. "It's a win-win for both Noah and me. He already provides pastures for the program, but his ranch is too far out to attract many buyers. Whispering Pines is in a more strategic location, and it'll attract buyers, but it might also attract campers."

"When do you start?"

Coy flinched. *You.* Not *we.* "My main goal is being ready for Fourth of July, so I'm focusing on the campground right now. I'll finish the application process after that."

Her brow furrowed. "So you won't need to contract with a veterinarian until you finish applying?"

He could see the wheels in her head spinning and wondered if she was already trying to figure out a way to get out of their deal. "Technically, no. But I still need to have horses ready for the Fourth."

She took a long drink from her coffee before setting the cup in the sink. "I better check on Maze and then get started on my rounds. I'll see you later."

He was tempted to follow her, but he knew she liked her space while she was working, so he sat at his desk and turned on the ancient computer. Stacy had told him how to access the program that she used when people booked rooms. He just hoped he could remember how to do it.

The screen finally lit up and after a few more minutes, everything finished loading. He opened the browser and went to the website that Stacy used for managing the cabin rentals. It only took him two tries to log in and he spent the next few minutes learning how to navigate the site.

A small chime sounded and a notification popped up on his screen. He grinned and picked up his phone to call Stacy.

"What's up?" Stacy answered on the first ring.

One leg bounced as excitement rushed through him. "I'm on the website and got a notification that a cabin was booked. Do I need to do anything?"

"Do you see a confirmation number?"

He squinted at the screen. "Yes."

"Then all you have to do is make sure the cabin is ready for them when they arrive. Can you see when they plan to check in?"

"This evening," he said.

"Great," Stacy said. "Guests stop at the market to sign in and pick up the keys, but I guess I should start having them go straight to the campground."

"Not yet, if you don't mind doing it a little longer." Coy wanted to wait until he was more comfortable with the system before she turned everything completely over to him. "I'm heading out to Noah's ranch soon and I may not be back until late this afternoon."

"Don't worry. If your guests get here before you, I'll make sure they're taken care of."

"Thanks." He disconnected the call and stared at the screen again. A total of six cabins would be rented out for the weekend.

He'd already planned on making sure campers were aware of all the activities that were available at Whispering Pines. But first, he had to acquire more horses. Scott had agreed to trade saddle-broke horses for good bucking horses. Noah's horses looked promising. Today he would find out for sure.

He stepped out of the office and into the main area of the barn. Maze stuck her head over the fence of her stall and snorted. He hadn't even heard Becky leave. After making sure Becky had removed the soak bag, he opened the gate and led Maze to the pasture with the other horses.

In the tack room, he gathered a few things he might need. A couple of ropes, some leather riggings, a halter and a saddle made specifically for bronc riding. He'd seen cowboys have their pelvic bone broken by the saddle horn while riding, so the hornless saddle would come in handy today. He knew firsthand how painful a broken pelvis was and he had no desire to go through that again. It was a bull's hoof that broke his, but he couldn't imagine that the pain would be any different if it was caused by a saddle horn.

He tossed his equipment in the back of the truck

and got into the cab. The drive to the Double S Ranch took almost half an hour and Noah was waiting for him at the barn when he arrived.

"Morning," Noah greeted him. "You're by yourself? I thought you might bring Caden with you."

Coy had competed against Caden in high school. Caden had been a champion team roper and he wasn't bad at bronc riding, either. After high school, he'd joined the army instead of the rodeo circuit.

"I thought about it, but he's pretty busy trying to get their house finished before the baby gets here." He grabbed his stuff from the bed of the truck. "Besides, I wouldn't want to be on the receiving end of Stacy's wrath if something happened and he got hurt."

Noah laughed. "Luke probably wouldn't be too happy about that, either. You know they're going into business together?"

He nodded. "I heard. Do they think there's enough business in Coronado to keep them open?"

"Absolutely not." Noah held open the barn door for him. "It'll be a part-time gig at the most. Fortunately, neither one of them is relying on it as a main source of income. I think it's more of a community service than anything."

Coy shifted the ropes over his shoulder and followed him to one of the corrals behind the barn. He dropped his equipment at the edge of the fence and watched the horses in the pen.

"How long have you been working with this group?"

Noah hooked one foot on the bottom rung of the fence. "I started working with these about a year ago, but after not making any progress for six months, I put them back out to pasture."

He opened the gate and stepped into the corral. The horses shifted nervously, but showed no sign of aggression. He scanned their undercarriage and was glad to see they were all mares. Stallions were too unpredictable, especially when in the company of mares.

For a few minutes, he walked around the edges of the corral, not attempting to approach any of them. Curiosity got the best of one roan mare and she stepped closer to him. She lifted her head and sniffed the air. Coy reached into his top pocket and pulled out a slice of an apple. He held it in his palm and extended his arm with his hand flat. The horse took another step forward and plucked the treat from his hand.

He glanced at Noah. "Are they all this friendly?"

"Nope." Noah nodded toward the end of the property. "We got a few that are meaner than snakes. They're in the back pasture. I wouldn't waste your time with them."

Noah was one of the best horsemen he knew, so he trusted the man's opinion when it came to horses. And with an entire herd of horses to choose from, he didn't need to waste his time trying to break horses that didn't want to be broken.

Coy's plan was to find out why these horses didn't want to be broken. Were they stubborn? Or did they just like to buck? There was only one way to find out.

He grinned at Noah. "Let's get to work."

BECKY STOOD AT the sink in Robert Watson's barn, scrubbing her arms with soap and water. Mr. Watson had already secured his cow and was waiting patiently for her to tell him if the cow was pregnant or not. She'd just slipped her waterproof apron over her clothes and was pulling the shoulder-length gloves on when her phone began to ring. She ignored the call as she coated the glove with a lubricant and approached the back end of the cow.

She was up to her elbow inside the cow, carefully palpating the uterus, when her phone rang again. It rang three more times while she was trying to confirm the size of the fetus.

One of Mr. Watson's sons stood to the side, watching the procedure with great interest. "Can you answer that for me?" She nodded at her phone sitting on the cabinet near the entrance to the barn. "Just put it on speaker and bring it over here."

The teenage boy did as she asked and held the phone close to her.

"This is Dr. Maxwell," she said, learning farther into the cow.

"Dr. Maxwell," a man's voice said, "this is Clarence Whitmire. I need you out at my ranch right now."

"What's going on?" It seemed like everyone who called expected her to drop everything and go to them. Rarely was it an emergency.

"One of my heifers is down. Her stomach's bloated something awful."

She pulled her arm out of the cow and removed her gloves. "How long has she been down?"

"That's just it." Desperation laced his voice. "I don't know. I've been out of town, so my neighbor was feeding my cows for me and I just got home. I don't know if she's been down ten minutes or ten hours."

"I'm on my way." She dropped the gloves into the trash bin and removed the apron. "I'll be there in fifteen minutes."

"Do you know where my ranch is?"

"Yes, sir." She'd been to his ranch at least a hundred times, but she didn't want to waste time explaining how she knew who he was.

She glanced at Mr. Watson.

"Don't you worry about us," he said. "We'll be here when you're done."

"Thank you." She washed her hands and arms as quickly and thoroughly as she could. "I'll be back to finish later."

She got into her truck and headed for the Lazy W Ranch as fast as she could on a dirt road. When she pulled into the barnyard, she was met by Clarence Whitmire, a weathered-looking man in his late sixties. She hopped out of the truck and tightened the ponytail holding her hair back.

"Take me to her." She grabbed her medical bag off the seat.

"She's out in the back pasture. I couldn't get her to the barn." He nodded toward a side-by-side parked next to the barn.

Becky had barely jumped into the UTV before Mr. Whitmire started down a path that ran next to the fence. "I hope she hasn't lain down."

"My wife is with her," Mr. Whitmire said. "She's trying to keep her up and moving."

The side-by-side bounced along the path and Becky held on to the seat to keep from getting knocked into the man. As they topped the ridge, Becky scanned the pasture for the cow, but only saw a woman frantically waving her arms.

She jumped out of the UTV before it had come to a full stop and tossed her medical bag over the fence. She ducked between two strands of barbed wire. Without waiting to see if Mr. Whitmire was following, she picked up her bag and sprinted through the tall grass to the woman.

"She lay down as you were coming in sight." The woman wrung her hands. "I'm sorry, I couldn't get her to stand back up."

Becky knelt down next to the heifer and ran her hands over the large, extended stomach. The cow looked at her with soft brown eyes and she struggled for breath. She said a silent prayer of thanks that the cow was on her right side.

"I got you," she murmured softly as she pulled a corkscrew trocar from her bag. She handed it to the woman. "Hold this a second."

With swift movements, she opened a bottle of alcohol and poured it on the cow's stomach. Under normal circumstances, she would take her time sanitizing the area, but time wasn't something the cow had a lot of. She poured more alcohol over her scalpel and then made a small X-shaped incision, pressing hard enough to go through the cow's hide. Even without taking the time to administer anesthesia, the cow barely flinched.

Her heart leaped to her throat. "Don't you quit on me now," she warned the animal under her breath. She took the trocar from the woman, doused it with alcohol as well and inserted the end into the incision as far as she could push and then began to twist it farther into the cow. The moment she removed the needle from the inside of the trocar, air began to escape.

Within a few moments, the cow's labored breathing began to ease.

"You did a trocar already?" Mr. Whitmire said from behind her, his breath coming in gasps.

His wife nodded. "It was the fastest thing I've ever seen."

Becky couldn't help but feel a surge of pride.

She pushed on the cow's abdomen, making sure the gas was still escaping. "It's the fastest way to relieve the pressure. I didn't want to waste time trying to tube her."

Mr. Whitmire wiped the sweat off his forehead with a handkerchief. "I have to admit, I was a little worried when Dr. Evans's office gave me your number. I haven't had the best experience with brand-new vets."

Becky stiffened. She didn't want to take it personally, but since most of the people around here knew her, it was hard not to. "I grew up on a ranch myself, so I know how urgent this can get. I'm just glad I got here in time."

"You definitely know your way around cattle. Where'd you study?"

"Arizona State and then Texas A&M," she said. "But I started working for Dr. Evans when I was sixteen, so between summers on my father's ranch and working for the clinic, I've got more experience than a lot of new vets."

Why did she feel the need to defend herself? George Walker must have gotten into her head more than she realized. The heifer lifted her head and rolled over in an attempt to stand. Becky moved to assist the cow if she needed it.

Once the cow was on her feet, Mrs. Whitmire rubbed her nose and wrapped a rope loosely around her neck. The animal was still weak, but she began to follow the rancher's wife without much argument.

"She'll need some time to recover, and I'm sure you already know this, but you'll want to keep her off feed for a bit—hay only for the next twenty-four hours. I'll leave you with some anti-gas meds in case the pressure isn't going down fast enough. I'll be back in about a week to remove the trocar."

The man reached out to shake her hand. "Thank you, Doc. Really. You were amazing."

"You're welcome." Her chest swelled as she accepted his handshake. The simple gesture carried more weight than just a simple thank-you. It was an act of respect and one that Becky hadn't seen a lot since she started. "I'm just glad I made it here in time."

He cocked his head and stared at her for a moment. "You look real familiar. Have we met outside of the animal clinic?"

She laughed. It was possible that she spent more time at his ranch than her own during rodeo season. In addition to being a rancher, Mr. Whitmire had been Coy's bull riding coach. "Yes, sir. I was at your arena almost every weekend."

"Arena?" His eyebrows furrowed for a moment. The moment he recognized her, his eyes widened. "That's right. You're Coy Tedford's gal, ain't ya?"

"I was." She nodded and gathered her things and put them in her bag.

"How is he?" Mr. Whitmire reached out to take

her bag for her. "I saw his ride in Fort Worth. It was a bad fall."

"I believe he retired," she said. "He's running Whispering Pines now."

Mr. Whitmire started walking toward the UTV. "That's a shame. I didn't realize the fall was that bad."

She hadn't, either. He'd suffered worse injuries and never considered giving up. So why now? She followed behind Mr. Whitmire as she thought about that. Did he do it for her?

He stopped at the fence and put one booted foot on the second string of barbed wire from the bottom and lifted the row of wire above it.

Becky lifted her leg and stepped through the gap before ducking down and sliding under the wire. Standing up, she turned and did the same for him.

They arrived back at the barn before Mrs. Whitmire did, so Becky followed him inside to help prepare a stall to keep the heifer in. One wall inside the barn was covered with pictures of all the cowboys Mr. Whitmire had coached over the years.

A large picture of Tommy Littlebear was in the center, surrounded by pictures of Tommy riding bulls, helping other cowboys get ready or hanging out in the pens. Coy appeared in more than half of the pictures.

One picture caught her eye and she paused. It was a picture of Coy and Tommy sitting on the tailgate of Coy's pickup truck. She and Maggie,

Tommy's wife, stood in front of them. It was taken at the last rodeo that the men attended together. Shortly after that picture, Coy joined the rodeo circuit and Tommy went to work full-time for the Hotshots.

Her gaze drifted to the rest of the pictures. A large portion of the wall was dedicated to Coy, complete with newspaper clippings about his wins. Most people thought Coy just loved riding bulls, but she knew it was more than that. He loved the challenge. And he loved being at the center of attention.

Which made her wonder, again, why he'd really retired.

# *CHAPTER SEVEN*

RIDING...TRYING TO ride a horse that was dead set on bucking you off wasn't easy. But after spending the afternoon trying to do just that, Coy knew his idea was solid. Adrenaline rushed through him as he headed toward his truck. Experience told him that as soon as it wore off, soreness and pain would set in.

He pulled his phone from his back pocket and scrolled through the contacts. He paused on one number, took a deep breath and hit the call button.

"Hello?"

"Hi, Scott." He kept his voice light. "This is Coy Tedford."

"What do you want, Coy?"

Apparently Scott still held a grudge against him. "I'd like to buy some horses from you?"

"Really?" Sarcasm laced the man's voice. "Why would you want some of my *inferior* horses?"

Scott Griffin bred horses for one purpose: to buck. Unfortunately, he hadn't hit on the magic formula yet and many of his horses weren't good enough for the circuit. Coy had told him so on more than one occasion.

Coy knew his request would have to be worded correctly to avoid insulting the man further. "I never said your horses were inferior. You've got great horses. I only pointed out that most of them weren't born to buck." He paused for a moment. "But I don't want bucking broncs. I'm looking for some gentle, saddle-broke horses."

"Right," Scott huffed. "For half of what they're worth. No, thank you."

Coy clenched his teeth. He knew Scott was always looking to sell the horses he couldn't use for the circuit. Just not to him.

"I'll give you a fair price," Coy said. "And I happened to find a few horses that were born to buck. I think they would be a great addition to your stock."

"Are you getting into the contracting business now?" Scott's voice was cold.

"Oh no," he said. "I have no desire to compete with you. I'm running my family's campground now. I need some good horses for trail rides and I have great bucking horses. I think we can make a deal that benefits us both."

"I'd have to take a look at them before making a deal," Scott said. "But I don't have time to go anywhere right now. You'll have to bring them to me."

Irritation flared in his chest. Scott wanted him to haul horses to Phoenix so he could have a look at them? His first inclination was to thank him for his time and hang up the phone. He took a deep cleansing breath. "Let me clear my schedule and I'll be there in a couple of days."

He disconnected the call and started the truck. By the time Coy got back to town, every muscle in his body ached and the longer he sat in his truck, the worse it got.

He stopped at the Coronado Market. He needed some ibuprofen and ice. Lots of ice. Despite the aches and pains, he was feeling better than he had in months and whistled as he limped inside.

Stacy stood behind the cash register. "What's wrong with you?"

"Nothing. Nothing at all." He winked at her.

Her green eyes narrowed. "Why are you whistling?"

"Because things are working out." He walked to the medicine aisle and scanned the items for the pain reliever he wanted.

He picked the biggest bottle he could find and hobbled back to the counter. "I need about six bags of ice, too."

"Seriously, what happened to you?" Stacy's voice was firm.

Coy handed her some money. "Relax, coz. I'm not hurt. Just sore."

Her brow furrowed. "Sore from what?"

"I'm out of shape. It's been a while since I rode horses all afternoon."

Before she could question him too much, he took

his change and headed out the door, stopping only long enough to get bags of ice from the ice machine outside. He opened his truck door and got into the cab, wincing slightly when his muscles protested the movement.

He opened the pill bottle and swallowed a couple of pills before starting his truck. The dirt road from the main highway to the campground was rougher than he remembered it being that morning and he felt every bump.

When the barn came into sight, he let out a sigh of relief. He parked and carried the bags of ice to the office and put them in the freezer section of the refrigerator. There were several oversize metal tubs sitting in the wash stall across from the office. Coy found the largest one and pulled it to the middle of the room.

After rinsing it out, he filled it halfway with cold water before adding the bags of ice to it. He pulled his boots off, followed by his jeans and the long-sleeve western shirt he wore over his T-shirt. Wearing only his boxers and his T-shirt, he stepped into the tub and sank into the cold water.

He groaned as the cold water rushed over him, but he inhaled deeply and let it out slowly, forcing his muscles to relax. After a few moments, the shock wore off and he leaned against the edge of the tub, with his arms on the edges. He let his head fall back and closed his eyes.

"What are you doing?"

Coy jumped. He looked up to see Becky standing next to the entryway. "I'm taking an ice bath."

"I can see that," she said. "Why?"

Irritation flared in him at her tone. Why was she looking at him like he'd committed a crime? She was the one who taught him how and when to use ice baths. "I'm sore."

Her mouth pressed into a hard line. "From what?"

"From working with horses at Noah's today." He started to stand up, then thought better of it. "Hand me one of those towels, please."

Becky glanced at the towels stacked close to the tub. She picked up the top one and handed it to him. "So you're really planning on training some of the wild horses to use at Whispering Pines?"

"Yes, but those aren't the ones I was looking at today." He unfolded the towel and held it as wide as he could before he stood up. He wrapped the towel around his waist and stepped out of the tub, then grabbed another towel to dry off with.

She reached up and tightened her ponytail with both hands. "Then what were you doing?"

He didn't want to answer her. Would she think it foolish of him to be testing out the bucking ability of horses that he had no guarantee of selling? "I'm going to try to sell them to Scott Griffin."

Her eyebrows furrowed. "I thought Scott contracted bucking broncs."

"He does." Coy rubbed the towel briskly over his legs to warm them up.

Her eyes narrowed. "Then why are you trying to sell him some of Noah's horses?"

He wrapped a third towel around his shoulders and tried not to let her hear his teeth chattering. "Noah has some horses with the bucking gene."

She rolled her eyes. "I'm pretty sure that doesn't exist."

He shrugged and looked around for his pants. A moment later, he spotted them in a crumpled pile on the ground next to his boots. "Let's agree to disagree."

"How do you test for that?"

Holding the towel around him with one hand, he picked up his pants and walked barefoot to the office. "Only one way that I know of."

She followed him. "Why doesn't Noah do it? He's the one selling the horses."

"I can't let Noah have all the fun."

"I thought you wanted to turn Whispering Pines into a world-class guest ranch." She lifted her chin. "How can you do that if you get hurt?"

He ran a hand through his damp hair. "I'm not going to get hurt. I know my limits."

"Do you?" she shot back, her voice rising. "Because it seems like you're always finding new ways to test them. If you miss the rodeo that much, go back."

"I'm not going anywhere," he said firmly. A slight breeze blew through the open aisle of the barn and he shivered. "Let me get dressed, then we'll talk."

He stepped inside the bathroom in the office and felt the warmth slowly return to his body as he pulled on his clothes and boots. Once he was fully clothed, he stepped back into the breezeway where she was exiting Maze's stall. When she saw him, she stood still, her posture rigid.

He leaned against the railing of one of the stalls. "I don't want to go back to the rodeo. I'm just trying to find a way to give Whispering Pines the boost it needs."

"Explain to me how riding wild horses is going to do that. I thought you were wanting ones you could train for the campground."

"I do. But that takes time. If I want to make the campground a place that draws people in, I need good horses now. I don't have the resources to buy ones that are already trained, but I can buy Noah's horses. Scott needs bucking horses and I need saddle-broke ones."

She nodded. "So you want to trade bucking horses to Scott for ones he already has trained."

"Right," he said. "I just need a few to get us started."

"Us?" She raised one eyebrow.

"Us." He reached out and took her hand, squeezing it gently. "I can build this campground into something great. Something to be proud of. I just need time."

Becky looked down at their joined hands, and pulled away. "You've traded one obsession for another, I see."

He frowned. "What do you mean?"

"It means that you're always chasing something. First a buckle, now a business. But once you get it, what will you do? You're never satisfied."

Coy dropped his hands to his sides. "What's wrong with wanting to be the best I can be? With being successful?"

"Nothing," she said. "But at some point, you have to stop chasing success and be happy with what you have."

"That's easy for you to say. Your future has never depended on your success."

"Excuse me?" It was clear he'd insulted her. "I'm pretty sure my entire future hinged on my graduating from vet school."

"No, it didn't. Your plans did. Your dreams did. But not your future." He shook his head. "The worst thing that would've happened was that you would have had to go back home and take over your dad's ranch."

She pressed her lips together. "I'm just saying that success is what you make it. You don't have to be a rodeo champion, a football star or own a thriving business to be successful."

"Try saying that when you're too poor to buy food."

She rolled her eyes. "Now you're being overly

dramatic. You may have worn a lot of secondhand clothes, but I don't recall you ever going without food."

"My dad didn't become sheriff until I was fifteen. Before that there were days we didn't eat and my dad was too proud to let my mom apply for food stamps. She volunteered at the food bank so she could get a box of food without anyone knowing about it," he said. "Most of my Christmas presents were given to my mother by members of the church. But you wouldn't understand any of that. Your parents are rich. You're rich."

Her eyes narrowed. Money had always been a bone of contention between them. "Is that why you were so determined to win the championship? For money?"

"Why else?" He gave her a crooked smile. "You don't think I liked riding bulls, do you? I was just good at it."

"Nice try," she said. "You loved every minute of it."

He chuckled. He did love it. He loved the excitement, the thrill. He loved having little boys begging him for his autograph. "I did. But what I loved most was that it gave us a way to be together."

"That's funny." Her voice was quiet. "I always thought it was what kept us apart."

He let out a heavy sigh. "Maybe in the end. But that's over now. We can start again."

Becky gave him a puzzled look. "Why did you really retire?"

Alarm bells went off in his head. She was treading into territory he didn't want to discuss. "I got injured."

"You've been injured lots of times. And a lot worse." She crossed her arms. "I've never seen one slow you down, much less stop you."

He shrugged. "I guess without you, it wasn't worth it anymore."

"I never asked you to quit doing what you loved." A hint of sadness filled her brown eyes. "Not for me."

"I know," he breathed. "This time I did it for myself."

Her gaze locked with his. "Good night, Coy."

He watched her walk away, her long ponytail swinging with each step she took. "Becky, wait."

She paused without looking back. "What is it?"

"Would you like to go to dinner tomorrow night?"

"I can't." She turned around to face him. "I'm going to the ranch for the weekend."

At least it wasn't a flat-out no. That gave him a glimmer of hope.

She bit her bottom lip. "What about breakfast?"

He simultaneously felt joy and disappointment. Her willingness to spend more time with him thrilled him, so he hated to tell her no. "I can't. I'm going to an auction in the morning with Noah."

"Okay. See you on Monday."

Coy watched her exit the barn, not moving until he heard her truck leave. He walked over to Shucks's stall. The horse lowered his giant head and pushed against Coy's chest.

He leaned his head against the horse's and stroked his soft neck. Coy's stomach had rolled itself into a knot when she'd asked him why he retired. She wasn't the first person to question his reasons for retirement.

Physically, the doctor had cleared him to return to riding six months after his injury.

Mentally was a different story. It wasn't that he was scared to get back on a bull. He wasn't even scared of getting hurt. It was something else. Something he felt so deeply that he couldn't explain it. The closest way to describe it was that the fire had gone out.

ON SUNDAY MORNING, Becky was up before the sun. She tiptoed down the stairs, pausing outside the kitchen in case her parents were already having their coffee. After hearing nothing but silence, she hurried through the room.

She stopped in the mudroom only long enough to pull on her boots and practically sprinted to the barn. A long horseback ride was the only thing that would relieve the tension building inside of her. And if she didn't release it, she might explode.

The last thing she wanted to do was say something that would hurt her parents.

The barn was dark, but she didn't need any lights to help her find her way. She did, however, need light to help her see when someone blocked her path.

"Oomph!" a voice cried when she ran into them.

"Felipe!" Becky gasped. "I'm sorry. I didn't see you there."

"It's hard to see in the dark." He laughed.

A second later, a light came on and she was surprised to see Felipe dressed in a pair of flannel pajama pants and barefoot. "Why are you sleeping in the barn?"

"Maria is due any day now," he said. "I want to be here if something goes wrong."

Becky frowned. "Would you like me to examine her for you?"

"That would be great, Miss Becky." The young man's green eyes lit up.

She walked through the barn and found the stall where Felipe's horse stood quietly. "Good morning, Maria." Becky let herself into the stall and ran her hands over the mare's abdomen. "Is she waxing?"

"Not yet." Felipe stood at the gate. "She lost her last foal. I don't want anything to go wrong this time."

Becky patted the mare's neck. "I think you have a few days to a week at least. But call me as soon as it's close and I'll be here to help."

"Thank you," he said. "What are you doing up so early?"

She sighed. "I feel like a sunrise ride."

It was on the tip of her tongue to invite him along, but she didn't. She doubted she would be very good company this morning.

"I'll saddle Gollum for you."

"No," Becky said, stopping him. "I can saddle my own horse."

Felipe nodded, but followed her to the tack room and then to Gollum's stall. He stood close by while she got the bay gelding ready for the saddle.

"Your father is putting a lot of pressure on you, isn't he?"

Becky nodded. "How did you know?"

"I know a lot of things." He gave her a grin, showing off the deep dimples in his chubby face. "Especially when your parents argue over it in the barn."

"They were arguing? About me?" She lifted up the saddle and placed it over Gollum's back. "What did they say?"

Felipe had been her biggest confidant when they were children. He'd worked on the ranch his entire life and he knew how to fade into the background when he needed to.

"The usual." He shrugged. "Levi wants you to commit to taking over the ranch. Your mother wants him to let you make your own decisions."

"He knows you could handle things if he wanted

to take a vacation, or even cut back on the work. You practically run the place now."

"Yes, he knows I'll take care of anything he needs. But it's not the same as knowing the ranch will stay in the family."

"Why is he pushing this now? Is there something he's not telling me? Is he sick?"

"No," he said, laughing. Then he gave her a look so serious that it reminded her of her father. "Why don't you want to take over the ranch?"

"You know why." Her gaze swept over his pajamas. "Change clothes and come for a ride with me."

He didn't say a word, but disappeared into the barn's sleeping quarters. Becky went to the stall of Felipe's second-favorite horse and saddled it for him. Ten minutes later, he reappeared, this time dressed in jeans, a western shirt and boots. A large white Stetson topped his head.

By the time they rode out of the barnyard, streaks of pink and gold were starting to paint the sky. They rode in silence for a long time. Felipe was good at that. He not only had a sixth sense with animals, he had one with her, too, and could sense when she was ready to talk and when she wasn't.

A heavy weight pressed down on her. Coming to Arizona was supposed to help her find closure. Instead, she had been served a heavy portion of guilt by her dad.

"Why is it selfish for me to want to establish my own career before even considering taking over the ranch?"

Felipe let go of the reins, letting them rest on the saddle, and leaned back on the horse's flank. "Levi is worried that if you don't start learning now, you won't be ready when the time comes."

"Don't you dare take his side!"

"I'm not," he said. "But I've seen how much of himself he puts into this ranch. It's his legacy. It's only right that he wants to share that with his only child."

"For five years I postponed finishing school to put Coy's bull riding career first. Now, when I'm finally able to focus on my own career and my own dreams, my dad wants me to put the ranch first." She let out a loud huff of air. "The entire Maxwell legacy is resting on my shoulders. Do you have any idea how much pressure that puts on me?"

Felipe gave her a long look. "Can't you find a way to compromise? You love ranch life. You love animals. But you don't want to be a rancher. Why?"

"Maybe I just don't want this ranch." She lifted her chin. "You said you heard my parents arguing in the barn. I've heard them argue in the barn, in the pasture, in the house, in the truck, in the store. Everywhere. I'm probably the only kid who ever wished their parents would divorce and put an end to everyone's misery."

In true Felipe style, he said nothing. He just waited.

"I hated coming to the ranch every weekend. I dreaded watching my parents pretend to be happy in front of me, only to hear them argue behind closed doors." She halted her horse at the top of the ridge they'd been working their way up. "Look at this. It's beautiful. And it's mine, as far as the eye can see. But I'd give it up in a heartbeat if it meant my parents could be happy together."

"They are happy, *mija*," Felipe said softly. "I know you don't see it, now. Over the last few years, they seem to have forgiven each other. But this—" he gestured to the land "—this is the one thing your father will not budge on."

Becky's eyes narrowed as she studied his face. "And you wouldn't, either, would you?"

"No." He sat up straight and faced her. "I was only five when my mother died and I came to this ranch to live with *mi abeulo*. From the moment I stepped foot on this land, I felt a deep connection to it. My *abeulo* felt it, too. That's why he worked this land his entire life. I will, too."

"Why? Why spend your entire life working for something that will never be yours?"

He shrugged. "Why spend your entire life running from something that is?"

Running? She accused Coy of running away from his problems. But she did the exact same thing.

She pressed her lips together. "Felipe, you have too much faith in me."

"Maybe. But I don't think so."

He turned his horse back toward the barn and Becky knew their time was up. He didn't mind riding with her for a while, but animals needed to be fed, ranch hands needed their orders for the day and her father would want an update on it all.

"Thanks for riding with me," she said.

"My pleasure," Felipe replied. He tipped his white Stetson back a little and turned toward her. "Do you want to go back to Texas because of Coy?"

How did he know that? She didn't bother asking because, somehow, Felipe knew everything. "No."

He shot her a look out of the corner of his eye.

"Okay," she said, sighing, "maybe. I'm not sure."

"Not sure if you want Coy or not sure if you want to go back to Texas?"

She licked her lips. "Not sure if I can be this close to Coy and not want him."

Felipe smiled and shook his head. "You wouldn't feel like that if things were really over."

Becky flinched. That was a truth she wasn't ready to face yet. "Race you back to the barn."

She let out a yell and Gollum burst into a run. Leaning close to his neck, she urged him faster, but Felipe caught up in no time. They were both laughing when they reined the horses in outside of the barn.

Her father stepped out of the barn and waited for them to dismount. "Who won?"

"I did, of course." Felipe laughed and gave Levi a high five.

Becky put her hand on one hip. "He cheated."

"Did he? Or are you a sore loser?" Levi grinned. "Your mother has breakfast ready for you."

She left the men to their work and headed into the house. Her mother was standing at the kitchen sink, staring out the window.

"Whatcha looking at?" She walked over to the kitchen table and sat down.

"Nothing." Autumn wiped her hands off on a towel, then filled her coffee cup and sat down across from her. "Are you okay?"

"Why wouldn't I be?" Becky spooned gravy over her biscuits. She wondered if her mother was concerned about the ranch, or her situation with Coy.

"I know your father is pressuring you to move back and take over the ranch," Autumn said.

Becky set her fork down. "He is. I just don't understand what the rush is. Does he want a break from the ranch? Is there something wrong?"

"Yes." Autumn nodded. "He's scared."

She sat up straight. "Of what?"

"Of you moving back to Texas."

Autumn's index finger circled the rim of her cup.

"It was fine when you were there for school. But if you take a job that far away, you might never come back."

"That's silly," she said. "I'll always come back."

"Say you move to Texas and build a fabulous career. Then, you meet some guy who makes you forget all about Coy. You get married and have children." Autumn leaned her elbows on the table and rested her chin on her hands. "If you build a life in Texas, you're not going to want to come back and take over the ranch."

She bit on her bottom lip as she considered her mother's words. "So he's scared I'm going to abandon the ranch."

Autumn leaned across the table and tucked a strand of hair behind Becky's ear. "Or maybe he's scared you're going to abandon him."

"Do you think he'll back off if I tell him I'm going to stay here?" Her stomach was in knots. "Dr. Evans offered me a partnership at his practice."

"That's wonderful!" Autumn's face beamed. "I'm so proud of you!"

"I haven't given him an answer yet."

Her mother pressed her lips together. "Because of Coy?"

She nodded. "I don't know if I can stay here and stay away from him."

"Are you sure you want to stay away from him?"

Becky's chest swelled as she took a long, deep breath. "I'm not sure what I want."

## *CHAPTER EIGHT*

DARK CLOUDS GATHERED on the horizon, matching her mood, as Becky drove back up the mountain road to Coronado. Her dad had never made it a secret that he expected her to take over the ranch, but she never thought he would try to push her into accepting the responsibility until much later. Was her mother right? If she began her career in Texas, would she want to stay? Knowing that her father's sudden need to force her into a decision was based more on his fear of her leaving than on his needing her to take over helped to relieve her tension a little.

Still, she needed to make some decisions and she needed to do it by the time Dr. Evans returned from his trip. When she thought of becoming a partner at the clinic, her heart raced a little. She would love to have her own practice. And she would love to be closer to her family and friends. But could she be this close to Coy without losing her heart again?

In the time they'd been apart, she'd realized two

important things. First, Coy wasn't a team player. He'd never viewed her as his partner. Sure, he left most of the responsibilities to her. She paid the bills. She kept him on track. When they went to a rodeo, she decided where they stayed. She even picked out all his clothes. When she asked him for his opinion, he would shrug and say whatever she wanted was fine. Coy didn't want to worry about anything except which bull he'd drawn and how many points he had on the circuit.

But most importantly, she'd realized that he didn't love her the way she wanted to be loved. Everyone assumed the two of them would get married after high school. Whenever someone would ask when they were going to get married, he'd shrug and say there was no rush. After a few years, it became a running joke between them and their friends. Finally, she'd asked him if he was just staying with her until someone better came along. He laughed and told her she was being silly.

The longer they went with him avoiding the topic of marriage, the more worried she became. It wasn't that she needed to get married right away, but she wanted some kind of reassurance that it would happen someday. She wanted...no, she *needed* to know that he was as committed to her as she was to him. She'd left her job with Dr. Evans. She'd put off college. And what had he given up for her? Nothing. It wasn't like she'd asked him to walk away from the rodeo, but she wanted him to be willing to make some compromises for her.

Then, after she told him she was pregnant, he couldn't get her to the altar fast enough. She was in such shock that he'd even suggested it, she went along with it. She tried to tell herself it was because he loved her, but she wondered if it was really because he was worried about how it would look to his rodeo fans if he didn't marry her. He could marry her for his fans. For the baby. Just not for her.

The more she thought about it, the more it hurt. Then it made her angry. Each day, she got more and more angry about it. Before she got up the nerve to question him, tragedy struck and she lost the baby.

Had the hurt and anger she internalized been the cause of her losing her baby? The possibility that it was her fault changed her bitterness to guilt. Between the grief, the guilt and the anger, she was glad when Coy announced he had to leave for the weekend to participate in a rodeo. As soon as he left, she felt like she could breathe. How was she supposed to make a marriage work when she was so angry with her husband she couldn't be around him? So she'd packed his things and when he returned, she told him she needed space.

Time had dulled the grief. Several months of therapy had helped her to let go of some of the guilt. She'd forgiven herself. When she saw Coy again, she'd expected the anger and bitterness to flare up again, but it hadn't. Her resolve to officially end things with Coy and start over grew weaker each time she saw him. Could she really risk staying while he was around?

The sky was getting darker and the wind was starting to pick up when she pulled into the campground. Instead of taking the direct path to the cabins, she took the long way around, driving past the barns first. Coy's truck wasn't there, so she pulled into the empty space at the entrance to the horse barn and parked.

There was something about the smell and the sounds of a barn that was soothing to her. When she was a little girl, she often slept in the hayloft above the animals when she was at the ranch. The scent of hay and horses had always been her comfort.

She opened the door to her truck and got out, stretching her stiff muscles. The sun had set long ago, but the dark clouds blocked any sign of the moon or stars and there was no movement in the air. With nothing to light up the countryside, the barn was nothing more than a dark shadow against the horizon. She pushed the sliding doors open and felt her way inside, her fingertips brushing the familiar rough wooden walls until she found the light switch. Light flooded the barn, and five horses poked their heads over the stall doors.

"Wait. Five?" she muttered to herself, frowning. The last time she checked, Coy had only four horses. She walked closer to the unfamiliar horse. His warm brown eyes watched her with interest, his ears flicking forward as she approached.

"Hello, fella." She reached up and touched his nose, feeling the softness of his muzzle against her palm. The horse welcomed her touch, his breath warm and steady. She continued to stroke him, noting the graying hairs around his muzzle, a sign of age. She gently opened his mouth and inspected his teeth, counting the rings of wear.

"What do you think, Doctor?" Coy's voice caused her to jump. She looked around, expecting to see him standing in the office. When he spoke again, his voice was coming from the overhead loft. "My guess is he's almost twenty."

"I'd say that's pretty close." She watched him swing his leg over the entrance to the loft and descend the ladder with practiced ease. "Where did you get him?"

He jumped from the ladder and landed barefoot on the ground, the thud echoing in the quiet barn. "At the auction yesterday. The only other person bidding on him was Wayne Kreps."

Her eyes widened. "He's still around?" Wayne had a reputation for buying all the horses no one else seemed to want. He claimed to take them to Mexico to sell them, but most people suspected he sold them to a meat market.

Coy walked over to the stall and stroked the

horse's nose with a tenderness that made her chest tighten. "I just couldn't let him buy Whiskey. There's something special about him."

Becky laughed softly. "Whiskey?"

"Yes." Coy scratched the horse between his ears, eliciting a pleased snort. "He's the color of an oak whiskey barrel and his eyes are the color—"

"Of warm whiskey," Becky finished, a smile tugging at her lips. "I thought the same thing. Were you sleeping in the loft?"

He shrugged, a hint of embarrassment coloring his features. "Yeah. I like sleeping here. It's calming. Besides, with the storm that's rolling in, I don't know if Whiskey will get spooked by it, so I wanted to be close by."

Becky's heart fluttered. That was the Coy she had fallen in love with. The guy who worried about others and was willing to be uncomfortable to help take care of them. To be fair, he was still caring of others, especially her. But there was a difference between caring about someone and taking care of someone. She swallowed hard, pushing back the emotions.

"I saw the clouds building on my way up here. It looks like it might be a doozy."

He nodded, his eyes darkening with concern. "The Hotshots were in the market this afternoon stocking up on water bottles and snacks just in case the lightning starts a fire and they're in the field awhile."

Becky shivered. Wildfires weren't anything to take lightly. The last one that hit the area threatened to wipe out the entire town. The Hotshots managed to save it, but some mountain towns weren't so lucky.

"I guess I better get to the cabin and unpack. I have a lot to do tomorrow."

Coy gave her a strange look. "You've been running from dawn to dusk. How did Dr. Evans manage to do this and still run an office in town?"

It was a fair question, but she couldn't help wondering if he was trying to find out if she was really working or just using it as an excuse to avoid him. "It's normally not this busy. Dr. Evans had a pretty good schedule with the ranches around here for routine things like vaccinations and checkups. The problem is, he's way behind because of his injury, so I'm trying to get caught up on those. Throw in your minor emergencies and I'm rushing all over the countryside."

His gaze held hers as she talked, and he smiled softly. "You love it, don't you?"

Her chest inflated like a balloon. "I do. I really do."

"At this rate, you're not going to have time to help me train horses." His brow furrowed.

"I should be caught up before the end of the week."

His hand stroked Whiskey's neck. "I'm glad your first week was a success."

She shrugged one shoulder. "There are a few old-school ranchers who think I'm too young and inexperienced to know what I'm doing."

Coy snorted. "That's ridiculous. You've been dealing with ranch animals your entire life."

"I know." She tried to keep the frustration from her voice. "George Walker's mare is due to foal soon and he's convinced I won't be strong enough to help if things go bad."

"Would you like me to ride out with you when it's time?" he asked.

Irritation flared in her. "That would be just great," she said sharply. "I'm trying to prove to him I'm a professional and know what I'm doing, so I bring my ex-boyfriend along just in case I need help."

"Husband." The word was spoken so quietly she almost missed it.

"Don't," she said, her voice breaking slightly.

"It's the truth," he said.

"Only because—" she took a deep breath "—of the baby." It was amazing how much pain one word could cause.

She gave him a hard look. "There's no baby now, so there's no need for a marriage."

He stepped back as if she'd punched him. The hurt look on his face was evident. "You're saying the only reason you married me was because you were pregnant?"

Her mouth fell open. Was he serious? His blue

eyes zeroed in on her with an icy stare. Her own gaze shifted away from his and darted around the room. She didn't want to talk about this anymore. A peal of thunder rolled through the valley and one of the horses kicked their stall. Coy turned his attention to the animals and walked down the aisle to check each one.

It was the best escape she could have asked for. She rushed to her truck and started the engine. For a moment, she rested her head on her forearms, but a shadow caught her eye. Coy stood at the entry to the barn.

She shifted the vehicle into Reverse and pulled away from the barn as fast as she could.

# *CHAPTER NINE*

COY BARELY SAW Becky for the next few days. She was gone from early morning until after dark. He knew she had lots of calls to catch up on, but he couldn't help but wonder if it was also a good excuse to avoid him. But not today. She could not avoid him today.

He'd been able to convince Scott Griffin to look at Noah's horses. He'd even agreed to trade some of his saddle-trained horses for bucking horses if he liked them. The only requirement he had was that a licensed vet look over the horses and give them a clean bill of health.

Becky had agreed to do that today.

Tomorrow morning he would take the horses to Scott's ranch outside of Phoenix and when he returned, he would go back to Noah's ranch and pick up the horses he wanted for the campground. He was confident that he and Becky could finish the training that Noah had started.

He just hoped he wasn't shooting himself in the foot, so to speak. She agreed to help him train horses in exchange for him signing the divorce papers. He had come up with the idea in an attempt to spend time with her. She needed to see that he was serious about turning the campground into a guest ranch. Once she saw that, she'd see that he was ready to settle down and give her the life she wanted.

He put his cowboy hat on and picked up the keys to his truck. Knowing Becky, she was already at the barn.

Sure enough, when he pulled up to the barn, Becky's truck was parked in front and the lights were on inside. Instead of parking next to the barn, he pulled around to the back. Several trailers were parked in a neat row. A flatbed trailer, a small utility trailer and a couple of livestock trailers. He made a big loop so that his truck was in front of the largest enclosed trailer.

When he got inside the barn, Becky was standing in Whiskey's stall. She moved her hands over his legs with practiced ease, her voice calm and steady.

"Morning," Coy said softly. "Is something wrong with Whiskey?"

Becky turned, a hint of surprise in her eyes. "I didn't hear you come in. He's fine. A little malnourished, but fine. I just wanted to check his joints, again."

"I'm going to start the coffee, then we can head to Noah's after I feed the horses."

"Make it loaded and I'll go ahead and start feeding," she said.

He laughed. "You got it. No decaf today."

She headed for the wheelbarrow sitting in front of a stack of hay bales. "One flake of hay each?"

"Yes, except Whiskey gets half a bucket of mash."

Coy was filling two thermoses with fresh coffee when Becky came into the office. "That was fast. Are you ready to go?"

She nodded. "I am, but I'm going to take my truck. I need to be able to get to George Walker's ranch right away if I'm needed."

Coy handed her one of the thermoses. "Sure. No problem. I just have to hook up to the horse trailer and then we'll head out."

Becky tucked her thermos under her arm. "All right, let's get going. I'll help you with the trailer."

Dawn was just beginning to break when they walked out of the barn. It would be a while before the sun peeked over the mountains, but streaks of pink and orange lit up the eastern horizon.

Coy jumped in his truck and adjusted his side mirror where he could see Becky standing off to one side. Using her hands, she directed him so that the hitch of his truck lined up perfectly with the tongue of the trailer. She motioned for him to stop and he put the truck in Park. By the time he got to the back of the truck, she was already cranking the jack of the trailer to lower it onto the hitch. He hooked up the brakes and lights.

"See you out there." Becky waved and walked toward the barn.

He got into the cab of his truck, trying not to be too disappointed that she wasn't riding with him. He put the truck into gear and was approaching the front of the barn when he saw her waving at him from next to her vehicle. Maybe she'd changed her mind. He stopped the truck and she hurried toward him.

"I almost forgot." She was breathless. "I made you a breakfast burro." She handed him a foil-wrapped burrito.

"Thanks." He took the warm package and waited for her to get into her vehicle.

He glanced at the burrito. She was always doing little things to make his life easier. It had been like that since they started dating. He'd taken it for granted for far too long.

It was a half-hour drive to the Double S Ranch. A half hour that he'd hoped to use to reconnect with Becky. He'd missed her. She'd been his best friend and closest confidante for as long as he could remember.

A few minutes later, he turned off the main road onto the long dirt road that would take him to Noah's ranch. A soft mist still hung in low spots and the dew on the trees and plants glistened in the light of the rising sun.

Noah was waiting for them outside the barn when they drove up. He waved for them to park by the corrals. Becky pulled in next to his truck and they got out at the same time.

"Morning, Coy! Becky! Right on time." Noah greeted them, shaking their hands.

"Morning," Coy said. "Do you have both sets of horses ready?"

"Both sets?" Becky gave him a puzzled look.

"Yes." Noah pointed to the first pen. "The ones for Phoenix and the ones for the campground."

A loud whinny, almost like a trumpet, sounded from a pasture in the distance. Noah led them past the main barn to the back, where several different corrals held horses. He pointed to a narrow pen farther back. "That's where your horses are."

Becky followed closely, her eyes scanning the horses as they made their way past the corrals. "I didn't realize your operation dealt with this many horses."

"Most of them stay in the pasture," Noah said. "The ones in the corrals are ones that I have separated to work with."

"How do you pick which ones you want to work with?" Becky seemed impressed.

"I start with ones that aren't too skittish. Some of them seem more curious about me than afraid of me. Then I start getting them used to being handled. They have potential, but it's a slow process. Now that Coy's on board, we can help more horses."

Coy's chest swelled with excitement. "Once

they're used to being handled, I'll move them to Whispering Pines where I'll start training them and get them ready for adoption."

He put his elbows up on the edge of the pen and watched the horses destined to go to Phoenix. Their coats gleamed in the morning sun. It was easy to see their muscles rippling beneath their sleek hides.

"And these horses?" Becky nodded toward the holding pen. "How did you decide these were the ones Scott might want?"

"These are the ones that fooled me." Noah laughed. "They aren't skittish. Most of them are quite friendly. They'll even sit still while I put a saddle on them. But the minute you try to ride them, they turn into a tornado."

One of the horses ambled close to the fence. Coy reached over the fence and scratched the mare's ears.

Becky, too, reached out to stroke the mare's neck. "How long did you work with them?"

Noah snorted. "Twice as long as all the horses I've saddle broke. They just like bucking more than they like being ridden."

"The bucking gene." Coy grinned at Becky. "I told you it was a thing."

She laughed. "Well, then, let's get started."

"I'll start moving them into the crowding pen. Then, when you're ready, we'll move one at a time into the loading chute. All the horses already have halters, so we can secure their heads and you should be able to do most of the examination without too much trouble. The only thing I'm not sure of is how well they will take to having their teeth inspected."

Becky nodded. "I brought a speculum, if we need it."

Coy waved at a table close to the panels. Several small boxes were on the table and a trash can was placed at the end. "Are those the vaccines?"

"Yes." Noah opened a gate and stepped inside the pen.

Coy prepared the first vaccine. He stepped over to the loading chute. Becky was standing close to the end. She had a stethoscope around her neck and held a clipboard.

"Here." She handed him something that looked like a tape measure. "Can you do the weight tape before you give him the vaccine?"

A flicker of worry went through him. The last time a veterinarian had worked with the wild horses, the veterinarian got hurt. He knew Becky wasn't in danger of getting kicked as long as the horse was in the chute, but he didn't want to get too far away from her.

"Measure the heart girth and body length." She pointed to a diagram on the clipboard. "Write the measurements down here."

Coy nodded. "Okay. Anything else?"

"You can run your hands over her back legs and let me know if you feel any swelling or warmth."

"Ready?" Noah called. "Horse number one-four-two."

Coy jotted the number down on the top of the paper. "Let's go."

Noah guided the horse into the chute. Coy tensed and waited for the horse to get into position. By the time the horse approached the end of the panels, Noah had jumped over the fence and was waiting next to the chute.

Becky and Coy waited for Noah to latch a lead rope to the horse's halter. He held on to the rope firmly and nodded.

They moved quickly. Becky took the horse's vitals while Coy took the measurements. Then Noah secured the horse's head while Becky checked the mare's teeth and gums. The horse didn't like that at all and kept trying to toss her head back. They had to wait a few minutes for her to settle down before Coy gave her the vaccine.

While Noah led the horse out of the loading chute and into a separate holding pen, Becky recorded the information on the clipboard and added a few notes before putting a new sheet on the front.

The next horse was easier to manage. She didn't fight getting her teeth checked and seemed to enjoy the attention. The next two horses were right in between. While none of them seemed aggressive, Coy still let out a sigh of relief when the last one was done and Becky no longer needed to stick her hands in the mouths of the animals.

After releasing the last horse back into the holding pen, they walked into the main barn. Noah opened a small refrigerator standing in the corner and removed several water bottles.

He handed them the cold drinks. "That went much better than I expected."

Becky took a long drink from the bottle. "I thought it went smoothly, also."

"That's because we make a good team," Coy said. He kept his voice too low for Noah to hear. Couldn't she see they were better together than apart?

THERE WAS NO doubt that Coy's words were meant for her ears only. There was also no doubt that Coy wasn't just talking about working with the horses. Her heart leaped into her throat and she kept her gaze averted from his.

She turned her attention to Noah. "The horses really weren't that much trouble."

"Wild horses get a bad rap most of the time," Noah said. "They usually aren't much more difficult than any other horse that hasn't been handled much."

She nodded. "Dr. Evans told me the same thing."

Noah's face was solemn. "I feel really bad about what happened to him."

"It wasn't your fault," she said. "He called last

night to check in and see how things were going and I told him I was doing this today. He said he got complacent because some of them seemed as tame as kittens, and he let his guard down."

"Still, I feel like I should have been more on my guard." Noah sighed.

Coy gathered all the supplies still on the table and handed them to Noah. He turned to Becky. "Want to take a look at the ones we'll be training?"

"Why not?" She followed him to the corral closest to the barn.

At the fence, she stopped. A few of the horses turned their heads to gaze at her.

Coy pointed out a horse that was watching. "I think the roan has some good potential."

She nodded and a knot started to form in her stomach. "She looks gentle enough."

He pointed at another horse, this one farther back. "Come see this one."

He took her hand and pulled her around the corner of the fence. By the time they reached the back of the pasture, he'd asked her a dozen questions, including which training methods she thought would be best for them to use and which names she liked.

The knot in her stomach seemed to grow with every question he asked her. Her answers got shorter, if she even answered at all. By the time they made their way back toward the barn, she wanted to jump in her truck and run away.

Just when she was starting to wonder if there

was a way for them to work things out, he reminded her of all the reasons she shouldn't. She didn't want to go back to being the one he relied on for everything.

"Did you see any you really liked?" He stopped at the back entrance to the barn. "Which ones should we start with?"

She clenched her jaw for a moment and took a deep breath. "I don't know, Coy. Which ones do you want to start with?"

Without waiting for an answer, she turned and walked through the barn.

"What's wrong?" He stopped her. "Is there something you're not telling me about the horses?"

She hesitated, her gaze dropping to the ground. "It's not the horses, Coy. It's...well, it's you."

"Me?" Coy frowned. "What do you mean?"

Becky sighed, brushing a strand of hair from her face. "Whispering Pines is *your* business. What do *you* think?"

Hurt flashed in his blue eyes, but she wasn't going to let him make her feel guilty. For the last ten years, she had made every decision for both of them. He needed to make some on his own.

Coy swallowed, the muscles in his jaw tightening. "I just thought... I thought you'd see something I might miss."

"No, you didn't." She crossed her arms over her chest. "You are one of the best judges of horseflesh that I know. You don't need my opinion, you just don't want to be responsible for anything."

His face tightened and he tilted his head to one side. "I'm sorry. I didn't realize valuing your opinion was a bad thing."

She groaned. "It's not. But for once, I'd like to see you value your own."

Without waiting for a response from him, she started walking toward her truck.

"There you are!" Noah stepped out of his office. "Becky, Abbie is in the house and she's dying to meet you. Coy, I have the papers ready to sign."

Coy's mouth opened, but whatever he was going to say, he changed his mind and turned to follow Noah.

Becky glanced at the house, then back to her truck. Leaving now would be rude, especially since Noah expected her to go inside to meet his wife. Besides, she was curious about Stacy's long-lost sister.

As she approached the house, the smell of freshly baked bread wafted through the air. Her mouth watered. She'd never met Abbie, but her bread-making skills were legendary. Becky knocked lightly on the back door before pushing it open and stepping inside.

"Abbie?" she called.

"In here!" came the cheerful reply.

Becky stepped into a large kitchen and found Abbie at the counter, drizzling some type of white icing on items that resembled a triangle-shaped cookie. Her face was flushed from the heat of the oven, but she looked content.

"You must be Becky." Abbie greeted her with a warm smile. "Just in time. I'm making scones. Want some?"

"Sure, that sounds great," Becky replied, taking a seat at the kitchen table.

Noah walked in a moment later. "Ignore me, ladies. I forgot my work gloves."

He picked up a pair of thick leather gloves lying on the end of the counter. His gaze landed on the plate of goodies and he frowned at Abbie. "Have you been baking again?"

Abbie rolled her eyes but nodded. "Just scones. I'm done now."

"Good. Sit down and eat." Noah guided her to the table. "Stay off your feet."

As soon as Abbie sat down, he carried the plate of scones and set it in front of them, followed by two empty glasses. Then he opened the refrigerator and removed a gallon of milk. He set that on the table as well.

"Do not—" he gave his wife a stern look "—I repeat, do not bake bread."

He pressed a kiss to the top of her head and disappeared through the door.

Becky watched him leave. As irritated as she was with Coy because he wanted her to make all the decisions, she suspected she would be even more irritated if Coy tried to wrap her in Bubble Wrap. She sighed. Maybe she was the problem. Maybe no one would ever make her happy.

She raised one eyebrow at Abbie. "He doesn't like your bread?"

"He loves it." She laughed softly. "But he's a little overprotective. He doesn't want me to exert myself with all the kneading, so he ordered a bread machine for me. It's not here yet."

Becky opened the milk and filled both of their glasses. "I've never tried baking before, but I didn't know kneading bread was that hard."

"It's not, really." Abbie took the glass of milk. "But kneading really works the abdominal muscles and ever since…ever since the miscarriage, he's been even more cautious."

Becky's heart ached for the woman she'd just met. "I'm so sorry, Abbie. I didn't know."

"Thank you," she said. "I don't talk about it much."

"We can talk about something else."

Abbie gave her a shy smile. "Most people don't understand. They think I should just get over it."

Becky nodded. "I know. People don't understand how you can grieve over someone you never met."

"Exactly," Abbie said. "They say things like, 'Just try again.' As if that makes up for the baby you lost."

Her stomach tightened as memories washed over

her. "Or, 'There was probably something wrong, so be grateful.'"

Abbie gave her a long look. "You, too?" Her voice was barely more than a whisper.

Becky's breath caught in her throat. "Yes."

"When?"

"A year and a half ago." Becky scanned the room, her gaze resting on the back door for a moment. "Please don't tell anyone. No one else knows."

"Of course." Abbie's face was full of sympathy. "It was hard enough to go through, but at least I had Noah and Stacy and my parents. I can't imagine trying to deal with it alone."

She swallowed. Coy was there, so she wasn't completely alone, although it might have been easier without him.

Abbie sighed. "Is that why you and Coy broke up? Because he wasn't there for you?"

"It's not so much that he wasn't there for me." She bit her bottom lip. "We both handled it differently."

"People told me that this would either bring Noah and me closer together, or rip us apart." Abbie toyed with the scone on her plate.

Becky wanted to tell her that it was the marriage that tore them apart, not the baby, but she didn't. That was harder to talk about than the baby.

"Your secret is safe with me. Now can I tell you

one? I'm dying to tell someone." Abbie's face was a mixture of joy and terror.

It wasn't hard to figure out what her secret could be. Becky leaned on the table with her forearms. "Are you pregnant?"

"Yes." Abbie nodded, her green eyes twinkling.

Becky's heart stuttered. If she and Coy had stayed together after her miscarriage, would they be ready to try again? She smiled at Abbie. "Congratulations! How far along are you?"

Abbie cast a cautious glance at the door. Her face grew somber. "Only eight weeks. But we're not telling anyone yet."

"I understand." She nodded. "That's probably wise."

"I'm scared to death that something is going to happen again."

Becky ran through the list of warning signs in her head. "Are you experiencing any cramping? Bleeding?"

"No." Abbie pushed her plate to the side. "Noah thinks I worry too much."

Becky reached across the table and squeezed the woman's hand. "From what little I can see, I think he's just as worried. The chances are good that everything will be fine this time."

Abbie nodded, her eyes brimming with tears. "I hope so. But it's hard not to worry."

"I get it," Becky said softly. "But try to focus

on the positives. You've got a strong support system around you."

"I know I do." Abbie's smile faded. "Please don't say anything to Stacy."

"I won't, but don't you think she'll want to know?" She picked up her scone and took a bite. "Wow. This is really good."

"I don't want to put a damper on her own pregnancy if something happens." Abbie took a bite of her scone. "She found out she was pregnant just a few weeks after I miscarried, but she was scared to tell me for almost three months."

"I'm sure she just didn't want to upset you," Becky said.

"I know. Everyone tiptoes around me like I'm made of glass." Abbie took another bite, followed by a drink of milk. "When I was little, I was sick for a long time. But even when I was better, my parents were so scared I was going to get sick again, they wouldn't let me do anything."

Becky frowned. "I'm afraid that's one subject I don't have in common with you. My parents were on the opposite end of overprotective. Sometimes I felt like they were shoving me out the door before I was ready to go."

"Really?" Abbie's eyes were wide with amazement. "I always felt like I was being smothered. I mean, I know they were just trying to keep me safe, but sometimes it was too much."

"Are they better now?" Becky didn't know

much about Abbie, other than that she and Stacy had been in an orphanage in an Eastern European country and had been adopted by separate families in the States. They didn't find each other until two years ago.

"They are," she said. "Although, as soon as they find out I'm pregnant, they'll be worse than Noah. I'll be lucky if they let me walk to the bathroom by myself."

Becky took a bite of her scone. Her relationship with her parents was complicated, so she had no business offering advice. "I don't really know you, but I think you're probably a lot like me. You try to keep the peace, but by doing that, you're not speaking up and letting people know how you feel. So you end up more frustrated than you should be."

Abbie lifted her chin. "You're right. I'm always worried about upsetting someone."

"Well, stop it." Becky gave her arm a soft squeeze. "One thing I learned recently is that nothing will change if you don't set it in motion."

Her phone buzzed and she picked it up off the table. "I'm sorry, Abbie. It looks like I have to go to work."

"So soon?" Abbie's face fell.

She stood up and took her plate to the sink. "I'd love to stay, but one of my patients is in labor, so I have to go."

"I understand." Abbie stood up and walked with her to the door. "If there's one thing I've learned as a rancher's wife it's that sometimes animals come first."

"Thank you for the scones." Becky gave her a quick hug. "Let's talk again soon."

As she walked away from the house, she felt a little lighter. It was the first time she'd shared the pain of the miscarriage with anyone. It was nice to have someone to talk to about it.

## *CHAPTER TEN*

COY WAS LOOKING over the documents that Noah had given him. The purchase agreement for the wild horses was straightforward. It was basically an affidavit that he was going to provide the horses with humane care and wasn't going to send them to a slaughterhouse or sell them to someone else who would send them to slaughter.

He glanced at his wristwatch. It was a little after eight, which meant that, if he left now, he'd be arriving in Phoenix around noon. He didn't like that at all. While Coronado only got up to about eighty degrees, it would be over one hundred and ten in Phoenix. Inside the horse trailer it would get even hotter.

The horses weren't used to temperatures like that. He needed to have them there in the coolest part of the day so they wouldn't be shocked by the heat.

He was signing the last document when he heard boots crunching on the gravel path outside. It sounded as if Becky was in a hurry.

The footsteps didn't stop at the barn but went past, and a moment later, his phone beeped with an incoming text. Disappointment flooded him. It seemed she didn't even want to stop and say goodbye. Was he that difficult to be around?

He pulled his phone out of his back pocket to read the text, unsure if he even wanted to know what it said.

Heading out. Walker's mare is in labor.

The tension in his shoulders relaxed a little. At least she had a good excuse for her hasty departure. He kept his response short.

Good luck. Thanks for helping today.

He placed the phone back in his pocket and signed the last paper.

"Everything okay?" Noah inserted the documents into a manila envelope.

Coy nodded. "George Walker has a mare in labor, so she had to take off."

"Which way was she going to take to get there?" Noah handed him the envelope. "It's a lot faster to cut through the back roads."

Most of the ranches in the area were connected with dirt roads that cut through public lands managed by the Bureau of Land Management. The problem was that some ranchers had started locking the gates connecting their land to BLM land, effectively blocking people from using the public roads.

"I'd hate to tell her to go that way and then have her end up turning around because of locked gates."

Noah grinned at him. "Unless you have a master key."

Coy's eyes widened. "You have one?" He knew that ranchers were required to allow BLM personnel to have access through their land to the public land, but he'd never actually met someone who had a key.

"Yep." Noah nodded. "Sometimes I have to go remove horses from a ranch, so I need to be able to get in."

"I'll call Becky and let her know." He removed his phone from his back pocket again. "She can't be very far down the road."

He was about to hit Send when she burst into the barn.

"Noah, can I borrow your truck?" Her face was tight. "George Walker's mare is foaling, and my truck has a flat tire."

Noah's gaze darted from Coy to her. "Of course. The keys are in it."

"Thanks." She turned and raced back outside.

Coy frowned at him. "Why didn't you tell her about the back way and give her the keys?"

Noah reached into his pocket. "I thought you might want to go along and open the gates with her."

He tossed the set of keys toward Coy and winked. "You better hurry and catch her."

Coy sighed and ran after her. He caught up to her just as she reached Noah's beat-up ranch truck. "You'll get to Walker's ranch faster if you take the back roads through the BLM land."

"True," she agreed, opening the driver's side door, "but aren't the gates locked?"

"Noah gave me the keys to the gates." He opened the passenger door and slid inside the cab.

"What are you doing?"

He fastened his seat belt. "I'm coming with you."

She whirled around to face him, her brow furrowed. "I don't need your help. I can handle this."

"Stopping to unlock and open the gates is going to slow you down." He sat back in the seat. "What are you waiting for? Let's go."

She hesitated for a split second, but in the end, she put the truck into Reverse. Instead of heading for the main highway, she cut across a rugged dirt road that seemed to lead deeper into the mountains. The truck bounced as she navigated the rough terrain. Coy didn't try to converse with her. He could tell by the look on her face that not only was she concentrating on the road, she was probably going through everything she would need to do when she got there.

As they approached the first gate, Coy jumped out while she was still driving and raced ahead. He had the gate unlocked before she came to a full stop and waved for her to keep going as she drove through. He closed the gate and wrapped the chain around it, but didn't take the time to lock it again.

Becky didn't stop after going through the gate, but kept moving at a snail's pace. When the gate was secure, he sprinted toward her truck, jumping onto the back bumper. As soon as he'd catapulted himself into the bed of the truck, she pressed on the gas, not slowing down until she got to the next gate, where he jumped out, sprinted ahead of her, and the cycle started all over.

When they arrived at the Walker ranch, George met them at the truck. "Her water broke fifteen minutes ago, but there's no sign of the foal yet."

Coy had been around enough pregnant mares to know that once the horse's water broke, the foal should follow in less than a half hour. They got here just in time.

Becky grabbed her medical bag and raced ahead of him to the barn.

When Coy got to the barn, she was talking to Mark Kirby, the ranch's foreman.

"The foal is upside-down." Mark stood with the mare, a worried look on his face. "I was able to get the legs repositioned, but I can't get the foal to roll over."

George shook his head. "Pete would've had that foal out by now."

"Yes," Becky agreed, "but the foal and your mare would probably be dead."

Pete Navarro had been George's right-hand man for fifty years. When a mare was having a difficult birth, he reached in and yanked the foal out, not worrying about the safety of the mare or the foal. Coy had only met Pete a handful of times, but he knew the man's reputation.

He also remembered a time when Becky worked as a veterinary assistant for Dr. Evans. Becky was at his house when Dr. Evans called her. He said George had a mare going into labor and wanted her to meet him there. Dr. Evans warned her that Pete might try to force the issue and for her to discourage him until he could get there.

Coy and Becky left immediately, but by the time they'd arrived, Pete had forced the foal through the birth canal, and ruptured the mare's uterus in the process. The result had been a tragic mess and Becky had been horrified that anyone would do such a thing.

He glanced at her as she slipped on her obstetric sleeves and approached the mare. She carefully examined the mare and the position of the foal. A moment later, she nodded at Mark. "You're right. It's upside-down, but not completely."

Mark rubbed the mare's neck in a soothing manner. "What do you want to do, Dr. Maxwell?"

"I need to get the mare to lie down, then stand up."

Her answer was swift and confident, but Coy didn't miss the way the corner of her mouth twitched. She was nervous. He couldn't blame her. George Walker had a lot of pull in the ranching community. If something went wrong, he would blame her and spread the news far and wide that she didn't know what she was doing.

George scowled at her. "That's it? That's all you're going to do?"

She stood close to the mare while Mark urged her to lie down. She cast a quick glance at George. "It might help the foal to reposition itself," she explained.

The older rancher shook his head. "The foal's stuck. Shouldn't you be doing something more... drastic?"

"It's not stuck, it's just turned. I think she can correct this herself," Becky said firmly. "If we intervene too much, we could complicate things."

George's face reddened with frustration. "You need to do something now! Sedate her and get the foal out!"

Becky looked George straight in the eye. "I will if either she or the foal is in danger. They're not, so let me do my job."

"I'll do it myself." George pushed her to the side.

He unbuttoned his western shirt and removed it before reaching for the large tub of lubricant.

"If you want me to leave, that's fine, but you're going to sign a waiver before I do." Becky stepped between him and the mare. "And you're going to scrub and sanitize your hands before you even think about touching her."

He snorted and raised his hands as if he was going to physically move her.

Coy stepped between them. "Back off, George. Let Becky do her work."

George glared at him, but took a step backward. "You better hope she's right, because if she's not, I'll make sure she never works in this county again."

Coy crossed his arms. "You do what you have to do, but don't put your hands on her."

George glanced past him to Becky, who had already moved over to check the mare. She was so focused, she didn't seem to be paying attention to them.

A moment later, the mare was lying on the ground, her stomach contracting with each breath. Becky checked the foal again. "Almost there, girl. Let's stand back up."

She nodded at Mark, who pulled the mare's halter and encouraged her to stand back up. Becky spoke in soothing tones while probing inside the mare to check the position of the foal again.

She smiled and stepped back. "Good, girl."

The mare shifted, and the front hooves of the foal appeared. Becky sighed in relief as the mare delivered the foal without further complications.

George didn't say a word as he watched the mare clean the new foal. Becky waited until the foal made a few awkward attempts to stand before removing her gloves and walking to the sink in the wash area of the barn.

When she walked back to the center of the barn, George still had a scowl on his face. "You got lucky."

Coy rolled his eyes. "You just can't admit that she was right."

"This time," George said. "What happens the next time when things don't go as smoothly?"

"Next time you can either trust that I know what I'm doing, or you can call someone else." Becky picked up her medical bag. "Let's go, Coy."

She whirled around and headed to the truck without checking to see if he was following or not. She got into the truck and slammed the door.

A moment later, Coy got into the passenger side. "Do you mind going back the same way we came? I closed the gates, but I didn't lock them."

Becky nodded, started the truck and put it into gear. They rode in silence until they reached the first gate. Coy got out and opened it. This time, she waited for him to lock it and get back inside the cab before moving again.

"You okay?"

"No," she admitted. "I shouldn't have lost my temper with him. I'm sure he's already complaining about me to his buddies."

"Nah." Coy shook his head. "Most likely, you've earned his respect. You did a great job. George knows that, too. He's just being stubborn."

The sun was high in the sky by the time they came to the gate adjoining Noah's property. It was definitely too late to head to Phoenix right now. He pulled out his phone and sent Scott a text.

Becky glanced at him. "Are you going to take the horses to Phoenix this evening?"

"Either tonight or early tomorrow morning." He nodded at his phone. "I'll let Scott decide what works best for him." He opened the door and got out to open the last gate.

More than anything, he wanted to ask her to ride to Phoenix with him. He knew she would resist, so initially, his plan was to ask her to come because he wanted her opinion on the horses he was going to bring back. Apparently, that was a no-no. She thought he was asking her for her input because he wanted her to make the decisions. In reality, he just wanted her to know that he valued and respected her opinion. After all, that was the reason his parents divorced.

He swore he wouldn't make the same mistakes with Becky that his father made with his mother. Frank never asked anyone for their ideas or opinions. Including his wife. Coy vowed that he would never make Becky feel the way his father had made his mom feel. He was so careful to ask for her input on everything, she believed he was too scared to make a decision on his own. Her biggest complaint was about the one thing he went out of his way to do. Now he had to show her that he did it out of respect and not fear.

"Come with me," he said when he got back into the truck.

"Why?" She pressed her lips together. "Do you want to discuss which training techniques I prefer?"

He ignored the sarcastic tone to her voice. "No. Because I want to spend some time with you. I want to get to know you again."

Her mouth dropped open, but no words escaped. "Um... I'll think about it."

BECKY DIDN'T SAY anything else on the short drive to the barn. She had purposely tried to push Coy's buttons. Instead of reacting to her overly sarcastic comment, he responded by inviting her to Phoenix so they could spend time together.

His invitation left her feeling guilty for trying to make him angry. The problem was that her emotions were in turmoil. The other night, at the barn, she realized how much she missed him. She couldn't fault him for what happened. But she didn't want to fall back into their old routine of him letting her do everything. So instead of talking to him about it, she became passive-aggressive and tried to force him to argue with her.

It didn't work and now she was left with even more emotional turmoil. The trip to Phoenix would be a good opportunity to tell him that their deal was off and he needed to sign the divorce papers. But she'd already said she would help. Whispering Pines was the first thing she'd seen him really excited about in a long time and she wasn't going to jeopardize that because she was too scared to be around him.

She glanced at him as they approached Noah's barn, trying to read his expression, but his face remained blank. His heavy silence hung between them and she wondered if he already regretted his invitation.

"Noah changed your flat tire," Coy said abruptly, pointing at her truck.

Becky followed his gesture and saw that her flat tire had indeed been replaced with her spare. The sight brought a rush of relief, mingled with a pang of guilt. She was more than capable of changing a tire herself, but now she could head straight home.

She parked Noah's truck next to hers and shut off the engine. "Thank you," she blurted out. "I'm not sure that George would've listened to reason without you being there."

"It was nothing." Coy's eyes locked with hers, sending a shiver down her spine. "I hope you'll consider going to Phoenix with me in the morning. We can stop by Kyle and Alyssa's."

Becky hadn't seen her friend Alyssa in almost six years. They had been friends in high school, despite living in different parts of the state. The two of them competed in barrel racing together both in high school and later, on the circuit. Then Alyssa fell in love with Kyle, who was a team roper. It wasn't long before they got married and quit the circuit to settle down and start a family.

"I would like to see her..." Becky's voice trailed off.

"They have four kids now," Coy said. "Three girls and a boy."

Becky sighed. She hadn't been a very good friend. The last time she'd talked to Alyssa, they only had two little girls. She got so caught up in school and her own problems that she'd neglected other people.

"Hello? Noah?" Coy's voice echoed through the barn. No answer. He peeked inside the office, then the tack room. "He must be in the house."

"Can you tell him I said thank you?" she asked, the words tasting bittersweet. "I'm going to head back to town. I want to chart everything for Walker's mare before I forget."

Disappointment flashed across Coy's face. "Okay, sure. Let me know if you decide to come with me tomorrow."

"I will." She forced a smile, then turned away.

She took her time driving back to Coronado. If she was being honest, she was scared to spend an entire day with Coy. She didn't trust herself not to forgive him and it would be too easy to fall back into their same old patterns.

On the outskirts of Coronado, she pulled into Bear's Garage. As she stepped out of the truck, the familiar scent of oil and rubber filled her nostrils. It reminded her of all the days she spent sitting with her dad while he worked on tractors in the barn.

"Well, aren't you a sight for sore eyes?" Harry Littlebear greeted her when she entered the small building, his grin warm and welcoming.

"Hi, Harry," she said, giving him a hug.

"I heard you were back in town. Are you taking over for Dr. Evans?"

"Just for the summer." Becky noticed a picture frame of a dark-haired woman and a young boy on the counter. She walked over and picked it up. "How are Maggie and Jacob?"

"They're good. Jacob looks just like his daddy. He'll be in second grade this year."

A smile touched Becky's lips. Jacob did bear a strong resemblance to Tommy as a little boy. "What does Maggie do now? Does she still work at the Bear's Den?"

"Only when they need help." A look of pride crossed Harry's face. "Maggie's a schoolteacher now. She teaches kindergarten."

"That's wonderful. Here in Coronado?"

Harry nodded. "Yes. After Tommy died, her parents tried to talk her into moving to Flagstaff with them, but she said this is where Tommy wanted to raise their son, so she stayed. Now, what can I do for you? I'm sure you didn't stop by just to say hello."

"I've got a flat tire I need to drop off."

"Sure." He nodded and followed her outside. "When do you need it by?"

Tomorrow was Friday and he was closed on the weekends. She knew he would get it done for her by tomorrow if she asked, but she didn't want to pile extra work on him. "Monday morning?"

"No problem." Harry reached into the bed of the truck and lifted the tire out as if it weighed nothing. "We'll have it ready for you."

"See you on Monday." She waved to him and got into the cab of the pickup.

Harry rolled the tire around the side of the building, but she didn't put her truck into gear yet. She stared at the building in front of her. On the wall, to the right of the entrance, was a large symbol with two crossed axes in front of blazing trees. The words Last Call were printed above it, and below it was the name of Harry's only son. Tommy had been a Mogollon Rim Hotshot and was killed while fighting a forest fire just before he turned twenty-one. The entire town had been devastated. If Harry hadn't had Maggie and Jacob, Becky didn't know if Harry would've survived the loss.

Maggie almost didn't. She spiraled out of control for a few months. It was rumored she'd started abusing prescription medication, and she was definitely drinking too much. She was almost killed after she drove her car over the edge of the mountain one night. Some people claimed that she did it on purpose. When Harry brought her home from the hospital, he let her know that in no uncertain terms was she allowed to leave Jacob an orphan. Together, they got through it.

As Becky drove away from the garage, she was hit with a weariness that was bone-deep. Her limbs felt heavy, almost as if a weighted blanket covered her. She prided herself on being able to stay calm and collected in almost any situation. Crying in front of anyone was out of the question. Even Coy had never seen her lose control of her emotions. But every so often, when she was alone, the emotions slipped through. Like now.

Talking to Abbie about her miscarriage had put a crack in her armor. Staying aloof while George Walker accused her of not knowing what to do had bothered her more than she wanted to admit. But seeing the tribute to Tommy outside of Harry's garage was just one more reminder of how precious life was. She didn't want to waste any more time. But how could she start building the life she wanted when she still wasn't sure what that was?

She parked in front of her cabin and trudged up the steps. The cabin's silence was comforting. As soon as she finished charting, she was going to take a nice long nap, and then she'd reread all the paperwork Dr. Evans had left for her. Then she would go talk to Coy.

She kicked off her boots and padded across the cool wooden floor to the kitchen counter. She dug through the drawer and found a box of matches. Her bare feet didn't make a sound as she walked into her bedroom and lit the lavender candle on her nightstand.

She stripped out of her jeans and heavy western shirt. They were replaced with a light cotton T-shirt and flannel shorts. She pulled the rubber band from her hair and tugged the ponytail loose with her fingers. It was amazing how freeing it felt to take her hair down. Once her long locks were free, she massaged her scalp with her fingers.

The aroma from the candle filled the little cabin with its calming scent. She blew out the flame and collapsed onto her bed, the mattress creaking under her. As she closed her eyes, images of Coy swirled in her mind. It would be so easy to melt into his arms. But how long would it be before she was putting all her energy into what he wanted? She couldn't lose herself again.

Of course, it would be a lot easier to stay the course if she knew exactly what it was she wanted. She'd always wanted to be a veterinarian—that had never changed. But when Coy made the rodeo circuit his life, she reasoned that specializing in equine medicine would allow her to do her job and keep traveling with Coy. And now that Coy wanted to stay in Coronado and convert Whispering Pines into a guest ranch, she could envision herself living there and taking care of all the animals.

Her dad wanted her to be close so she could take over the ranch. Becoming Dr. Evans's partner would allow her to do that and have the added benefit of making both her parents happy.

Every decision she made had been based on what someone else was doing. She stared at the ceiling, trying to think of a time when she'd been proactive instead of reactive.

She couldn't think of one.

## *CHAPTER ELEVEN*

When Becky woke up, the inside of the cabin was dark, with only dim light seeping through the curtains. She sat up in bed and stretched. A glance at the clock said it was after five o'clock. Wow. She'd only meant to take a short nap.

Her stomach growled and she tossed the covers back and got out of bed. The cold wooden floor sent a shiver up her spine. She wrapped her arms around herself, rubbing her hands along her arms to ward off the chill. The floorboards creaked slightly under her weight and she opened the blinds over the kitchen window to bathe the room in a soft golden light.

She picked up her phone from the counter. How many times had Coy texted her to see if she was going to Phoenix with him in the morning? The screen lit up, but there were no missed calls or text messages.

Odd. Becky stared at the screen, her brows knitting together in confusion. Coy hadn't called once.

The realization brought an unexpected pang of disappointment.

Opening the top freezer of the refrigerator, she pulled out a TV dinner and tossed it into the microwave. The hum of the appliance filled the small kitchen as she turned her attention to her laptop.

It sat open on the dining table and she moved her fingers across the touch pad to wake up the screen. She read the offer from the veterinarian's office in Abilene again. It was a great opportunity. She would be working with ranch animals as well as smaller pets in the office. The thought should have filled her with excitement, but it didn't. She felt a strange lack of enthusiasm.

The papers from Dr. Evans lay in a file next to the computer. She didn't need to open it again to go over the details. She practically knew them by heart now. If she stayed with Dr. Evans's office, she would have her own practice. How many veterinarians did she know who had their own practice less than a year after graduating from school? None. It was an incredible opportunity, too. While she felt a surge of excitement for the job, something held her back.

It was because it was here. And Coy was here.

The microwave beeped, breaking her train of thought. She retrieved her dinner, the smell of processed meat and vegetables less than appetizing. Sitting back down, she pushed the bland food around with her fork before taking a bite.

Becky finished eating and tossed her paper plate in the trash can, then began to pace the cabin. The nap hadn't cleared her head. If she were at the ranch, she would saddle up her horse and go for a long ride before sunset to clear her head. She paused her pacing, struck by an idea. Why couldn't she? There were several horses right down the road.

She hurried to the bedroom to change back into her jeans and grabbed her boots next to the kitchen door. She wrapped her hair into a messy bun and headed out the door. Instead of driving to the barn, she decided to walk. The physical exertion would help where the nap hadn't.

It wasn't that far, but by the time she got there, she'd broken into a sweat, her hair sticking to the back of her neck. She lifted it up off her neck, letting the cool evening breeze soothe her heated skin.

As she approached the barn, the sound of giggling caught her attention. Instead of going inside, she walked around the side to the enclosed pen that connected to the stables. In the middle of the pen, a little girl sat on Maze, Stacy's horse. Her tiny face was deep in concentration as she tugged back on the reins with all her might. A moment later, Maze took a step backward. Then another.

"I did it!" the little girl squealed, her voice filled with triumph. She pulled back on the reins again and Maze backed up a few more steps.

"Good job, Khatia!" Coy reached up and high-fived the girl. "Now I want you to circle the pen three times. At a trot."

"A trot?" Khatia's mouth dropped open, her eyes wide with fear. "Can't I walk?"

"No," Coy said gently but firmly. "You're ready."

The little girl lifted her chin defiantly. "I can't."

Becky leaned against the barn and watched, curious to see how Coy would handle the situation. He reached up and took Khatia's hand, his tone soft yet commanding. "Khatia, look at me."

His voice even caught Becky's attention.

He squeezed the girl's hand reassuringly. "Does Maze do everything you tell her to?"

"Uh-huh." She nodded.

"Have you scared her?"

Khatia looked at him with wide eyes. "I wouldn't do that."

"So, she trusts you," Coy said. "Now it's your turn to trust her."

Khatia's face scrunched in thought as she considered his words. "How about this," he suggested. "Walk her for one round. Then trot for a little ways, then walk. Then trot. But the last round, you trot."

Becky was impressed. She had no idea Coy could handle a child so well. His patience and understanding warmed her heart.

Another giggle caught her attention. Close to the entrance of the barn was another little girl, this one smaller. Whiskey stood next to her, nosing her head and cheek. The little girl reached into her pocket and held out her palm. Becky recognized a small white sugar cube in her chubby hand. Whiskey removed the cube gently and nuzzled the girl again, causing more giggles.

"Marina." Coy's voice caused the little girl to snap to attention. "Are you feeding Whiskey sugar cubes again?"

"No." Marina shook her head.

Coy walked over to Whiskey and Marina, scooping the girl up into his arms. "You love Whiskey, don't you?"

"Uh-huh." She reached over and placed her hand on the horse's neck.

"Remember that Whiskey came to us from a home that didn't take good care of him. We're trying to make him better."

Marina nodded solemnly. Coy tapped her nose gently. "What would happen if you ate candy all day?"

She rolled her eyes dramatically. "I know. My teeth would rot out and I would get sick because I didn't eat good."

"Right. And I know he likes it, but we have to get him healthy. And when we do, you can let him have a little, sometimes."

"Okay," she said, sighing, the disappointment clear in her voice.

Coy put her down and smiled. "Whiskey really likes to have his hair brushed. Why don't you get a currycomb from the tack room and I'll stack some hay bales so you can brush him?"

"Okay," she chirped, disappearing inside the barn.

Coy shook his head, a fond smile on his face, and turned. Becky's heart skipped a beat when his eyes met hers. "What are you doing here?"

She moved closer, the evening light casting a golden hue over everything. "I thought it was a good evening for a ride." She nodded at the girl riding Maze. "You're really good with them."

He shrugged. "I wasn't in a good place when I came to Coronado. The girls helped me. That's part of the reason I stayed so long."

Becky averted her gaze. What did he mean about not being in a good place? Could he have had as much difficulty dealing with the loss of their baby as she did? It didn't seem possible, but his face was so intent that she believed him.

She cleared her throat. "It's a bit late to go for a long ride tonight. I'll do it another time."

Coy's eyes watched the little girl working her way around the edge of the pen. "I have a better idea," he said. "Jasper is already saddled. Go for a short ride in the pasture with Khatia."

"Okay." She nodded.

She climbed over the fence and followed Coy to the back entrance of the barn. As she was coming around the corner, Marina ran right into her.

"Sorry," the little girl said. She looked up at Becky with curious brown eyes. "Who are you?"

"I'm Becky." She held out her hand to the little girl.

Marina switched the currycomb to her other hand and shook Becky's. "You're pretty."

She blushed. "Thank you."

Warmth flooded her limbs. She'd always thought of herself as plain. There certainly wasn't anything striking about her features. Plain brown hair. Plain brown eyes.

Coy moved toward the stack of hay bales, but Becky moved farther in the barn to the palomino mare standing in the breezeway.

She adjusted the stirrups on the saddle, patted Jasper's neck and swung herself into the saddle. When she rode Jasper out to the round pen, Khatia stopped her horse close by.

"Hi, I'm Khatia."

Becky detected the faintest hint of an accent in the girl's voice. "I'm Becky."

"Coy said you were going to ride in the big pasture with me."

She nodded. "If that's okay with you."

"Sure." Khatia guided her horse over to the gate. "I've never got to ride out of the corral before."

Becky leaned down and opened the latch on the gate with her hand. She urged Jasper forward to push the gate open, then held it until Khatia got all the way through.

She let the little girl take the lead and for a while they rode side by side, the clopping of the horses' hooves dulled by the tall grass.

"You're doing really great," Becky said. "Ready to go a little faster?"

She urged Jasper into a trot and it wasn't long before Khatia and Maze were trotting, too. The little girl clung to the saddle horn as the horse bounced her.

"Relax and don't stand up in the stirrups. You're putting your weight on your toes. Squeeze your legs and put your weight more on your heels," Becky told her. "Move with your horse."

Khatia did what she said and soon she didn't look as if she'd bounce off the horse at any moment. "Like this?"

"Very good," she said. She was itching to let Jasper loose and run. She wanted to feel the wind in her hair.

Instead, she let the horse slow down to walk again. Khatia followed suit.

"Are you Coy's girlfriend?"

Becky frowned, unsure how to answer that. "Not anymore," she said.

The girl's face tightened. "Are you the one that broke his heart?"

"What makes you think his heart was broken?"

Of the two of them, Coy was much more open with his emotions. Still, she couldn't imagine him talking to anyone about their problems, especially a small child.

"My mom said that Coy's different. He used to love going out and being with people and now all he does is sit in his cabin."

"Your mom told you that?"

"I heard her talking to my dad," Khatia admitted. "She said she didn't know if Coy would ever get over his broken heart."

Becky swallowed. She'd been so focused on the pain she felt, she never gave a thought to Coy's pain. Guilt pressed down on her.

She glanced toward the barn to make sure Coy and Stacy were within sight. "Khatia, you can head back to the barn. I'm going to let Jasper run a little. I'll catch up to you."

She turned the horse toward the far end of the pasture and urged her forward, hoping to outrun the ache in her chest.

COY HELPED MARINA brush Whiskey, but couldn't stop himself from glancing toward the pasture at where Becky and Khatia seemed to be enjoying themselves. What were they talking about? Khatia was at the age where she repeated everything she heard, whether it was appropriate or not. More than once, he'd started talking to Stacy about Becky only to be interrupted by one of the girls piping up and asking a question.

Marina was standing on top of the hay bales

and was at shoulder height with the horse. Marina wrapped her arms around the horse's neck and sighed. "I love Whiskey."

Coy laughed. "I know you do."

Her face scrunched up. "Why were people mean to him?"

"They weren't mean to him," he said. He'd worked with enough abused horses to know that wasn't the type of home Whiskey had been rescued from. "I think they loved him, but they weren't able to take good care of him. He didn't get enough to eat and his hooves weren't taken care of."

Her angry face smoothed. "Why not?"

He shrugged. "Maybe they didn't have enough money. It costs a lot of money to take care of them."

"Dada... I mean, Mom says pets are big 'sponsity." She nodded seriously.

"Yes, they are a big responsibility."

"Dad says that we can get a kitten when we move into our new house." She ran the brush down Whiskey's neck. "But Max has to like him."

Max was Caden's service dog. He didn't go anywhere without the dog. Max even rode on Caden's motorcycle with him. "I'm sure Max will love any kitten you get."

"I am, too," Stacy said from the barn entrance.

"Hey, coz." Coy nodded. "I didn't hear you walk up."

She looked around. "Where is Khatia?"

"In the pasture."

Stacy straightened up, her gaze drifting to the pasture. "Do you think that's a good idea? She hasn't been riding that long?"

"Relax." Coy waved at her. "She's with Becky."

"Oh." Stacy walked over to where Marina was standing on the hay bales and sat down on one. As she did, she let out a soft moan.

"You okay?" He gave her his full attention.

"I'm fine," she said. "Just uncomfortable."

"Gray-gray sits on her tummy and makes her pee her pants." Marina spoke up.

"Marina!" Stacy's face turned dark red.

The girl gave her mother an innocent look. "That's what you told Daddy last night."

Stacy chuckled. "You don't have to repeat everything you hear."

Coy laughed with her, but he glanced at the pasture, wondering if Khatia was doing the same thing.

"Mom!" Khatia's voice traveled from across the pasture. "Watch."

The little girl squeezed her legs and leaned forward, urging the horse to start moving. Within a few seconds, Khatia and Maze were trotting. Becky and Jasper raced to their side and the two of them trotted to the corral together.

Khatia brought the horse to a stop next to the fence and she barreled over the edge. "Did you see me?" Her voice brimmed with enthusiasm. "I galloped."

"I saw you." Stacy moved to the edge of the hay to stand up.

Coy reached under her arm to help her stand. He succeeded in getting her to her feet a split second before Khatia got to her. Khatia wrapped her arms around her mother. "I did good, didn't I?"

"You were wonderful," Coy said, giving her a high five.

Becky opened the gate between the pasture and the pen and led both of the horses through the gate.

"How did you talk her into that?" He met her halfway across the pen and took the reins from her.

"It wasn't that hard." Becky grinned at Khatia. "She's a natural."

"Becky said when I get a little bigger, I might want to barrel race, just like she did." Khatia turned to her mother. "Can I? Please?"

"We'll talk about it." Stacy nodded toward the horses. "First, you have to remember to take care of your horse."

"Yes, ma'am." Khatia turned around and took the reins from Coy. "Come on, Maze."

Marina scrambled off her hay bale and followed her sister into the barn.

"I'm sorry," Becky said to Stacy. "I hope I didn't start something. She asked me when I learned to ride horses and…"

"I know." Stacy laughed. "Once she gets something in her head, it's almost impossible to distract her."

"I better go take care of my horse." Becky led Jasper to the barn.

Coy watched her disappear inside.

"When are you two going to kiss and make up?" Stacy nudged him.

"I'm trying," he said. "I don't think she's interested in it."

"She is." Stacy crossed her arms. "Trust me."

He hoped she was right. He glanced toward the barn. No sign of Becky. Just in case, he kept his voice low. "Can you help me? Has she talked to you?"

"No." Stacy shook her head. "Maybe you should—"

"Coy! I'm ready!" Khatia's voice rang out.

"Coming," he called back. "Talk later?"

His cousin nodded and followed him inside the barn.

Khatia stood patiently next to Maze. The straps to the saddle had been undone and hung down. Coy lifted the saddle from the horse's back and carried it to the tack room to put in its place. When he turned around, Khatia was placing the saddle blanket in its spot. She picked up a brush from the table and went back to brush Maze down.

Becky entered the tack room, carrying Jasper's saddle. She nodded toward Khatia. "I offered to help her, but she insisted that she had to do it all herself. Except for lifting the saddle off."

"Stacy and Caden told them if they want to learn to ride they have to help with everything."

"That's good," Becky said. "I know a lot of people who just show up to ride and then leave."

He stepped aside to let Becky put the saddle away. "Will you go with me in the morning?"

She frowned. "I don't think so."

Disappointment flooded him, but he knew it would be useless to argue with her. He nodded and went back to check on the girls.

Khatia was still brushing Maze, but Marina was standing next to her mother. Stacy had a pained look on her face.

"Are you okay?" Coy rushed over to her.

"I'm fine," Stacy said. "This little boy just likes to use my ribs as a punching bag."

He wrapped one arm around her and put the other hand on her tummy. "Are you sure you're okay? Don't lie to me."

"I'm not," she assured him. "I promise you, I'm fine."

Coy bent close to her stomach. "Grayson Murphy, this is your cousin, Coy. Stop beating up your mom, okay? You're making her grumpy and she takes it out on me."

The girls giggled and Stacy gave him a playful punch on his arm. "I'm not grumpy."

"Ow. See!" He rubbed his arm dramatically, causing the girls to giggle even more.

"All right, girls," Stacy told them, "put Maze

in her stall so we can go home. Coy has to get up early in the morning. Tell Coy good-night."

A chorus of goodbyes echoed as she herded her children out of the barn. At the door, she gave a quick glance toward Becky and winked at him. *Good luck*, she mouthed.

He shook his head and followed them to the front of the barn. He waited for them to get in their SUV before closing the barn door. When he turned around Becky was in the middle of the barn with a hay bale in the wheelbarrow.

"I thought I would help you feed." She shrugged. "As long as I'm here, anyway."

"Thanks." It was a nice gesture, but he didn't want to read too much into it. At least she wasn't avoiding his company.

He was mixing up mash for Whiskey when she finished tossing all the horses a flake of hay. Her eyes darted to the bulletin board where all the horses' feed requirements and amounts were listed. She opened the grain bin, filled a bucket and started taking it to the feed troughs.

"Is something wrong with Whiskey?"

"Nothing that good food and some TLC won't take care of."

"Oh, good," she said. "I was afraid I missed something."

Coy scoffed. "I don't think so. You're a great veterinarian."

"Thanks." She tucked a long strand of hair behind her ear. "You're great with kids and horses, it seems."

"I don't know about that." He dropped the mash into Whiskey's trough.

She put the grain bucket back in the bin and leaned against the side of the barn. Her long hair hung down her back in soft waves. Coy could feel her watching him. When he was done, he turned to see her openly staring at him. He didn't say a word. He just stared back, drinking in the sight of her.

He could stare at her all night, but he still had work to do. Pulling his eyes from her, he carried the empty bucket to the washbasin and picked up the bottle of dish soap to wash the bucket.

Becky picked up a toy from the ground. "Someone lost a toy."

Coy recognized the miniature doll. "That's Marina's. Do you mind putting it on my desk?"

"No problem." Becky carried the doll into the office.

She hadn't come back to the main center of the barn by the time he scrubbed the bucket, rinsed it and placed it upside down on the drain board. He looked around, but there was still no sign of her. His stomach tied itself into a knot. She had left without saying goodbye.

So much for getting to talk to her alone. Or trying one more time to get her to go to Phoenix with him. He double-checked all the stalls and made sure all the horses had fresh water. The light in the office was still on, so he went to turn it off and lock up.

He paused at the doorway. Becky was standing inside, studying his kanban board again.

She saw him there and smiled. "You added a new column."

He walked inside to join her. "I started advertising for the trail ride, so I needed a way to keep up with it."

"I've never seen you put this much effort into anything besides bull riding." She let out a soft laugh.

Coy swallowed. "There's one thing I would put even more effort into."

Her brown eyes widened. "What's that?"

"You." He cupped her face with one hand. "Whatever it takes. As long as it takes."

Her breath hitched and when he saw her gaze drop to his lips, it was all the invitation he needed. He brushed his lips across hers, giving her the chance to pull away. When she didn't, he pulled her closer, deepening the kiss.

Becky's arms wrapped around his neck and welcomed his embrace. Coy's heart was racing when he finally broke the kiss and pulled away.

Her brow furrowed. "I better get going. What time are you leaving in the morning?"

"Four," he said. He started to ask her again to

come with him, but changed his mind. She knew she was welcome. If she wanted to come, she'd come.

"I better let you go, then," she said. "Good night."

# *CHAPTER TWELVE*

COY GRABBED HIS keys off the kitchen counter. It would be a long day and he should have gotten more sleep, but the kiss he shared last night with Becky kept him up all night long. She couldn't be as eager to be rid of him as she claimed to be if she could respond to his kisses the way that she had.

He had a feeling there was something she wasn't telling him. He couldn't quite put his finger on it, but he wanted to find out what it was. As he opened the door to the cabin, cool air rushed into his lungs. There wasn't any light in the sky because clouds covered it up. It looked like they might be in for another storm. It wasn't unusual this time of year

Monsoon season usually started in the middle of June and lasted until September, bringing with it lots of rain. However, it was unusual for the clouds to build up overnight. Typical monsoon storm clouds started building early in the morning and peaked in the late afternoon, so this was a rather rare chain of events.

He hoped he could get to Noah's ranch and have

the horses loaded up before the weather hit. His boots echoed on the wooden planks of the porch as he crossed it to get to his truck.

"Good morning!" a voice called through the darkness, startling him.

Coy was not expecting to hear anyone that early in the morning. He squinted in the darkness and saw Becky standing at the back of his truck. "Don't you know better than to scare the life out of someone in the dark?" he said.

She laughed. "It's not like I was hiding. You just don't pay attention to your surroundings."

"What are you doing here?" There was only one reason she could be here this early in the morning: she was going with him. His heart fluttered a little.

"My tire won't be fixed until Monday, and I'm not driving up and down the mountain on a spare tire so I figured I might as well go with you."

She walked around to the passenger side of the truck and opened the door. Coy settled into the driver's seat and started the truck, then turned to face her.

"I think we need to get something straight," he told her. He'd lain awake all night thinking about it and as long as it was fresh on his mind he might as well blurt it out.

She didn't say a word but looked at him with her warm brown eyes.

"Do you think I'm weak-minded?"

Confusion crossed her face. "No. Why do you ask that?"

He paused, trying to get his words together. "It's just that you seem to think that I can't make my own decisions without your help."

She bit her bottom lip for a moment and shrugged. "You have to admit, I was the one who took care of everything when we were together. Whenever I asked you for your input, you always just told me to do what I thought was best."

Coy nodded. He knew he had gotten lax about letting her do everything. She had always been a very in-charge person so he assumed she liked it that way.

"It's okay," she said. "I get it. Your parents had just gotten divorced. It was a shock to you and all you wanted to do was get out of the situation, and it was easier for you to let me be the one to worry about paying the bills and where we would stay and everything else."

"You're wrong," he said, reaching across the cab and taking one of her hands in his. He opened it up and traced his fingers across her palm. How could this woman—the woman who knew him better than anyone else in the world—not know this about him?

"One of the reasons my mom left was because I was out of the house and no one needed her anymore. My dad never needed her, or at least she didn't feel like he did. He was the one who dictated everything in our home. Whenever she tried to offer her opinion on something, he was quick to shut it down."

Becky cocked her head to the side. "I knew he did that with you, but I never realized that he did it with Rachel, too."

"He was worse with my mom." Coy laced his fingers through Becky's. "Even when I was a kid, my mom would tell me to make sure I married someone who mattered to me. I never realized what she meant until the day she moved out of the house."

That day was burned into his memory. Frank had stood off to the side, watching her haul her suitcase to the car. He never tried to stop her. He just said that she would be back because she didn't know how to survive without him. Rachel had looked him straight in the eye and said, *It's because you never gave me a chance to.*

With his other hand, Coy traced Becky's jawline. "I swore then that I would never make you feel like I didn't care what you thought. I wanted so badly to be good that way, but I guess I went a little overboard."

She covered his hand where it rested on her cheek. "You could say that," she said softly.

"I'm sorry," he said. "As time went on, I probably—" he paused "—I did take you for granted. I didn't mean to make you feel like you weren't appreciated."

"What you just said explains a lot," she said. "Back then my parents seemed to live separate lives. Most of the time we were in Coronado, just Mom and me, and when we were at the ranch all my parents did was argue. I always thought that it was my parents who should be getting a divorce, not yours. Yours never fought or argued. I always thought they had the perfect marriage."

"I did, too, and look how things turned out. Your parents are still together and mine are not. It just goes to show that you can't judge a book by its cover."

Letting go of her hand, he turned and put the truck into gear. For a while, they drove in silence through the dark. A couple of streaks of lightning lit up the sky and he pushed his foot harder on the gas. He really wanted to have the horses loaded before the storm hit.

When he pulled into Noah's ranch, he noticed that Noah's truck was hitched up to his trailer. He parked next to the vehicle and got out.

"Are we taking Noah's truck?" Becky shut the door and nodded to the trailer.

The horses were already loaded. Coy scanned the area looking for Noah. He saw a light on in the barn so he went inside.

"Noah?"

"Back here," he hollered from the last stall.

They followed the sound of his voice and found Noah cleaning muck out of a stall.

"What's going on? Why is the trailer loaded and hitched to your truck?"

Noah leaned his pitchfork against the side of the barn. "The horses get spooked easily during a storm. Their instinct tells them to seek shelter, so I figured it was better to load them up before the storm rolls in. I hope you don't mind taking my truck to Phoenix."

"That's fine." Coy nodded. "It'll save us some time, anyway." He glanced at Becky. "Might as well head out, then."

"We're probably safer in Noah's truck than your old relic," she teased.

"Show some respect to your elders. That truck is older than me and you both," he quipped.

"Exactly." She laughed.

After checking the lights and brakes, Coy climbed into Noah's much larger truck where Becky was already sitting. "Need anything before we leave? I don't want to stop once we get on the road, especially when we get out of the mountains."

"I'm good." She held up a tote bag that he hadn't noticed earlier. "Question is, do you need anything?" She rummaged through the bag. "I have snacks, gum, water and a book."

"I don't know how you can read in a vehicle," he said.

Coy had suffered from motion sickness most of his life, which was why he preferred to drive when he could, especially when taking the winding roads through the White Mountains.

"Here." She handed him what looked like a hard candy. "Suck on this."

He pulled off the wrapper and popped it in his mouth. He didn't recognize the taste. It was good, but it definitely wasn't candy. He gave her a questioning look.

"Ginger chews," she explained. "Ginger is good for motion sickness."

"Thanks, but you do realize you're doing it again."

"Doing what?" she asked.

"Taking care of me." He glanced at her out of the corner of his eye. "This is why it was so easy for me to kick back and let you make the decisions. You know what needs to be done and you do it without being asked."

"I'll make sure to let you fend for yourself from now on," she said, giving him a crooked smile. Then she leaned against the headrest. Her eyes fluttered closed, so he turned his attention back to the road. He felt a smidgen of hope.

He'd learned from the mistakes his dad had made. Frank wasn't much for communicating, especially if he thought he might be the one in the wrong. But Coy knew the only way to solve a problem was to talk about it, and he would talk Becky's ear off if that was what it took to fix them.

He cast another glance at her out of the corner

of his eye. She was clearly trying to sleep, so he decided not to bother her any more at the moment. Then he shifted the truck into a lower gear and started the descent out of the mountains.

THE SUN HAD risen over the horizon when Becky opened her eyes again. Her neck was stiff from sleeping sitting up.

"Did you have a good nap?" Coy asked, grinning at her from behind the wheel as she stretched.

"Yep," she said, smiling back at him, her voice a little groggy. She looked out the window and noted that the pine trees and aspens had been replaced by junipers and mesquites, although they were still in the mountains.

The sky was overcast with clouds. Becky leaned back into her seat. "I love monsoon season, but I don't like the humidity it brings," she said.

Coy gave her an amused look. "This coming from the woman who wants to stay in Texas?"

She laughed. "I've only been back in Arizona a little over a week and I already forgot how bad it was."

"That's probably a sign that you shouldn't go back," he said.

"I don't know if I'm going to. I haven't made up my mind yet."

He gave her a long look. "You haven't made up your mind about Texas or about me?"

"I made up my mind about you a long time ago,"

she said. "Now I just have to decide if we can coexist."

A look of hurt flashed across his face, but it was quickly replaced with one of hope. "Does that mean you're considering working for Dr. Evans?"

"No," she said, "but he did offer to make me a partner at the clinic."

"That's great!"

"I haven't decided yet," she said as she peered out the window at the passing scenery. "My dad is pushing for me to stay and take over the ranch—"

"And I'm pushing you to stay with me," he finished for her.

"Yes," she admitted. "And while I love the ranch and you, I have to decide what's best for me."

He smiled. "You admitted you still love me. That's a start."

"Let's take this one day at a time," she said.

He nodded. "I'm not giving up on us. I'm not going to push you to make a decision right now. There's still a while to go until Independence Day."

"Thank you."

The closer they got to Phoenix, the heavier the traffic became. She opened her tote bag and pulled out her book. Coy needed to concentrate on his driving and she didn't want to distract him.

"How long has it been since you've seen Alyssa?"

She frowned. "I think the last time I saw her was

when she and Kyle got married. What about you? When is the last time you saw Kyle?"

"In October," he said. "I bought a load of hay from him and came down here to pick it up. I used the hay for the Harvest Festival and then took it to Whispering Pines."

Guilt hit her again. "I doubt if she will be too happy to see me," she said. "I pretty much neglected everybody over the last year and a half."

"We've...you've had a lot going on," he said. "Between school and losing the baby, I'm sure you weren't feeling very social."

"It didn't stop you," she mumbled underneath her breath.

"You didn't leave me with much choice," he said. "At least you could hide away at school. I was the one who had to face all of our friends and listen to people constantly asking me where you were and what had happened between us. I wasn't even allowed to grieve the loss of our baby."

She had never considered what Coy might be going through while she was safely out of the spotlight in Texas. They had both agreed not to tell anyone about the baby, so he couldn't talk to anyone about it.

"I'm sorry," she whispered. "I guess I wasn't very fair to you at the time. I didn't think it could possibly have affected you the way it did me."

His face tightened and he pressed his lips together. "You may have been the one carrying our baby, but it was my child, too."

They rode in silence for a little bit as they entered the outskirts of Phoenix.

"Do you want me to drop you off at Alyssa's while I deliver the horses to Scott?" he asked.

Although she had never been a big fan of Scott Griffin, she didn't want to impose her company on Alyssa, especially since she hadn't spoken to her in a while. "I haven't talked to Alyssa in a long time. I don't want to show up unannounced."

"You won't be," he said. "I called Kyle and talked to him while you were sleeping. Alyssa can't wait to see you and promised to have breakfast waiting for us when we get there."

"Really?" Becky smiled. "In that case, take me to Alyssa. Unless it's too far out of the way."

"Actually, I have to drive right by there to get to Scott's," he said. "I know you don't care much for Scott, anyway."

She snorted. "You do? How many times haven't you almost gotten into a fistfight with that guy? I'm really shocked that he'd even consider buying horses from you."

"It took some persuading," he said. "He's still convinced that I told Larry his horses were inferior."

"You did," she reminded him.

Larry Goldberg was one of the men in charge of hiring stock contractors for the rodeo. When Larry didn't renew Scott's contract, Scott was convinced it was Coy's fault.

"I did not," Coy said. "I just said that he had great horses but they weren't born to buck, and he looked at them and made up his own mind."

"Still, you're the one who brought it to his attention," she said. "If you ask me, he was always jealous of you. When the two of you competed for the high school championship, you beat him in every event."

"I had to." Coy gave her a crooked smile. "He told everyone he was going to steal you away from me."

Becky rolled her eyes. "He was more interested in my dad's ranch than he was me."

Coy chuckled. "He always was a money-hungry guy, but this time that worked out in my favor. He may not like me, but he's smart enough to know a good deal when he hears one."

A few miles later, they turned off Highway 60 into the community of Gold Canyon. Becky couldn't believe so many houses could be crammed into one tract. It gave her claustrophobia just driving through it. Coy turned onto another road, leading through an older residential area. The houses here were larger and sat on several acres, so at least she could breathe again.

"Is this where Alyssa and Kyle live?" The home was one of the fanciest she had ever seen. "They've done well for themselves."

"Kyle went back to college and got his engineering degree," Coy told her. "He works for Lockheed Martin."

"And what does Alyssa do?"

"She stays home with the kids," Coy said. "I think she's homeschooling them."

He pulled into the circular driveway and parked in front of the house. Becky had barely opened the truck door when the front door opened. Three children flew out, followed by Alyssa, who was carrying a toddler on her hip.

The older children surrounded Coy, jumping up and down in circles around him. Becky watched the interaction with interest. They obviously knew him well. He tossed the youngest girl up into the air, causing her to squeal with delight.

"My turn!" her older sister said.

"Becky!" Alyssa wrapped her arms around Becky and gave her a big hug. As she pulled away, she gasped and wiped at a spot on Becky's blouse. "I am so sorry," she said. "Paige wiped ketchup all over you!"

"It's okay." She bent over to look at the little girl's chubby face. "She looks just like you."

Alyssa laughed. "The other three are the spitting image of their dad."

"They may look like me, but they're all as stubborn and hardheaded as their mother," a man said, appearing from around the side of the house.

"Hi, Kyle," Becky greeted him. "Nice to see you again."

"You, too." Kyle winked at her. "I thought you had fallen off the face of the earth."

She could feel her face turn red at his words. "I know I haven't been much of a friend."

"Oh, girl, please." Alyssa waved one hand at her. "We all grew up and got a life. I know you've been busy. Now, come inside and have some breakfast before these little vultures eat it all!"

She had taken a few steps toward the house when she stopped to look back at Coy. He was talking to Kyle.

"Are you coming?" she asked him.

He shook his head. "No, go ahead. I'm going to get these horses to Scott before he changes his mind."

# *CHAPTER THIRTEEN*

Becky bounced Paige on her hip while watching nine-year-old Corbin show off his roping skills. His sisters cheered when his rope landed over the head of the roping dummy. She shifted the toddler to the other side and wiped the sweat off her face with the back of her hand.

Alyssa laughed. "Hey, it's not even hot yet."

"It is to me," she sighed. It was amazing the difference in temperature between Coronado and Phoenix. "No wonder people flock to the mountains in the summer."

They heard a loud truck coming down the road and Becky didn't need to see it to know that it was Coy. He'd only been gone a couple of hours. Either things had gone very well or it had been a disaster. She and Alyssa went to the front of the property just as Coy was parking.

"Scott must not have wanted all the horses." Alyssa nodded at the two horses in the trailer.

Becky walked toward the truck. "No, those

aren't the same horses we brought. He must have been able to talk Scott into trading a couple."

"Hi." Coy got out of the truck and walked around the end of the trailer to meet them. "Are you ready?"

"So soon?" Alyssa frowned. "You just got here."

"I'd love to stay for a while," Coy told her, "but I want to get out of this heat and get the horses settled."

Becky kissed Paige's chubby cheek and handed her back to her mother. Then she said goodbye to Alyssa and her children and climbed into the truck.

"I guess things went well with Scott?"

Coy grinned. "After Scott had a couple of his men try to ride them, he couldn't make a deal fast enough."

"Then he should have traded you across the board." Becky glanced over her shoulder at the covered horse trailer. "You gave him four good horses, but he only gave you two."

He laughed. "True, but I got to pick the two I wanted."

She shook her head. "How often do you plan to do this?"

"Not often. I'd rather spend my time working with horses I can use at Whispering Pines. If Noah finds some that Scott would like, I'll do it again. But it'll be an even trade then."

"Now you have six horses, if you don't count Whiskey," she said. "How many do you need?"

"After I drop these off, I'm going to pick up six from Noah. That's a pretty good start. It'll be enough for a trail ride."

"You're picking them up today?" She glanced at the clock on the dashboard. "It'll be after five o'clock when we get home."

"I know, but the sooner I get them to Whispering Pines, the sooner they can get settled."

"Are you going to start this weekend or give them a few days?" She opened her phone and looked at the growing list of things she needed to do. All of her Thursday afternoon appointments had been rescheduled so she could take care of George's mare, then her flat tire and today's trip had put her even further behind.

"It depends. If they've adjusted well, I might take them out for a ride on Sunday afternoon."

"Let me know if you do and I'll come help," she told him. "I'm a little behind in my schedule, but I should be able to start working with the horses by Wednesday."

He didn't respond and Becky could see him studying the rearview mirror, probably watching for a break in the traffic. She glanced up. Ahead of them, a semitruck was driving with its blinkers on. If they weren't able to get to the next lane and got stuck behind the semi, they would slow down almost to a crawl. With horses in the trailer, it was important to keep moving to provide enough airflow to keep the horses cool.

She didn't say anything more, letting him concentrate on the road. He was just starting to pull into the neighboring lane to pass the semi when his cell phone started ringing.

His attention remained focused on the road. "I'm not connected to Noah's Bluetooth. Can you answer that for me?"

She reached across the seat and picked up his phone. "It's Luke. I'll put it on speaker."

Coy was still trying to navigate traffic and wasn't paying much attention so she spoke first when Luke picked up. "Hello?"

"Hello? Who is this?" Luke obviously wasn't expecting anyone else to answer Coy's phone.

"This is Becky," she said. "We're on our way back from Phoenix and traffic is pretty heavy so he couldn't answer. I have you on speaker, though."

Coy relaxed as he got past the semi and was able to pull back into the slower lane of traffic. "What's up?"

"I wanted to see if you were coming to the Watering Hole tonight. I'm trying out a couple of new songs and need all the support I can get."

"It'll be pretty late by the time we get back and unload, but I'll try."

"Don't try. Just do." Luke's laughter was still coming through the line when he disconnected the call.

The tension seemed to leave his body as he leaned back against the seat. Becky frowned. He'd been pulling horse trailers since he got his driver's license. They'd pulled a trailer much larger than this one through Houston, Texas, in rush hour traffic, through Las Vegas, and every major city in between. Phoenix was a cakewalk in comparison.

"Are you okay?"

He glanced at her. "I don't like driving other people's vehicles."

She didn't buy it completely, but she didn't push him for another answer and decided to change the subject. "So, have you met Matt Spencer?"

Matt Spencer was one of country music's biggest stars, and Coy's best friend, Luke, had written at least half a dozen songs for him. Rumor had it that Matt often spent weekends at Luke's house when they were working on a new album.

"A couple of times." He shrugged.

She shook her head. "I can't believe that we're friends with someone who is friends with someone famous."

He laughed. "Matt's just like any other guy. He wants to do his job and be left alone."

"Are you going?"

"Where?" His brow furrowed for a moment. "You mean tonight?"

"Yeah," she said. "Are you going? It might be fun."

"We can go if you want," he said. He nodded at the upcoming town. "Too bad we don't have time to stop at the Top-of-the-World."

"Is the Trading Post still open?"

He shook his head. "This morning it looked like the place had closed up. The jerky stand is still open, though."

She glanced back at the horse trailer. "Another time."

"Especially if you want to go dancing tonight."

She gave him an innocent look. "Who said anything about dancing?"

He gave her a crooked smile and turned his attention back to the road.

One of the things she missed about the rodeo circuit was the post-rodeo nightlife. While Coy enjoyed the attention he got from being a bull rider, when the rodeo was over, he was ready to go home and relax. She, on the other hand, was ready to let loose after a long weekend of watching him risk life and limb on the back of a bull.

She sighed. "Do you miss the rodeo?"

"Not as much as I miss you."

She gave him a pointed look.

"No." He shook his head. "I miss parts of it, but I wouldn't want to go back."

"That surprises me," she said.

Coy raised one eyebrow. "I only did it because I didn't know what else to do."

"There were lots of things you could've done. You didn't have to resort to bull riding." She knew that his ultimate reason for joining the circuit was to get out of Coronado for a while, but it didn't explain why he stuck with it for six years.

He rubbed the back of his neck with one hand. "I didn't have many options. I couldn't afford to go to college, so my choices were to get a job, join the military or join the rodeo. None of the jobs I could get in Coronado paid much more than minimum wage. I went to talk to a recruiter a couple of times before deciding the military wasn't for me. So I did the only thing I was ever good at."

"I didn't know you thought about joining the military," she said.

"Until the recruiter told me there was a chance I could get stationed somewhere that you couldn't come with me."

"So you picked the rodeo."

"Seemed like the right thing to do. I thought I might win some fast cash. I also thought it might impress your parents if I became a world champion."

Becky blinked at that. "Why would you want to impress them?"

"Your mom made it pretty clear that she expected me to provide you with the lifestyle you were accustomed to. I couldn't do that without money."

Her heart skipped a beat. He hadn't been chasing the thrill of competition. He'd been chasing stability. For her.

"I thought you loved it," she murmured, more to herself than to him.

"I loved being with you," he corrected, his voice steady but gentle. "The rodeo was just a way to make it work."

Coy hummed as he dried himself off after getting out of the shower. If his feet lifted off the ground right now and he floated away, he wouldn't have been the least surprised. Today had been perfect. He and Becky hadn't argued once about the past and she hadn't mentioned the divorce papers in a while. Maybe she was ready to try again?

He put on his best pair of jeans and buttoned the western shirt Becky had given him for his birthday two years ago. He glanced at the clock on his bedside table. It was seven thirty. Considering that they didn't get back to Coronado until five thirty, he was making good time.

All the new horses were unloaded and settled for the night and he had been pleased with how well they seemed to take to their new environment, even the once-wild horses he'd picked up from Noah.

Fifteen minutes later, he knocked on Becky's cabin door. His insides quivered like this was their first date. In a way, it kind of was. Maybe this could be a whole new beginning for them.

"Hi." She opened the door and stepped outside.

Coy let out a soft whistle. It wasn't often that Becky wore her long hair down. It hung past her waist and looked so silky and shiny he was tempted to wrap his hands in it. She'd applied just a touch of makeup, accentuating the dark lashes that framed her eyes.

"You look beautiful," he told her.

Becky laughed. "You look pretty handsome yourself."

He took her hand and led her to the truck, and opened the door for her.

"I hope we didn't miss Luke's set," she said.

Coy shook his head. "He doesn't even start until eight, so we'll get there in plenty of time."

The parking lot in front of the town's only tavern was almost full. Once again, he took her hand as they started toward the entrance. Just before he pushed open the door, she pulled her hand away.

The Watering Hole buzzed with the familiar hum of chatter, clinking glasses and laughter. On the stage, the band were getting ready to start. Luke noticed them and nodded at him.

Becky leaned back against the bar, her gaze drifting over the room. "Where do you want to sit?"

He pointed toward one of the empty tables closest to the dance floor. It would be loud, but he doubted they would be sitting much. Nostalgia hit him hard. The worn wooden floors, the cowboy hats, the smell of beer and sawdust—it was the same all over the country, but the Watering Hole was different. It was home.

Luke's wife, Emily, hurried over to the table. "Hi, Becky!"

"Hi," she greeted her. "Where is your little one tonight?"

Emily's bright blue eyes sparkled and she ran one hand through her blond curls. "My aunt Tricia is watching him. How'd you manage to get this one out of his cabin?"

Coy stiffened when Emily nodded at him. It wasn't like he never left the campground.

Becky grinned. "It wasn't easy."

Emily looked around the bar. "Millie's here!"

A moment later, Emily had dragged Becky over to Millie's table. Coy listened to their laughter from across the room and wondered what they were talking about.

"Wedding stuff," a voice said behind him.

Coy turned to see Randon, Millie's fiancé, towering over him. Goodness, the man was big. "What did you say?"

Randon sat down at Coy's table and took a drink of his soda. "Every time Millie gets around other women, all they seem to want to talk about is the wedding. I don't understand how they can talk about the same thing over and over."

Coy laughed. "How much longer do you have?"

"One hundred and thirty-four days," he said.

"Sounds like you may be just as anxious as Millie."

Randon gave him a sheepish grin. "I've been waiting for this since I was eight years old."

Coy's stomach twisted. Like him, Randon had been in love with Millie since he was a kid. The only difference was, Randon had no qualms about getting married.

His gaze drifted back over to Becky and he was surprised to see that she was watching him. His gaze locked on to hers for a heartbeat longer than necessary and his breath hitched. As far as he was concerned, she was the only person in the room, the only thing that mattered.

The band started to play and Becky pulled herself away from the group of women. She stopped at the bar and bought two beers before heading to his table.

"Want a beer?" She sat down next to him and placed the glass in front of him.

"Thanks." He took a drink as the music cranked up even louder.

Millie joined them a moment later. Like Randon, she sipped on a soda instead of beer. "I'm on call at the nursing home," she explained.

Becky's fingers drummed on the table, keeping time with the music. "Luke sounds amazing."

"Yeah." Coy leaned in close to her so he didn't have to shout. "Have you heard him sing 'Emily's Song'?"

"No. I've heard Matt Spencer sing it on the radio."

"You have to hear Luke sing it," Millie told her. "It's like nothing I've ever heard."

Luke's first song kicked off, a fast-paced song that got several people out on the dance floor. Becky bumped into him as she swayed with the beat of the music. His pulse quickened. The next song was a bit slower.

"You want to dance?" He tried to keep his posture casual, but there was nothing casual about the way she made him feel. He couldn't believe that she didn't feel it, too.

Becky didn't hesitate. She jumped up, and this time, she let him take her by the hand to pull her onto the dance floor. He drew her into his arms and sighed. He hadn't realized how much he missed dancing with her.

The song ended, and just as she started to step away, the familiar notes of Luke's love song to Emily began and Coy pulled her back to him. His hand fit perfectly against the small of her back and her hands rested on his shoulders.

"I don't know if this is a good idea," she said softly, though her body had already leaned a little closer to his.

"It's just a dance." Coy was careful to keep his tone light.

When the last note ended, she didn't even try to step away. "That was beautiful."

"It's a great song," he said.

Becky bit her lip and let out a long breath. "It's

not the song. It's the way he sings it. It's the way he looks at Emily when he sings it."

"He wrote it at a time he thought he might lose her." Coy's fingers curled around hers and he led her back to the table. Couldn't she see that he felt the same way about her?

The music stopped for a moment and Luke introduced the band. Then he introduced Emily and the crowd cheered. When she got onstage with him, Becky let out a loud whoop.

"I didn't know Emily could sing, did you?" She clapped as loudly as the rest of the crowd.

"Luke mentioned it, but I don't think I've ever heard her."

Emily looked a little nervous when one of the band members handed her the microphone. Luke took her by the hand and they sang "Louisiana Woman, Mississippi Man" together. When the song was over, Emily handed the microphone back to Luke and hurried off the stage.

"That was great!" Becky waved her over. "You sounded just like Loretta Lynn."

"Thanks." Emily's face was red. "I was so nervous."

Millie squeezed her hand. "You two should sing together more often. You were fantastic!"

The band started a fast-paced song and Coy didn't hesitate to drag Becky back out on the dance floor. Immediately, they fell into rhythm together. They twirled and spun and she never missed a beat.

She knew him well enough to know which way to spin and when to stop. By the time the song was over, they were both breathless.

The music slowed, and Coy pulled her into his arms again. He wondered if he could pay Luke to only play slow songs for the rest of the night. She let her head rest against his shoulder as they swayed together. The scent of her—lavender mixed with something slightly sweet—engulfed him.

As soon as the song ended, Becky pulled away from him and hurried to the table. By the time Coy got to the table, she and Millie had hightailed it to the bathroom.

"You got it bad," Randon told him, grinning. "It's not too late to make it a double wedding, you know."

"Yes, it is," he said.

Randon gave him a puzzled look, and it was on the tip of his tongue to explain that he'd already married Becky once. Somehow, he doubted she would be very appreciative of him telling anyone, though.

But why? His gaze traveled to where the women had disappeared. Why was it such a big secret? They were two consenting adults. Was she ashamed of him? He stood up from the table and walked past the bar to where the bathrooms were located. He leaned against the wall, waiting for Becky to emerge.

"Come on, honey," a man at the bar slurred. "Just one little kiss."

The bartender, a tall, stocky woman with bright red hair, blew the drunk man a kiss. "How about I call a ride home for you?"

The man didn't seem to be satisfied with an air-kiss and reached across the bar to grab the woman's arm. Coy pushed himself off the wall to intervene. Before he had even taken a step, the bartender took the man's arm, twisted it and had him practically lying across the bar. It happened so fast that Coy wasn't sure exactly how she did it.

As she was leading the man toward the entrance, Becky and Millie appeared.

"What happened?" Becky nodded toward the crowd that had gathered around the man.

"I'm not sure," Coy said. "One minute the man was trying to flirt with the bartender and the next minute, she had him on the bar."

Millie nodded. "The guy must have broken the number one rule here—Don't touch Caroline."

"She moves fast, that's for sure," Coy said.

"No one messes with her," Millie said. "At least, not more than once."

"I can see why."

Millie walked past and Becky started to follow. Coy stopped her, careful not to grab her arm. He didn't want to appear as if he was trying to manhandle her the way the man had Caroline. "Can we talk outside?"

Becky glanced at Millie before nodding. She followed him out the back door of the bar. The area was obviously for the smoking crowd, but at least it wasn't so loud that he couldn't hear anything.

She lifted her hair up from the back of her neck and held it there for a moment. "What is it?"

"I don't want to keep our marriage a secret anymore," he said. "I don't want to have to keep tiptoeing around my words, afraid I'm going to let something slip."

She stared at him for a moment, her teeth worrying her bottom lip. "No," she finally said.

"No? Why not?" His heart thumped in his chest.

"What would it accomplish?" she said. "It's not like it was ever a real marriage to begin with."

Her words slammed into his chest like a two-ton bull. He swallowed and took a step away from her. Turning, he went back inside the bar.

Randon and Millie were sitting at the table, their heads almost touching as they talked. Coy picked up his keys from the table. "I've got a lot to do tomorrow. Have a good night."

As he spun around to leave, he almost ran into Becky. "I'm going. Are you coming with me or are you staying?"

She lifted her chin. "I'm staying."

## *CHAPTER FOURTEEN*

BECKY STOPPED HER truck in front of the barn and shut off the engine. She felt drained. It was only Wednesday, but she'd had to be at the office in Springerville every morning this week. That meant leaving the cabin by 5 a.m. And thanks to lying awake thinking about Coy every night, she wasn't getting much sleep. Her eyes lingered on the fast-food wrappers scattered on the passenger seat. Eating junk food and running on minimal sleep—no wonder she felt so run-down and terrible.

Somehow, she suspected that even if she'd been getting eight hours of sleep each night, she would still feel terrible. She hadn't seen or talked to Coy in four days. She could still see the look of hurt on his face when she told him she didn't want to tell people about their quickie wedding. The truth was, she was embarrassed. She'd tried for years to talk him into getting married and once they were, she wanted a divorce. No one would understand the reasons behind it.

They needed to talk about this and put it behind them.

Coy wasn't inside the barn. That meant he was probably in the round pen with one of the new horses. She sighed and grabbed her bag, trudging toward the back entrance of the barn. Her muscles ached with each step, the physical exhaustion mirrored by the emotional fatigue gnawing at her.

She walked around to the side of the barn, facing away from the entrance to the campground. As she neared the round pen, she spotted Coy standing in the middle with a long lead rope attached to the chestnut filly. The horse moved in graceful circles around him while he continuously talked in a low, soothing voice. Every other circle, Coy would shorten the rope until the horse was close enough for him to reach out and touch. But he didn't. He continued speaking until the filly realized how close she was and stopped.

Becky held her breath, waiting to see if the horse would shy away from him or try to interact. The filly tossed her head, sniffing the air. A moment later, she nuzzled the pocket of Coy's shirt, searching for the sugar cubes he kept there. He laughed and pulled out a sugar cube, offering it to the horse.

"I thought I heard your truck." Coy glanced over at her. "You okay?"

"I'm really tired," she said, her voice betraying her exhaustion. "I had to go in to the office again, so it's been a long day."

"That's every day this week." He frowned. "I thought another doctor was managing the office."

She shrugged. "She is, but I still have to take care of the livestock, and some people prefer to bring their animals to the office."

He nodded. "Go to the cabin and get some sleep. Caden's helping me this week and Noah's going to help me this weekend."

His tone made her bristle. "I'm sorry, but my job comes first. My *real* job."

"I know," he said, keeping his voice low and calm. "But I'm running out of time. I've already started advertising for the trail ride, so the horses have to be ready."

She could tell that he was still angry with her, but trying hard not to let it show.

"Can I ask you something?" she said. "Why don't you just buy some horses? Ones that are already trained and ready."

Coy led the horse out of the round pen and let her go into the pasture with the rest of the horses. "Come and see."

She followed him into the office, where he pulled a ledger out of the drawer and slapped it on the desk. When she opened it, one side of the ledger was filled with expected expenses, and the other side was projected income. She scanned the expenses—new saddles, harnesses, helmets and other riding equipment. Insurance was a large portion of the expenses, not to mention the additional cost of grain and hay.

"I can't afford to buy a horse that's already trained," he told her.

Her heart fluttered. "You didn't read the papers I gave you, did you?"

His face hardened. "If you're talking about the divorce papers, no."

"Just sign the papers and you'll have enough money to cover all these expenses."

"Excuse me?"

"The settlement," she said. "It would be enough to cover most of your expenses."

His eyes narrowed into hard blue stones. "You want to pay me to divorce you?" Anger laced his words.

"I wouldn't call it that," she said, struggling to keep her voice steady. "I was just trying to be fair."

"By reminding me that I didn't have the means to support my family, but you do?"

"Then don't think of it as a settlement. Think of it as a loan. You can pay me back when you get on your feet."

"There's just one problem with all that," he growled. "If I sign those papers and take that settlement, I'm saying that money is more important than you. And it's not. It wasn't eight years ago, and it's not now."

He stomped past her and out of the office. Eight

years ago? She shook her head, bewildered. What was he talking about?

She stormed after him and stopped him before he got out of the barn. "You better explain that comment."

The muscles in his jaw clenched and his mouth pressed into a thin line. "Forget it. It doesn't matter, now."

"It matters to me," she said. "Did my mother offer you money to break up with me?"

His brow furrowed and the surprised look in his eyes brought her a small measure of relief. She knew her mother was against his traveling ways, but she didn't want to believe that she would go so far as to try to buy him off.

Coy shook his head. "I had a sponsorship offer, but only if I traveled alone."

Becky's mouth fell open. It was the second time she'd found out that he turned down something to stay with her. "Why didn't you tell me?"

His blue eyes turned icy. "It doesn't matter. It's not like this was a real relationship, anyway."

He turned and walked out of the barn.

His words punched her in the gut. But they weren't his words. They were hers. She followed him to the corrals, determined to talk this out, but he'd already started working with a different horse. She stood there, watching him work. His eyes never left the horse, and she was a little baffled. In all the time they'd been together, he'd never dismissed her. She couldn't recall him ever getting mad at her. Every time they had ever argued, it was always her that instigated it. Why was that?

She glanced at him one more time, his posture stiff and rigid. Her presence wasn't welcome, that much was clear. "I'll talk to you tomorrow," she said before turning and walking away.

Back in her truck, Becky gripped the steering wheel, her knuckles white. It had never occurred to her to question why Coy had never stood up to her. He always let her take the lead in their arguments and always apologized first.

She'd seen him angry. She'd even broken up some of the fights he'd been in. No one could ever accuse him of being a pushover. He'd never backed down from a fight, whether he was defending himself or standing up for someone else. But he never stood up to her.

The weight of their conversation pressed down on her as she drove to the cabin. Once inside, she collapsed onto the couch. She glanced at an envelope on the coffee table—her copy of the divorce papers. It was what she still wanted, wasn't it?

Her mind drifted back to the kiss last week at the barn. She thought about how it felt when he held her in his arms and they danced together. Coy was taking every opportunity to remind her that they belonged together.

If he'd been as outspoken about how much they belonged together in the past as he was now, she would never have doubted him. Where had this side of him been hiding for the last eighteen months? If he was as determined to stay together as he claimed now, shouldn't he have done more than text her? He didn't even show up for her graduation from veterinarian school. If he really loved her, he should've been there.

She picked up the laptop from the coffee table and opened her email account. Last week she'd received a job offer from the clinic in Abilene that she'd interviewed with on her way to Coronado. She opened the email and reviewed the job offer again. Now she had two job offers. Well, three if she counted Dr. Evans's offer. Part of her wanted to accept the offer in Abilene and leave as quickly as she could.

She set the laptop back on the coffee table and picked up the papers with Dr. Evans's offer. She would have to be crazy to turn it down. Wasn't it every veterinarian's dream to have their own practice? And this one was already established. She wouldn't be starting from scratch, trying to build clientele. It was everything she should want.

COY KEPT HIS attention on the filly circling him. From the way she tossed her head, he knew she was picking up on his anger. He would never make progress working with the horses in this state. He led the horse to the gate and released her into the pasture with the other horses. As he stood there, one foot hiked on the bottom rung of the fence, he watched the horses graze.

Noah had saddle broke them, but they needed to be ridden a lot in order to be trustworthy enough for strangers to sit on their back. He didn't need Becky's help training them. It was just an excuse to spend time with her. He'd been desperate for a way to change her mind about wanting a divorce.

Her words still echoed in his head when he lay in bed at night. *Not a real marriage.* It was the second time she'd made a comment like that. Maybe he should give up and give her what she wanted. But the thought of saying goodbye to her for good felt like shards of glass ripping into his heart.

He pushed away from the fence and walked to his truck. His cabin was at the far end of the campground. There were two ways to get there. There was a road that led from the barn around the back side of the cabins, and there was the main road that entered the campground from the highway. Instead of going the back way, he chose to return to where the road to the barn split off the main road. The last thing he wanted to do was drive past Becky's cabin.

As he traveled on the main road, he tried to look at the campground as if he'd never been there before. What would attract someone to stay there? What would make a person decide not to stay there? The cabins were scattered throughout the property with lots of space, offering each cabin a semblance of privacy. Tall pine trees provided shade and scenery. The common area was neat and well-groomed. There were grills stationed at each corner of the common area for large cookouts, as well as horseshoe pits and cornhole boards for those that wanted to play games.

Stacy had done a great job managing the campground. It was a warm, inviting place for families. Its only downside was that it was a long drive into town and some people didn't want to be that far away from amenities. Of course, there was a trail that cut over the ridge and led from the common area to the Coronado Market, but not everyone wanted to walk that far.

Coy stopped the truck and looked at a large empty area between the common area and the caretaker's cabin. When he and Stacy helped their grandfather run the campground, she'd suggested building a store, reminiscent of an old-fashioned general mercantile, a sort of sister store to the market. He'd suggested adding a western-style saloon for refreshments—nonalcoholic, of course. The campground was family-friendly after all. If he was going to convert this place from a campground to a guest ranch, he needed to add all the things he and Stacy had talked about when they were kids. The problem was, he needed money to do it. Right now, the campground made enough money to keep it in the black but not enough to pay for expansions. He needed a way to make some money fast.

Coy parked in front of his cabin and went inside. On the refrigerator was the business card Barrett Montgomery had given him. Maybe that was it. An extra source of income that he could use for the campground. Taking a deep breath, he dialed the man's number.

"Mr. Montgomery," he said when the man answered the phone, "this is Coy Tedford. We met a couple of weeks ago in Coronado."

"Yes, I remember." His voice was enthusiastic. "Have you decided to take me up on my offer?"

"Yes and no." Coy hoped he was doing the right thing. "I'm still not looking for a new job. However, if you have any horses that need to be trained, I'd love to discuss it with you."

"If you're willing to come to Eagar for a few days to look over my operation, we can certainly talk about it."

A few minutes later, they'd made arrangements to meet, and Coy felt a surge of relief. He could do this. He could make Whispering Pines into the guest ranch he wanted. And he could do it without the Maxwell money.

He leaned against the kitchen counter, his thoughts drifting back to Becky. He had to admit that part of his drive to make Whispering Pines successful was to prove to her that he could provide for them, something her mother never thought he would be able to do. What good was it to prove Autumn wrong if Becky wasn't part of it? Did he even want to continue without her? He looked around the cabin and a feeling of contentment settled over him. Yes. This was where he wanted to be. This was what he wanted to do. He would much rather have Becky be part of it, but he was committed to Whispering Pines with or without her.

He straightened up. Wow. He'd finally found who he was. Maybe there was hope after all.

Speaking of, he had to go back to the barn. He'd left in a hurry because he needed to get away, but the horses had to be brought in from the pasture and put in their stalls before their evening feed.

Again, he took the long way around to the barn. He still didn't want to drive by Becky's cabin. After parking, he walked down to the pasture and let out a soft whistle. The horses lifted their heads and most of them started moving toward him. After a moment, the others followed.

He leaned against the fence, watching them as they ambled toward him. They were beautiful creatures. He'd always had a way with horses and probably should have pursued roping or cutting instead of bull riding. It just happened that he was a good bull rider, and he enjoyed the prestige. But this— he nuzzled Shucks's nose when the horse stuck his head over the fence—this was what he really loved.

When he was done with the horses, he stood in the office, studying the kanban board. He'd divided his ideas into categories based on importance and price. Once he started showing a sizable profit with the campground, he could apply for a loan in order to build the store and the saloon. He needed to create a business plan that would wow the loan officers at the bank. And he needed some rough sketches of his vision for Whispering Pines, including the store and saloon. Trouble was, he couldn't draw a stick figure. It was a good thing he knew someone who could.

He texted Stacy. Can you get me Randon's number?

A second later, his phone rang. "Hi, Stacy."

"What do you want Randon's number for?" she asked.

Until he was more sure of his plans, he didn't want to tell her what he was doing. "I have a project I need his help with."

"Hmm," she said. "I'll send it to you now."

"Thanks." He hung up the phone and waited for the text.

Randon was the newest art teacher at the middle school. He'd also painted the large mural on the side of Stacy's store. Coy only hoped that Randon wasn't so busy preparing for his upcoming wedding to Millie Gibson that he wouldn't be able to help.

He held his breath as he waited for Randon to answer the phone.

"Hello?"

"Hi, Randon. This is Coy."

"Oh, hey. What's up?"

Coy stared at the kanban board. "I'd like to take advantage of your art expertise. I'm working on a business plan to present to the bank in the next few months. I would like to include some drawings of my vision for Whispering Pines. Interested?"

"Sure. I can come out tomorrow morning."

"Sounds great. I'll see you then." He disconnected the call and sighed. He was one step closer to getting what he wanted.

# *CHAPTER FIFTEEN*

THE STREETS OF Coronado were more crowded than usual. Becky had to circle the Coronado Market three times before she could find a parking place. She was used to the market being busy in the mornings, but the afternoons weren't supposed to be this bad.

She ended up parking almost a block away and walking to the market. Inside wasn't much better. Vince—Stacy's father—and Millie were behind the registers and there was a long line for each one. Stacy and Donna were working behind the deli counter.

"Hi," Stacy greeted her. "I never see you in here this early in the afternoon."

"I finally caught up with all of Dr. Evans's backlogged calls and got off early," Becky said. "Why is it so crowded?"

"It's always like this in the summer." Stacy handed an ice cream cone to a little girl waiting near the counter. "Here you are, sweetie."

Becky frowned. She'd been so wrapped up in

her own world, she was missing out on everything that made the area so special. She stepped back to keep from getting run over by people wanting down the next aisle.

"Can I get you something?" Stacy nodded at the menu.

"I'll come back when it clears out," she said. "I thought I might buy Coy some cream soda as an apology before I start working with the horses. I was supposed to start helping yesterday, but I was just too exhausted."

"You're apologizing for being too tired?"

Becky shook her head slightly. "I upset him the other night and he's still mad at me."

"Donna, I'm going to the back to get more cones." Stacy walked around from behind the deli counter. "Coy's not here."

"What do you mean? Where is he?"

Stacy motioned for her to follow her to the back of the store. "He went to Eagar for a couple of days and asked Caden to take care of the horses for him."

They got to the back and Becky waited for Stacy to open the door to the storage area. "What's he doing in Eagar?"

"I don't know," Stacy said, waddling to the far end of the room. She pointed to a couple of boxes containing ice cream cones. "Here, help me carry these back to the deli. They're not heavy, just large."

Becky pulled out her phone and swiped up to see the text messages. "I told him I'd be at the barn this afternoon. Why didn't he tell me he wasn't there?"

"I don't know." Stacy frowned and rubbed her large stomach. "Maybe he needed some space."

*Space.* A sour taste filled her mouth. That's what he'd told her he was giving her when he left to go to a rodeo event a year and a half ago. She'd thrown the word back at him when he returned to find his suitcases sitting outside her apartment.

She swallowed. "Is that what he said? That he needed space?"

"No." Stacy didn't seem as concerned about the word as she was. "I just thought it might be why he didn't tell you where he was going."

Becky's stomach hardened. He'd done it again. When things got difficult, he did what he always did. Ran away. How could they ever work things out if he wasn't willing to stay and fight for them? She let out a loud huff. He couldn't fight *with* her, so why should she think he'd stick around long enough to fight *for* her?

"He's talking to a man about training horses."

Becky jerked her head around and saw Caden in the doorway, wearing an apron and food service gloves. "When did he leave? When will he be back?"

Caden shrugged. "He left early this morning and said that depending on how things go, he'll either be back Saturday or Sunday."

Over his shoulder, Becky could see that the once large storage area had been converted into a kitchen.

She glanced at Stacy. "I didn't know y'all had installed a kitchen back here."

Stacy shook her head. "Where do you think we cook the hamburgers and pizza?"

Caden grinned. "Stacy makes me do all the cooking so she can sit in the front and look pretty."

Stacy shook her head. "Don't listen to him. He begs to be put on cooking duty. Crowds bother him."

Becky shifted the box in her arms and followed Stacy back to the front of the store. *Eagar.* Something teased the back of her mind, but she couldn't quite put her finger on what it was.

She followed Stacy around the deli counter and set the box on the back counter. "Do you need me to get anything else for you before I leave?"

If Coy wasn't around, she didn't need to worry about buying his favorite soda for him, so she might as well get to the barn and start working with the horses.

"I'm good, thanks." Stacy put both hands on her back and stretched.

"Okay. I'll see you later, then."

She walked out of the store and stopped in front of the large community bulletin board attached to the wall. There were flyers for everything from community events to missing pets. A bright yellow paper flapped in the breeze, catching her attention.

It was an advertisement for the upcoming Round Valley Rodeo, held during the Fourth of July weekend. It was one of the biggest local rodeos in the area and a stepping stone for any Arizona cowboy wanting to make the transition from local rodeos to professionally sanctioned events.

She caught her breath. That was it. Floyd Taylor lived in Eagar. Floyd was a brother-in-law to Mr. Whitmire, Coy's bull riding coach. Floyd was a stock contractor for many rodeos in the area and often hosted bull riding competitions at his ranch.

In the weeks before a large rodeo, it wasn't unusual for his ranch to be flooded with cowboys looking to get in some extra practice, or who wanted to get familiar with the bulls they might draw for the rodeo. The Round Valley Rodeo was two weeks away. Which meant that this weekend, Floyd was sure to be hosting a minicompetition for cowboys eager to prove themselves. Coy had participated in it enough to know it, too.

Becky pressed her lips together. Coy talked about needing money for the campground. He got into bull riding because he thought it would be a way to make money fast. Did he still think that? Was he going to try to finance the campground with bull riding?

The drive from the market to the campground wasn't that long, but it felt like forever. Coy had made it pretty clear that he no longer needed her help, but she'd made a deal with him and even though he didn't seem interested in keeping the deal, she was.

She parked at the barn and went inside. After grabbing a lead rope, she went into the office. On Coy's desk she found the notebook with the riding schedule for the new horses. She flipped it open. He kept extremely detailed records. Even more detailed than when she charted things regarding her patients. She looked to see which horses needed to be worked with and closed the book.

The movement of air caused by the closing of the book ruffled other papers on the desk, and one paper floated off the desk onto the floor. She picked it up to set it back on the desk.

The words on the page jumped out at her and her blood turned to ice. *Bull Riding Participation Waiver.* She picked it up and read it again. It was from Floyd's ranch. Her fingers started to shake. Was he so desperate for money that he was willing to risk getting hurt? Or maybe it wasn't the money at all. Maybe he wanted to see if he still had what it took to be competitive. Did he want to get back on the circuit after all?

She wadded the paper into a tight ball and tossed it in the trash before storming out of the office. It took her three laps around the barn before she felt like she had calmed down enough to work with horses. The last thing she wanted was for them to pick up on her agitation. They would be leery enough of her as it was.

It only took a few minutes for her to locate the gelding she needed to work with and lead him to the tack room. She took her time brushing the dark chestnut's coat and talking to him. The action did more to soothe her than all the walking she'd just done.

The horse was calm and didn't appear to have picked up on her emotions, so she replaced the halter with a bridle. When she put the saddle blanket on him, he barely flinched, but he spooked a little when she put the saddle over his back.

"I know how you feel, buddy. I hate not knowing what's going on, either." She rubbed his neck and spoke in low tones. Soon he had settled down enough that she was able to finish saddling him.

Taking the reins in her hands, she led him to one of the empty corrals. She clutched the reins and part of his mane with one hand while she put one foot in the stirrup and mounted. Immediately, the horse jumped. She kept a tight hold of his mane and squeezed her legs around him while he bucked a couple more times.

After a few seconds, he stopped jumping, but was still skittish. Becky rode him around the corral a few times until he settled into a comfortable pace. The small pen was too confining to get much of a feel for the horse, so she urged him over to the gate. She leaned down and unlatched it so she could enter the larger pasture.

The moment the horse sensed that he was no longer confined, he bolted. Becky expected it and was ready. She let him run to the end of the pasture before turning him around and letting him run back toward the barn. After two more laps, sweat dripped from the horse's neck and his chest was heaving, but he responded easily to her commands.

She slowed him down and they walked a few more laps before she decided he'd had enough for the day. When she reached the corrals, she dismounted and led the horse back to the tack room. After putting the saddle and blanket away, she brushed the horse again. This time both she and the horse were relaxed and she felt sort of a kinship with the animal.

After putting him back into his stall, she went to the office to make notes in Coy's book and looked to see which horse she needed to work with next. At this rate, she was going to have all her frustration worked out and might sleep well for the first time in weeks.

COY HAD BEEN at the Montgomery Ranch for two days. Not only had he convinced Barrett to let him train some horses for him, he also wanted to send some of his staff to Whispering Pines to learn from Coy.

When he told Barrett about his plan to train wild

horses and get them ready for adoption, the man expressed interest in buying some of the horses after they were trained and promised to let the local ranchers know that Whispering Pines would be a good place to purchase a horse for their operation.

His excitement built with every person he talked to. His biggest regret was that he'd wasted his last nine months in Coronado. He'd been too scared to make plans without Becky and too scared to confront her and put an end to their separation.

He said goodbye to Barrett and was walking to his truck when his phone rang. He glanced at the screen. "Hey, Floyd. I was just about to call you."

"Hi," the man said. "Did you get the waiver I sent you?"

"I did." Coy opened the door to his truck and got in. "I wanted to see if you have a medical release form as well."

"I do. And I also have a photo and video release form that I require so that I can use their pictures on my website."

"That's a good idea." Coy started the engine to his truck. "I really appreciate you helping me out with this. I'm leaving Barrett Montgomery's ranch right now. Do you mind if I swing by?"

"Not at all," Floyd said. "There are some boys here who would love to meet you."

"I'll be there in about half an hour." He pulled away from the Montgomery Ranch and headed farther out of town until he came to the turnoff going to Floyd Taylor's ranch.

When he pulled up, he was greeted by Floyd and six teenage boys. Floyd introduced him to each of the boys, who in turn shook his hand and told him what a big fan they were. A few of the boys even asked for his autograph.

"Are you going to make a comeback?" a dark-haired boy with a mullet asked.

"No, I'm officially retired," Coy told him.

"All right, boys." Floyd ushered the teens away. "Jake is waiting for you at pen three."

They groaned, but turned and headed toward the practice pens.

"Thanks for meeting with me." Coy nodded at the retreating boys. "I would love to have the opportunity to influence boys the way you and Clarence have influenced me."

"I hope I'm not digging my own grave." Floyd clapped him on the shoulder. "I really shouldn't be helping you go into competition with me."

"I won't be competing against you." Coy paused at the entrance to the office building. He looked at the pictures of cowboys on the wall. "Your camp is for experienced cowboys who've ridden for a while and are serious about bull riding. I just want to offer a bull riding experience for my campers. I'll be using a drop barrel, not real bulls."

Floyd laughed and opened the door to his office. "So it'll be the city-slicker version of bull riding."

"Bull riding, barrel racing, roping." Coy's chest swelled. "I'd really like to get it set up for the fall season."

"I think it's a great idea." Floyd opened a file cabinet and pulled out several different permission forms. "Here. These ones should give you a pretty good idea of how to set things up. I wish I could send you the file on the computer, but my daughter is out of town and I don't even know how to turn the contraption on."

Coy took the forms from him. "No, sir. This is great."

A few minutes later he was in his truck and headed back to Coronado. He cranked up the radio and sang along. How many times had his dad told him that bull riding was a waste of time? Frank said he'd never be able to make a living from it. Now his entire future was shaping up thanks to his bull riding.

While he wasn't going to make any more money by riding bulls, the contacts he'd made and the skills he'd developed were going to help him build a guest ranch that his grandfather would've been proud of. He hoped it would make his dad proud, too.

His entire life he had been compared to his dad. Part of the reason he liked bull riding was that it was something his dad never did. His dad was a star football player, a great basketball and baseball player, and a decorated veteran. The coaches at the high school pushed Coy to play football, but he knew he would never be half the football player that his dad was. So instead of trying to live up to his dad's image, he participated in things that were the opposite of what his dad did.

When Tommy Littlebear talked him into trying to ride a steer the first time, it had been kind of a joke. But then he discovered that this was the one sport where his short, stocky stature was an advantage. He excelled at it, and for a while had the same level of respect and recognition that his dad enjoyed everywhere they went.

He stopped to get gas and check his text messages. He kept waiting for a text from Becky, expressing anger for him leaving and not telling her, but it never came. Each time his text notification went off, he hoped it was her. And each time, he was disappointed because it wasn't. Why hadn't she texted or called? Why wasn't she mad that he left without telling her?

It wasn't that he was purposely trying to anger her. He'd thought about telling her before he left, but he'd still been too fired up to have a casual conversation. When they did talk again, it would be anything but casual. They would clear the air and she would tell him why, after years of hinting that she wanted to get married, she was so anxious to get a divorce. Not a real marriage? What did she know about marriage?

Neither one of them had a great example of what

a good marriage should be. His father had ruled the home with an iron fist until his mother got sick of it and left. Her parents pretended to have a great marriage in public, but behind closed doors couldn't stand to be in the same room.

The question was, how did he and Becky get beyond their pasts to build a future together?

# *CHAPTER SIXTEEN*

ALL THE WAY back to Coronado, Coy replayed the events of the last couple of days. Things were working out well. Too well. When things went this well during a rodeo, it was a sure sign of disaster.

It was late when he got home. Funny, he hadn't allowed himself to think of the cabin as home, but he supposed it was now. He walked inside and looked around. The walls were bare. There was nothing anywhere that indicated someone lived there permanently.

A knock on the door startled him. Caden had been taking care of not only the horses, but the cabins as well, so unless there was an emergency, he doubted it was one of the campers. The only person it might be was Becky.

He opened the door and his heart leaped in his chest. "Hi, Becky."

"Where have you been?" She brushed by him as she stepped inside the cabin.

"I was in Eagar," he said. "I'm sure Caden told you."

Her brown eyes sparkled with anger. "The question is, why did I hear about it from Caden? Why didn't you tell me yourself?"

"You really need to make up your mind," he said. "First you tell me I need to stop relying on you for everything and to make my own decisions, now you're upset because I didn't discuss this with you."

Her nostrils flared and she clenched her jaw. He didn't get it. "I don't want you to ask me about every decision, but I'd like to be included in the process."

"I'd be more willing to include you in my plans if I knew you wanted to be a part of them." He crossed his arms. "One minute you're kissing me and the next minute you're offering me money to divorce you. I don't know what you want from me."

"I want…" Her mouth opened and then closed and she let out a heavy sigh. "I don't know what I want."

"Besides—" he lifted his chin "—you made it pretty clear the other night that what we had between us wasn't real, so I didn't think you cared."

Her face tightened and her eyes narrowed. "I never said that. Don't put words in my mouth."

He was tired and the last thing he wanted to do was argue with her tonight. "Did you come over just to argue with me?"

"No." She handed him a manila envelope.

His chest tightened. Was she trying to give him divorce papers again?

He tried to push it away. "I already told you no. Not yet."

She sighed. "Randon dropped it off and said it was very important that you get it right away."

It was from Randon? He grinned and took the envelope. "I can't believe he finished already. What great timing!"

He started to open the envelope.

Becky leaned closer. "What is that?"

He removed the drawings from the envelope and spread them out over the kitchen table. "Pictures of my vision for Whispering Pines."

The drawings were amazing. Randon had perfectly captured the atmosphere of the campground. "Look." He pointed to the first drawing. "Here's the saloon and the store. He even added hitching posts to the front."

Becky leaned over to get a better look. "These are beautiful, but what are they for?"

"If I can get Whispering Pines to be a little more profitable by the end of the summer, I'll apply for a loan to get enough money to build all the things I want to add to the campground. Randon drew these for me as part of my business proposal to take to the bank."

She touched one of the pictures. "What if you didn't have to wait until the end of the summer to get the loan you need?"

He stiffened. "I'm not taking your divorce settlement. Even if things don't work out between us and we end it, I will not take a dime from you."

The lines around her eyes tightened. "I wasn't talking about that. I'm talking about getting an investor. Someone who believes in your vision and will give you the money up front."

Coy frowned. "An investor would also want part ownership in the campground and I'm not willing to do that."

"Okay." She shook her head. "Not an investor in that sense. But someone who will invest in it, but only until you pay them back. I know my dad would be excited to help you with this."

That's all he needed. One more chance for her father to hold money over his head. Asking him for money, whether it was a loan or an investment, would only remind her dad that he didn't have enough money to take care of his daughter. "No thanks," he told her.

"Just think about it," she said. "Good night."

Without another word, she walked out the door.

She was right. If he wanted to get Whispering Pines off to a good start, he needed more money than he had now. Everything came down to money and he hated that.

He looked back down at the drawings lying on the table. His plans for Whispering Pines were coming together nicely. But to do it on his terms would take a long time. By that time, he could risk losing her for good, and would any of it be worth it without her?

BECKY TIED HER sneakers and opened the door to her cabin. The cool morning air burned her lungs, but in a good way. She hadn't jogged since arriving in Coronado and her muscles wouldn't be happy with her tomorrow. After a few stretches, she headed for the trail that circled the edge of the campground.

Only a few rays of light peeked over the horizon but it was enough to illuminate the trail she was on. Loud, rhythmic clangs echoed through the forest. The closer the path got to the barn, the louder the clangs got.

She slowed down to a walk and stepped off the trail to go over to the barn. Coy was in the farthest corral and was driving a large metal post into the ground. She wasn't sure what he was doing or why he was doing it. He had a look of deep concentration, so she didn't want to disturb him.

She turned around and jogged back the other direction. She had to admit that she was impressed he was following through with his plans for the campground. Her family's money had always been a sore spot with him, even though he tried to pretend it wasn't. She shouldn't have tried to get him to borrow money from her father.

When she approached the common area of the

campground, she turned off the main trail and followed the narrow path over a ridge and between the trees. The path leveled out and on one side of the trail, the trees had been cleared out and a large house stood in the middle of the clearing.

The Coronado Market loomed ahead in the breaking dawn. She slowed down and walked to the front of the store. For once, the store wasn't packed. She pushed open the door and the jingling of a bell announced her arrival.

Standing next to the registers, two older ladies held coffee cups and were chatting with Stacy. Both of the older women had bright-colored hair. One pink and the other blue.

"Good morning." She nodded at the Reed sisters, Margaret and Edith. She couldn't remember which sister was which.

"Well, if it isn't Rebecca Maxwell!" The blue-haired woman smiled. "How are you, dear?"

Her pink-haired sister spoke up. "Or are you Rebecca Tedford yet?"

"Um…" She turned to the coffee machine and poured herself a cup of coffee. With caffeine. When she turned around, they were both smiling at her.

She knew the Reed sisters well enough to know that she had about thirty seconds before she started getting the third degree about her relationship with Coy. "Actually, it's Dr. Maxwell now."

Stacy raised one eyebrow across the counter.

Becky shrugged. She didn't want to pull the doctor card, but it was the best way to distract them from the direction they were going.

A few dozen questions later, the two women shuffled out of the market.

Becky poured another cup of coffee and carried both cups to the counter. "Why am I always exhausted after being around those two?"

Stacy laughed. "We all are. I only hope I can have that much energy when I'm almost eighty."

"They're eighty?" Becky gasped. "I didn't think they were in their seventies yet."

"They are seventy-seven this year." Stacy rang up the coffee and nodded at the cups. "Two cups?"

Becky nodded. "One's for Coy."

"Is this still about whatever happened before he left for Eagar, or something else?"

"Something else. He's coming up with all these ways to make money for the campground and I suggested that he get a loan from my dad."

Stacy let out a soft whistle. "Oh no."

"I know," she said. "My family's money is a sore spot with him."

"It's not about the money." Stacy sat on the stool behind the counter. "It's about respect. He wants your dad's respect and he can't have that if he's asking him for money."

Becky counted out money for the coffee. "It's a loan, not a handout."

"If you ask me, I think that's one of the reasons Coy never wanted to get married."

Her brow furrowed. "His parents' divorce really rocked him. I always thought that's what made him leery."

"Have you ever actually asked him?" Stacy handed her the change.

She frowned. "Of course. He always had the same answer. It wasn't the 'right time' to get married."

Stacy raised her eyebrows. "When was the right time supposed to be?"

"I don't know. He'd never give me an answer. He said we would just know."

Stacy shifted on the stool and rubbed her tummy. "One thing I do know is that he's loved you for most of his life, so it wasn't because he had any doubts. He was waiting for something."

"Maybe. But what?" Becky took a sip of her coffee.

"Status? Money?" Stacy's voice went up an octave. "It could be he felt like he couldn't marry you until he had a certain amount of money."

Becky had toyed with the same thought before. "I've never pressured him about money. He knows…at least he should know…that money has never been that important to me."

"Maybe not to you," Stacy said. "But he could

think it's important to your family and he didn't want to disappoint them, either."

"My mom," Becky gasped. "He made a comment the other day about my mom expecting him to give me a certain type of lifestyle."

"That could be it." Stacy stood and stretched, her hands on her lower back. "You should've just gotten pregnant. That would've given him an excuse to marry you without the pressure of money."

The air in her lungs froze. "Why would that be?"

Stacy laughed. "Your parents are old-school. They would be more concerned about how it would look for you to have a baby out of wedlock than how much money Coy made."

Becky worried her bottom lip. Had a giant burden been lifted from him when she became pregnant? One hand came to rest lightly on her stomach. She thought he only married her because he had to.

"Are you okay?" Stacy's voice penetrated Becky's thoughts. "You know I was just kidding, right? I don't think you should try to get pregnant on purpose."

"Of course!" She faked a laugh. She picked the coffee cups back up from the counter. "I better get this to him before it gets cold."

The haze surrounding her thoughts followed her to the truck. Before she confronted him with her newfound information, she needed to talk to her mother.

The sun was barely up, but Coy was already exhausted. Partly because he hadn't slept much the night before and partly because he'd been working since 4 a.m. The coffeepot in the office was finished brewing, so he poured himself a cup.

He took a sip as he moved some Post-it notes around on the kanban board. After one more sip, he made a face and dumped the rest into the sink. Stacy's decaf wasn't too bad, but this morning it had no appeal.

He collapsed into his office chair and leaned back to survey the workflow board. A sense of pride rippled through him when he saw how many tasks he'd been able to move from the "To do" row to the "Done" row.

"Knock, knock."

He turned to see Becky standing in the door frame and his heart gave a little leap. "Good morning."

She held up a Styrofoam cup. "I brought a peace offering."

He stood up and met her halfway across the room. "If that is the real deal, I might just kiss you."

She laughed. "I saw you working this morning, so I thought you could use it."

"When?" He hadn't heard her come to the barn.

"About five o'clock." She walked to the wall and stared at the board. "You've got a lot done."

"I didn't hear you drive up this morning." He took another drink of the black gold.

"I wasn't driving. I was jogging. The trail loops all the way around the campground, including the barn."

"When did you take up jogging?" When he was competing, he jogged every day as part of his fitness routine. More than once, he'd asked her to join him, but she always refused.

"After you left." Her eyes avoided his gaze. "I fell into a pretty deep depression and I needed to get active again. I didn't have a horse to ride, so I started jogging."

His heart ached for her. "I'm sorry. I should have been there. I shouldn't have left."

She shook her head. "It doesn't matter now. We both handled things badly and we can't change the past."

"No, but we can move forward." His pulse pounded in his ears. "The question is, can we move forward together?"

"I'm thinking about it," she said. "I'm not making any promises. There's something I have to do first."

Coy's chest swelled. "After a year and a half of you not answering my phone calls, I'll take 'thinking about it' any day."

She took another drink from her coffee. "So what were you building back there? Are you dividing the corral up into smaller sections?"

He shook his head. "It's another way to attract campers to Whispering Pines. I'll show you when I'm done."

"About that," she said. "I'm sorry I tried to push you into borrowing money from my dad. I know how you feel about it and I shouldn't have done it."

"Thanks," he said. "I appreciate that."

"It's none of my business," she said. "You should really think about getting investors, though. It doesn't have to be my dad."

Coy frowned. None of her business? Didn't she know that everything he was doing, he did for her? For their future? "I don't know that I want to be in debt to anyone."

"Even if it will pay off in the long run?"

"It depends," he said. "What will I lose in order to gain a quick buck?"

She leaned against the corner of the desk and took another sip of her coffee. After a moment, she tossed the cup in the trash can and gave him a long stare. "Can I ask you something?"

He didn't see that he had a choice, so he just nodded.

"If I hadn't gotten pregnant, would you have ever married me?"

There was a hint of pain in her brown eyes that punched him in the gut. Did she really not know how much he loved her? "Of course. I never wanted anyone but you."

Her phone buzzed and she jumped. "I almost

forgot. I have to be at the Cordova Ranch by nine this morning."

"On a Sunday?"

"Yes," she said. "It's the only day that Brady has available. He's meeting me there."

"Who's Brady?" He recognized the name, but couldn't remember exactly who he was.

"The veterinarian out of Flagstaff who worked at Dr. Evans's office the summer we stayed here."

Now he remembered. He'd cracked his pelvis when a bull stepped on him, so he and Becky came home for a few weeks while he recovered. Becky worked for Dr. Evans and Brady was a brand-new vet who helped out over the summer. He'd also attempted to help himself to Becky.

He tried to keep the jealousy out of his voice. "Why are you meeting him?"

"The Cordovas are raising coos cows and Brady's family happens to breed them. Brady is bringing down some semen and we're going to artificially inseminate the Cordovas' cows."

"Sounds like fun," he said dryly.

"It'll be my first AI as a vet." She grinned. "Hey, what about Brady? He might be interested in investing in Whispering Pines."

"No." He shook his head. "Please don't mention anything to him."

"Okay." She gave him an odd look. "Talk to you later."

He waited until he heard her drive away and

then walked out of the barn to watch her truck disappear. His stomach was in knots. She claimed money wasn't important to her, but she was spending a lot of energy on helping him succeed. Maybe she would rather have someone like Brady.

# *CHAPTER SEVENTEEN*

Becky answered her phone as she got into her truck. "Hey, Dad. What's up?"

"Are you busy?"

"Not really. I just got finished administering antibiotics to some sheep with pneumonia." She opened the console of her truck and opened the package of baby wipes. She pulled a couple of sheets off and began scrubbing her hands with it. One downside to taking care of animals in the field was a lack of running water.

"I talked to George the other day and he said you did a great job delivering his mare's foal," Levi said.

She chuckled. "That's good to hear."

"What are your plans this week? Will you be coming home at all?"

Her father rarely called just to chat, but she would let him beat around the bush until he got ready to tell her why he really called. "Sorry, Dad, I doubt it. I met with Brady O'Rourke yesterday and he'll be back later this week to check on the cows we artificially inseminated, and I'm helping Coy train some horses, so I have to be in Coronado every afternoon."

"That's what I called to talk to you about."

She started her vehicle and waited for the Bluetooth to connect. "How did you know I was helping Coy with horses?"

"He called me this morning."

Her father's announcement took her by surprise and her heart started to beat faster. He wouldn't call her parents and tell them about the marriage, would he? "What did he want?"

"He wanted to talk to me about an investment opportunity," Levi said. "He said you were helping him with some horses and that you suggested he talk to me."

Her pulse quickened. He took her advice and called her father! "He wants to turn Whispering Pines Campground into a guest ranch." Becky didn't put her vehicle into Drive, so she could concentrate on the conversation. "I hope you heard him out. He's got some really good ideas."

"I agree. That's why I invited him to the ranch this weekend," Levi said. "He's bringing me a business plan and everything."

She couldn't believe Coy actually called her dad. That could only mean he was much more serious than she realized. Unless he was using it as an excuse to try to win her back.

"You know," Levi said, "if you and Coy were to

get married and take over the ranch, he wouldn't need a business plan."

"Careful, Dad," she warned. "It sounds suspiciously like you're trying to buy me a husband."

"I know you have no desire to run the ranch," he said. "Do you blame me for hoping that you'll at least marry someone who does?"

Worry tickled her insides. "Do not make his business proposal about the ranch. He's worked really hard on this."

"Sounds like you're pretty invested in it, too," he said. "Will you be coming with Coy on Saturday?"

"I don't know. I didn't know he was going. He might not want me there." She was almost certain he wouldn't want her there. He would want to do this all on his own.

"So, you two have been spending time together?"

"A little," she said. "I have to go, but I'll talk to you in a couple of days."

When she arrived at the campground, she saw that Caden's SUV was parked in front of the barn. He must be helping with the horses today, too. With the Fourth of July trail ride less than two weeks away, Coy had recruited every cowboy he knew to come help.

It was a great move on his part. The more often the horses were ridden, the calmer they would be. Additionally, being ridden by different people each time would help them to adapt to the different riding styles of all the people who would ride them while guests at the ranch.

She went into the tack room. When Coy had gone to Eagar for a few days, she had transferred the riding schedule from his notebook to the whiteboard on the wall at the entrance to the tack room. It was just easier, since she wasn't the only one working with the horses.

There was no sign of Coy, Caden or the little girls, so she went to the corral to find the horse she needed. Maybe they had gone on a ride on one of the trails. She quickly saddled the mare and led her to the pasture.

Other than one quick sidestep, the mare didn't seem to mind when Becky mounted. "Good girl," Becky cooed, patting her neck.

She urged the horse to the end of the pasture. More than once, the mare tried to turn and go back toward the barn. Becky patiently turned the horse back in the direction she needed to go. When they got to the end of the pasture, she turned the horse to head back.

The horse's ears pricked forward, sensing that they were headed back to the barn. The mare started to pick up the pace, but Becky pulled back the reins and slowed her down.

The horse wanted to run back to where the food was, but she kept a tight hold on the reins. By the time she got to the barn, her arms ached from fighting the horse. She turned the mare to circle the pasture again.

After a couple more laps, the horse seemed to be content to let Becky be the guide. She guided her to the gate and opened it. The trail that led from the end of the pasture to the river bottom that cut through the valley was the closest and probably the one that Coy and Caden had taken, so she turned her horse toward the trail.

The path was wide and smooth. It was obvious the weeds and brush had recently been cut. Soon, Coy wouldn't have to worry about controlling the overgrowth. The more times the trail was used, the more packed it would become and nothing would grow on it.

As she made her way toward the river, she noticed that small numbered stakes had been driven into the sides of the trail marking the path for both hikers and riders. Her chest swelled. Coy had been busy. How had he had time to do all this? He spent the early mornings at the barn, feeding, mucking stalls and riding horses. After that, he cleaned vacant cabins, took care of the grounds around the common area and all the cabins, and repaired anything that needed doing.

Once the guest ranch took off, he was going to have to hire staff. She could help with the horses, but he really needed to find someone else to help with things like cleaning and maintaining the cabins.

She pulled the horse to a stop. When had she

started making plans to help? She gazed over the valley. In the distance, she could see the waters of the Black River cutting through the mountain. The aspen trees in the river bottom swayed with the slight breeze. She tilted her head back and felt the warmth of the sun on her face.

The horse shifted slightly under her and Becky took another look at the area. This was where she needed to be. She felt it in her soul. The moment she acknowledged it, she knew it was the right decision. If only she could be this sure about Coy. At least one of her decisions had been made.

She guided her horse to the bottom of the trail and made a quick loop around the flats, looking for tracks or any sign that Coy had passed in that direction. When she couldn't find any sign of other horses having been there recently, she headed back up the trail.

As she approached the barn, she heard some loud metal clunks, as well as yelling. No, *cheering*.

She dismounted and tethered the mare before she followed the sound to the side of the barn. The post she'd seen Coy pounding into the ground had been joined by three more posts. Each post had chains coming from it that supported a large barrel hanging in the middle of it all.

Old mattresses had been thrown in a large area under the barrel and a long rope was attached to the barrel, with another rope wrapped around its middle.

Her heart lodged in her throat when she saw Coy sitting astride the barrel. His hand was tucked under the rope and Caden stood a distance away, with the longer rope in his hand.

Caden was pulling the rope, causing the barrel to wobble and jump around, emulating the movements of a bull. Khatia and Marina stood next to their father, jumping up and down and cheering.

After a few seconds of jerking the rope, Coy motioned for him to stop. "That's better, but it needs more. I think we're going to need another rope, maybe two, being pulled at the same time."

Caden nodded. "With just me, it's rhythmic. That's not a good way to train for bull riding."

Becky gasped and both Coy and Caden glanced at her. She couldn't believe that he was training again.

Instead of looking guilty, Coy grinned. "What do you think?"

Her mouth fell open. "What am I supposed to think? I thought you were committed to the guest ranch. Instead, you're training again?"

"What? No." Behind him, Caden herded the girls together and headed back to the barn.

She crossed her arms. "That's what it looks like."

"It's not for me," he said. "It's for guests who want to get the rodeo experience, without the fear of getting trampled on."

"Rodeo experience?" Her gaze strayed back to the barrel. "I thought you were doing trail rides and family activities. When did you decide to add a rodeo experience?"

"Floyd gave me the idea in Eagar." He stepped closer to her. "I'm not going back to the rodeo. Ever."

His blue eyes bore into hers and she sighed. "If that's what you really wanted to do, I could understand, but whatever you decide to do, I want to hear it from you, not someone else."

She turned and went around the corner to get the horse. When she entered the barn, Coy was waiting for her.

"What's going on?" His blue eyes were somber.

"Nothing." She removed the saddle from the mare and hefted it up to its spot.

"Did you really think I was going to abandon all my plans to go back to the rodeo?"

She shook her head. "My dad told me you talked to him. When I saw you on that barrel, I thought your pride may have gotten in the way and you were looking for the quick buck again."

"I guess I have no pride when it comes to you." He stood in front of her, blocking her way out of the tack room.

His smell wrapped around her. It was a mixture of hay, horses and Irish Spring. Her heart pounded in her chest. Her gaze darted to his mouth and she licked her lips and swallowed. If he pressed her for an answer now, she wouldn't have the strength to push him away.

"I better get the next horse ready." She moved away from him, breaking the spell.

Coy checked the list and went to get the next horse. He finished saddling his horse around the same time that she did. Together they led their animals to the pasture for a warm-up.

"Do you think they'll be ready for the trail ride?" Becky put one foot in the stirrup and stepped up, throwing one leg over the saddle.

"I think most of them will be," he said. "There's one that's still a little skittish. He's fine after a couple minutes, but he's not ready for an inexperienced rider, for sure."

After circling the pasture a few times, he opened the gate. "Let's ride through the campground. I want them to get used to seeing people."

Becky nodded. "The campground is full, so there will be a lot of people to see."

They started on the road that led from the campground to the cabins. The horse he was riding pulled at the bit, anxious to go faster, but Coy kept her to a slow pace.

Becky's horse pulled up next to his. "What are your plans after the Fourth?"

"For the campground?" He turned to follow the road that led past most of the cabins. "I'm hoping the trail ride will be such a success that we'll have to do them weekly."

She nodded. "Where does your fake bull fit into it?"

He laughed. "I'm not foolish enough to think that the campground will be packed with campers every week, so I'm planning different things for the offseason."

"I see," she said. "Like what?"

"Family reunions. Youth groups." He grinned. "Apparently, some large companies pay big money for team-building retreats. What could be more team-building than learning to ride a horse?"

Becky's phone buzzed. She looked at a lengthy message on her phone screen. "I'm sorry, Coy. There's an emergency and I need to go."

She turned her horse around and headed back up the road toward the barn at a gallop.

"Looks like it's just me and you." He patted the palomino mare's neck.

"Mr. Tedford!" A woman waved frantically at him from the porch of her cabin.

"Yes, Mrs. Jackson?" He stopped the horse in front of her cabin.

"I accidentally knocked my wedding ring off the counter and it went down the drain in the bathroom sink." Her eyes brimmed with tears. "Can you help me?"

He nodded. "Of course. I'll go get my toolbox right after I take the horse back to the barn. I'll be back in about a half hour."

A panicked look crossed her face. "That long?"

"Is that a problem?"

"My husband will be back by then." She bit her bottom lip. "He's going to be so mad at me. He's always telling me not to leave it on the counter."

He nodded. "I'll be right back."

This would be a good test for the horse. How would she react to Coy carrying a large, bulky toolbox with him? As he trotted past the common area, several families were gathered. The adults were playing cornhole while the kids tossed a Frisbee in the grass.

"A horse!" One of the boys dropped his Frisbee and ran toward them.

Coy stopped the horse before holding up his hand to the two boys running toward him. "Wait!"

His tone must have scared both the kids and the horse because the kids froze and the horse tossed her head. He dismounted the horse and rubbed her neck. "You can come over here now, but walk, please."

The boys did as they were told.

"Never run up to a horse, or any animal that you don't know," Coy told them. "You never know how they might react."

Both boys nodded their head. "Can we pet her?"

"Of course," Coy said. He reached into his pocket and pulled out several sugar cubes. "Feed her this and she'll love you."

He showed them how to hold their hand flat so

that the horse could pluck the sugar cubes from their palm.

"Her nose is so soft." The younger boy giggled.

The older boy rubbed his hand up the bridge of the horse's nose. "Is she yours?"

Coy noticed the parents walking over to see what was happening. "Well, she belongs to Whispering Pines."

"I didn't know you had horses here," the man said.

"We're expanding our focus," Coy told him. "In addition to the regular activities here in the common area, we'll have trail rides and even riding lessons for those who are interested."

"I want to do it!" The oldest boy turned to his dad. "Please?"

"When is the next trail ride?" the boy's father asked.

"The first trail ride isn't until the Fourth of July," Coy said. "We're in the process of getting the horses ready."

"Oh man!" Both of the boys groaned.

"If you'll excuse me, I need to fix a sink for one of the other tenants." Coy waited until the boys walked away a safe distance before mounting the horse again. He urged the horse into a trot.

At the shed, he held the large toolbox in one hand and took a deep breath. He put one foot in the stirrup and held the toolbox as close to his body as he could before swinging his leg over. The horse tossed her head and shuffled sideways, trying to look back at the box. Coy patted her neck and spoke in soft, low tones. Finally, he turned the horse back toward the cabins.

This time, the boys stayed in the grass and waved as he rode by. He dismounted just as carefully as he mounted and went into the cabin.

It only took a moment to remove the P trap under the sink and retrieve the woman's ring for her.

"Here you are." He placed the ring on the counter. "It's a little dirty."

"Thank you so much." She smiled with relief. "How can I thank you?"

"No need," he said. "It's part of the job."

Coy whistled as he walked out of Cabin Three, his toolbox in his hand. He mounted the horse and went back to the shed.

The smell of grilling burgers hung in the air and his stomach rumbled. The father waved from the barbecue, while the children played. On the other side of the grassy area, a group of young adults were gathered around a picnic table. One man sat on top of the table, playing a guitar.

Coy waved at the group and was making his way slowly toward the barn when his phone rang. He thought it might be Becky, but it was a number he didn't recognize.

"Hello?"

"Hello, Coy Tedford, please."

Coy definitely didn't recognize the voice. "That's me."

The man's voice continued. "I'm Tucker Kent. I work for Ms. Maxwell's attorney."

Coy's heart skipped a beat. "What do you want?"

"I'm sorry to bother you, but I'm on a bit of a timeline here. You haven't returned the documents yet, so I just wanted to know if you had any questions regarding the settlement."

He swallowed hard. "No."

"When can I expect them?"

His mind swirled with questions. Did Becky put him up to calling? Was it a passive-aggressive way of trying to get him to sign the papers? "You can't. I'm not signing them."

"The settlement is very generous, Mr. Tedford." The attorney's words were clipped.

Coy stopped the horse and dismounted. He didn't want the horse to pick up on his anger while he was riding her. "I don't care about the settlement."

"Just so you know, most dissolutions for a marriage as short as yours don't even offer a settlement, but Miss Maxwell said you needed the money and she wanted to offer the maximum allowed. I doubt a judge would award you any more than that if you go to court."

He clenched his fists. "I just said, I don't care about the settlement."

"It's also my duty to inform you that if you choose not to sign the documents, Miss Maxwell can have the papers served by a law enforcement agency, in which case a signature will not be necessary."

"Goodbye, Mr. Kent." Coy tried to keep the anger out of his voice. "Don't call me again."

He disconnected the phone and ran his fingers through his hair. His emotions were in turmoil as he walked toward the barn. He wasn't sure what he was more angry about, the fact that she'd had her lawyer call him to try to intimidate him, or the fact that Becky told the man that he needed money.

Maybe the problem wasn't that her parents wanted her to have a certain lifestyle, maybe it was her all along.

# *CHAPTER EIGHTEEN*

BECKY PRESSED THE gas pedal down as far as she dared on the bumpy dirt road. Her heart lodged in her throat. Her phone rang and she glanced at the screen on her dashboard. It was Coy. She pushed the decline button. She needed to keep the line free if Abbie called her back.

It had been fifteen minutes since Becky called her to let her know she was headed that way. That's when she realized how bad the situation was.

Noah was out of town for the day, so when Abbie started spotting a little blood, she panicked and texted Becky to come to the ranch. When Becky called just a few minutes later, the cramping had started and it took everything she had to keep Abbie calm. Then she lost cell phone service and Abbie hadn't called back.

She let out a sigh of relief when the Double S Ranch house came into sight. She parked her truck, jumped out and ran to the house.

"Abbie." She burst through the front door.

"Back here."

She followed the sound of the voice and found Abbie on the floor of the bathroom. "What are you doing down there? Let me help you up."

"No!" Abbie shook her head. "I don't want to move. What if it makes it worse?"

"Okay, I'm going to get you a pillow for your head and a blanket."

She jumped up and ran into the living room to grab a throw pillow from the sofa. Next, she pulled a quilt from the quilt rack and took the items back to the bathroom.

"Here." She tucked the pillow under her friend's head and stroked Abbie's hair. "How are you feeling? Any more cramps?"

"A...a...few," Abbie said between sobs. "Becky, I'm so scared."

She put her fingers on Abbie's wrist to check for her pulse. "Your pulse is a little fast, so I need you to take some deep breaths."

It took a few minutes, but she managed to get Abbie to calm down. "Have you called your doctor?"

"Yes. She told me to go to the hospital."

Becky nodded. "Okay. Then let's get you there."

"I'm afraid to move. What if standing up and moving causes me to lose the baby?"

Becky could see that Abbie was still in panic mode and she knew that no amount of reasoning would change her mind. "Did you call an ambulance?"

"No. You're the only one I could think of to call." Her eyes widened. "Do you think it's too late?"

Becky had one hand on Abbie and could feel the woman's anxiety increasing. "No. Now listen to me. Right now, your baby is fine, but we need to get you to the hospital to check things out. I'm going to go pull my truck as close to the front porch as I can, then I'll carry you to the truck if I have to."

She stood up. "Don't move."

When Becky opened the door to the truck, her phone was ringing again. In her hurry to get inside, she'd left it on the seat. She ignored the call and started the engine. She maneuvered the truck so that the passenger side was close to the front porch. She left the truck running and walked around to open the passenger door. Then she pushed the seat controls to lay the seat down as far as it would go, before sprinting back into the house.

A large yellow tomcat was sitting next to Abbie, his paws on her chest. She paused. Abbie had one hand on the cat's head, stroking it softly, and the cat was kneading his paws on her chest. The cat was doing what she'd failed to do: calm Abbie down.

"Who's your friend?" She knelt down next to her.

"This is Tom," Abbie said. "He used to be Noah's cat. Now he's mine."

Becky took the quilt and laid it out next to Abbie. "I want you to roll over onto the quilt, okay?"

The woman looked puzzled, but she managed to roll onto the quilt.

"I'm going to pull you on the blanket into the living room," she explained. "That way, we don't have as far to go to get to the truck."

Abbie nodded, clutching the cat to her chest.

Becky stood up and grabbed the end of the quilt. Fortunately, the ranch house was old and had all wooden floors. The quilt slid easily with Becky pulling it and she got Abbie to the living room in no time.

"Ready?" Becky slid her arms under Abbie and used all her strength to lift her friend off the floor.

Abbie wasn't a very large woman, and years of moving hay bales and tossing steers around had built up Becky's muscles. She carried Abbie through the front door, down the steps, and placed her into the truck. She shut the house door and got back into the truck.

As soon as they were on the road, her phone rang again. And again she ignored the call. As soon as the line was free, she called Springerville Hospital.

It took a few minutes, but she was eventually transferred to the emergency room. "Hello. I'm bringing in a patient for Dr..." She glanced at Abbie.

"Dr. Ortega."

She kept her eyes on the road. "I'm bringing in

a patient for Dr. Ortega. The patient is about ten weeks pregnant and experiencing some slight spotting and cramping."

After giving the hospital all the information they asked for, she glanced at Abbie. She wanted so badly to promise her that everything was going to be okay, but she couldn't. She'd been ten weeks along when she lost her baby. All the emotions that Abbie was expressing mirrored what she had felt at the time.

"Have you called Noah?"

"No," she said. "I don't want to call him until I know that everything's okay."

"Don't you think he's going to want to know?"

Abbie nodded. "There's nothing he can do about it from Phoenix, so there's no sense getting him worked up."

The hospital staff was waiting when they pulled into the emergency drop-off area. They removed her from the truck, loaded her on a stretcher and disappeared.

Becky parked her truck and started to get out when she spotted her phone. She picked it up and glanced at the screen. Eight missed calls.

While she sat in the waiting room, she stared at the screen. What was so important that Coy had called eight times in a row? She sent him a text.

Can't talk right now. Is everything okay?

She waited. No response. It must not have been too important, then. She put her phone on silent and picked up a magazine to leaf through.

An hour and a half later, a nurse called her name. She hurried across the waiting room.

"You can see her for just a few minutes. We'll be transferring her to a room shortly."

Becky followed the nurse back through the maze of beds in the triage area, separated by thin curtains. She was afraid of what she would find out when she reached her friend.

Abbie saw her and smiled and all of Becky's anxiety lifted. "You're going to be okay."

"I'm fine and the baby is fine." Abbie squeezed her hand. "They're going to keep me overnight as a precaution, but the doctor said it is a subco— something hemorrhage."

"A subchorionic hemorrhage," Becky supplied. "That's good. Are you going to call Noah? I don't want to be responsible for how he reacts when he finds out what happened."

"I already did." A troubled look crossed her face. "He's leaving and coming home now, even though I told him I was fine. Even the doctor told him I was fine."

"You can't blame him for being worried."

The nurses came in and told her they were moving her to a room.

"There's no need for you to stay," Abbie said.

"Noah will be here before they release me tomorrow."

"Are you sure?" She took Abbie's hand in hers. "I don't mind staying with you. Really."

Abbie squeezed her hand. "It's okay. At least one of us should get a good night's sleep. Thank you for everything."

"You're welcome."

It was well after dark when she made her way back to her truck. Since it was so late, she decided to drive to the ranch rather than go up the mountain. She called her parents to let her know she was on her way and then tried to call Coy. There was no answer.

The lights were still on in the ranch house when she got there. She slipped her boots off in the mudroom and entered the kitchen.

Both her parents were sitting at the kitchen table. "Hi, honey." Autumn stood up. "Are you hungry?"

"A little," she said. "I can heat up some leftovers."

"Nonsense," Autumn said. "You sit and relax."

"Thanks, Mom." She sat down at the table. "Hey, Dad."

Levi looked up from the newspaper he was reading. "You had to work awfully late. Must have been an emergency."

"It was," she said.

"What was it?"

Both her parents stared at her with concerned

eyes. She let out a heavy sigh. "It wasn't actually an animal emergency," she said. "A friend of mine needed to go to the hospital, so I took her."

"Oh goodness," Autumn said. "I hope everything is okay."

"It is." Becky nodded. "They're just keeping her overnight out of precaution. She's fine now."

"What was wrong with her?" Levi asked, holding her eye.

She was hesitant to answer, but since they didn't know Abbie or Noah, she felt it was okay to give general details. "She's ten weeks pregnant and she thought she was losing her baby. Her husband is out of town and she didn't know what to do, so she called me."

Autumn set a plate of food down in front of her. "Is the baby okay?"

"Yes. She and the baby are fine." Becky picked up her fork.

"I'm glad," Autumn said. "It's nice to have someone who understands what you're going through, so I'm sure she was grateful you were there."

Becky stared at her mom, not quite sure if she'd heard her right. How would her mother know that she could understand what Abbie was experiencing? Maybe she was referring to the fact that Becky had medical training. It was training for animals, not people, but she didn't think her mom would make the distinction.

"Ten weeks..." Autumn pinched her lips together. "That's about how far along you were when you lost your baby, isn't it?"

Becky choked on the food in her mouth. She started to cough. "What did you say?" Her heart sped like it was going to jump out of her chest. How did she know that?

She stared up at her mom. "You knew?" she whispered. "How?"

Her father answered. "You're still under our health insurance. You may pay your own bills, but we still receive copies of all the EOBs."

Her chest tightened. While she'd made sure that her parents' information wasn't on any of the paperwork at the hospital, not once had she thought about them receiving an explanation of benefits from the insurance company.

"I never meant to disappoint you," she whispered.

Autumn sat next to her and took both of Becky's hands in hers. "You didn't. I'm sorry you felt like you had to go through it alone," Autumn said. "Why didn't you call us?"

"I'm sorry, Mom." Her voice was thick with emotion. "I didn't want to talk about it to anyone."

Levi snorted behind his newspaper. "You should have been able to talk about it with your boyfriend. If that boy had any sense of decency he would be standing with you right now as your husband."

Becky buried her face in her hands and took deep cleansing breaths. She tried so hard to hide the truth from everyone and they already knew. "He is."

"He is what?" Her father frowned.

"My husband." She leaned back in her chair. "He insisted on getting married as soon as we found out."

Her mother frowned. "I don't understand. He's been in Coronado for the last few months. Why wasn't he with you?"

"I told him to leave," she said. "The only reason he married me was because I got pregnant."

"Why do you think that?" Autumn asked. "You've been together most of your lives. Why wouldn't he want to marry you?"

"If he really wanted to marry me he would have asked me a long time ago." She took a deep breath, fighting off the emotions that were beginning to rise in her chest. "Once I lost the baby, there wasn't a reason to stay together."

"So he left you?" Her father's eyes crackled with anger.

"Actually, I was the one who kicked him out." She pushed the plate in front of her away. "I didn't want him to be stuck with me for no reason. He obviously didn't want to get married and I essentially forced him to. The last thing I wanted to do was make him resent me for it later."

Her parents exchanged a look before they both stood up. "It's late," Levi said. "We'd better get to bed."

Becky stared after them as they exited the room, their heads close together. *At least my situation seems to have brought somebody together.*

THE NEXT MORNING Becky still hadn't returned to her cabin. Where had she gone and why hadn't she answered her phone? Coy couldn't believe that after all the discussion about his plans for the campground and the hours they'd spent working together she'd never once mentioned her lawyer.

At least now he knew how she really felt about him. She'd always claimed she wanted to get married but once they did, she must have realized how much she would be giving up. She knew that once they were married he would not want her living off her parents' money. Yes, it was prideful, but that's how he felt about it.

No wonder she'd had his bags packed and out the door when he returned just a few days later.

He had already fed the horses and was walking back to his cabin when he saw her truck coming down the road in the distance. Because he was walking through the trees, he knew he was hidden from her view. He stopped and leaned against a tree to wait for her to get out of her truck.

A shiny black SUV was following right behind her. The SUV parked behind her at the cabin. The driver exited the SUV at the same time that she got out of her truck. Coy's blood began to boil.

Brady walked around to the passenger side of

the SUV and opened the door. He held it open until Becky got into the vehicle. Coy waited until Brady drove away before stepping out of the trees.

Coy walked back to his cabin in a daze. Was that why she hadn't answered his phone calls last night? Had she been with Brady? He never would have believed it if he hadn't seen them together with his own eyes.

If he didn't do something with all his pent-up anger he might explode. When he was riding bulls he never had to worry about that. He pulled out his phone and called Clarence.

"'Lo!" the old man answered.

"Good morning, Clarence. This is Coy," he said. "Do you still have a bull riding event going on this week?"

"Sure do," he said. "You thinking about entering?"

"No, but I'd like to come ride one of your bulls if I could."

Clarence laughed. "Anytime, man. Anytime."

"I'm on my way."

His knuckles turned white as he gripped the steering wheel, and it took every ounce of control he had not to floor the gas pedal. He got to Clarence's ranch in record time. As he walked over to the arena, he scolded himself. This was probably one of the dumber things he had ever done. There were so many things he needed to be doing and some of them would help him get out his frustrations, but right now all he could think about was getting on the back of a bull.

Clarence greeted him when he made his way into the bunkhouse that doubled as the dressing room for visiting cowboys. He borrowed a pair of chaps and picked up some gloves from the basket. By the time he got to the loading chutes, he felt the familiar adrenaline shooting through him.

A couple of teenagers stood at the chutes and grinned at him. "I knew you were going to make a comeback," one of them said.

Coy shook his head. "Boys, what you're about to witness is the act of a foolish and desperate man."

The boys grinned, thinking that he was joking around with them. They whooped and hollered as Coy climbed onto the back of the chute. He stepped over the lip and slid onto the back of the bull. As soon as he had his hand in place, he lifted one arm over his head and nodded.

It had been almost a year since he had ridden a bull. And while his mind knew what he was supposed to be doing, his body seemed to have forgotten. He held on by sheer willpower. Every jump, he felt like his arm was getting ripped from its socket. When the horn sounded, he let go in an attempt to make a graceful exit off the back of the bull. It didn't work.

His legs came out from underneath him as he flew through the air and he landed hard on his back, knocking the wind out of him. He rolled over to all fours so he could stand up, pleased with himself for staying on as long as he did. The boys on the fence began to scream and he turned just in time to see the two-ton bull bearing down on him.

He threw himself to the ground and rolled out of the way, narrowly avoiding the bull's sharp horn. The bull whirled around and came back for a second try. Coy wasn't about to give him a better target. He stood up and ran for the fence as fast as he could.

He and the bull made it to the fence at the same time. The animal slammed into him, crushing him against the fence. The boys on the fence jumped into action. Two of them jumped into the pen, luring the bull away from Coy. Another boy helped Clarence haul Coy up and over the fence.

Once away from the pen, he allowed himself to sit down and assess the damage. His shoulder throbbed, and already his knee had swollen up to twice its regular size. Clarence handed him an ice pack. "You still have it," he said. "That was a heck of a ride."

The boys standing around him echoed his sentiments.

Coy shook his head. "I'm glad I retired. I'm getting too old for this."

Laughter erupted from the boys around him because they were sure he was joking again. He looked to Clarence, who nodded and knew exactly what he meant.

It took him an hour before he felt ready to sit in the truck for the twenty minutes it would take to get home. Thank goodness it was his left knee that was hurting, otherwise he wouldn't be able to drive.

When he got to his cabin, he limped inside and collapsed onto the couch. He knew he needed to get his jeans off and put some ice on his knee. He moved to take off his boots and his shoulder screamed with pain. By the time he got his jeans off, he was sweating.

He glanced up at the loft that was his bedroom. There was no way he would make it up those stairs. He groaned and looked around the small cabin. His laundry basket sat on the floor by the end of the sofa. He scooted closer to it and dug through the clothes for a pair of pajama pants. He sighed with relief when he found some.

He stood up to hobble to the bathroom and his knee gave out on him. Gritting his teeth against the pain, he managed to get to the bathroom and find some pain reliever. He opened the cap and took the maximum dose before making his way back to the sofa.

Would his knee be fine with a few days of rest? Or was something more serious going on? He wished there was a way to tell. He leaned back on the sofa and closed his eyes for a moment. He was going to have to call Caden and ask him to take care of the horses for him today. His phone was on the coffee table next to the pictures Randon had drawn.

Of course! Millie was a nurse. Would he be able to get her to come out and check his knee? He didn't have Millie's number, but he had Randon's. He breathed a sigh of relief when Randon answered the phone.

"Hey, Randon. Is Millie working at the nursing home today?"

"No. What's going on?"

Coy grumbled. "I messed up my knee bull riding this morning and wondered if she could come take a look at it for me, but I don't have her number."

"I thought you retired," Randon said.

"I did," Coy answered. "I was trying to work out some frustration and it backfired."

Randon chuckled. "I'll let her know."

"Thanks." He started to disconnect the call and caught himself. "Randon, tell her not to tell Stacy."

There was no response. He hoped Randon had heard him. He scrolled through the numbers and called Caden.

"Morning!" His friend's cheerful voice answered the phone.

"Hey, it's Coy. I hate to ask you this, but can you take care of the horses for me today? Maybe tomorrow morning, too."

"Sure. You going out of town?"

He huffed. "No. I did something reckless and

hurt myself. Not bad, but I'm not going to be able to run around the barn for a while."

"You okay?"

"I'll be fine," he said. "I know you're busy finishing up the house so you can start moving in this weekend, but can you stop on the way and pick up a couple bags of ice?"

"You got it. I'll be right there."

Fifteen minutes later, he heard a car pull up in front of his cabin. "Come in!" he yelled when the person knocked on the door.

Stacy and Millie barged through his door and he groaned. "Who blabbed? Randon or Caden?"

"Both. What happened?" Stacy had already put ice into a smaller baggie and brought it over for him to put on his knee. "Did you get kicked by a horse?"

"No. I got crushed by a bull."

She glared at him. "Then you deserve it."

Millie poked and prodded both his knee and his shoulder before declaring that he was suffering from nothing worse than stupidity and some bruises. "But if that swelling doesn't go down by the morning you should probably go have it looked at."

"Thanks, Millie."

Stacy sat next to him on the couch. "Why? Why would you do that?"

Coy shook his head. "I don't want to talk about it."

"I have to get back to the market." She stood up. "Get some rest. I'll bring you some lunch as soon as the rush hour is over."

"Don't bother. I have lots of leftovers."

When Stacy and Millie had left, he picked up his notebooks from the coffee table. He couldn't work outside so he might as well get some other work done.

He looked at the list of things he needed to buy for the Independence Day barbecue that he was hosting after the trail ride. He had already purchased enough meat to feed fifty people. Caden and his brothers promised to come over the day before to pit the meat. The sides and desserts were covered, while Luke had offered to supply the entertainment.

A loud knock took his attention from the list. It was probably Stacy coming back to yell at him some more. "Come in."

Becky walked in, her face full of concern. "Stacy said you got hurt. What happened?"

His anger flared again. "It's a little late to be concerned about me now, isn't it? Where were you all night?"

"I stayed at the ranch with my parents," she said.

"Hmm." He nodded. "Then why did you show up at your cabin early this morning with Brady?"

Her face tightened. "I was on my way here when he called to let me know he was in town to check on the cows at the Cordova Ranch, so I asked him to pick me up here."

He crossed his arms over his chest. "And that's all there was to it?"

"What are you implying?"

"You know what I'm implying," he said. "Tell me something. What's the real reason you want a divorce?"

She gasped. "You think I want a divorce so I can be with Brady?"

"Of course not." He shook his head. "I don't think you've been with anybody but me since we split up. But maybe you want a divorce so you can find somebody better. Somebody like Brady."

She crossed her arms and glared at him. "You're being ridiculous."

"According to Mr. Kent, I need money pretty badly. Did you finally figure out that I'm never going to be able to give you the lifestyle you want?"

"Mr. Kent?" Confusion clouded her eyes.

"Tucker Kent," he reminded her. "Your attorney."

Her mouth dropped open. "Tucker isn't an attorney. He's a paralegal who helped me file the divorce papers. What does he have to do with anything?"

"He called yesterday to remind me to sign the papers and let me know that if I was waiting because I wanted to take you to court, it was doubtful that I could get more money. Should I be grateful that you insisted on offering me the maximum settlement?"

"You've got it wrong." Her voice was almost a whisper.

"Yeah," he sighed. "It seems I got a lot of things wrong. Come back tomorrow and I'll have the papers signed."

Her face paled. "That's what you want?"

"It doesn't matter what I want. I can't fight you and your money."

Without another word, she turned and left the cabin, slamming the door behind her.

# *CHAPTER NINETEEN*

BECKY WALKED OUT of Coy's cabin in a daze. What had just happened? And why was Tucker Kent contacting Coy? She got in her truck to drive the short distance to her cabin. Her throat was thick and she found it hard to swallow.

Inside her cabin, the faint scent from her lavender candle still hung in the air. Why was she so upset? Wasn't this what she wanted? So why was her heart breaking?

Her phone buzzed and she glanced at the text message. Her heart skipped a beat when she saw Coy's name.

I need another copy. I threw mine away. Remove the settlement from the agreement or I won't sign. I don't want anything.

She sank onto the sofa. Her hands shook as she started to reply to his text.

Okay.

Her fingers hovered over the screen. What could she say? Would anything she said make a difference?

She found the number for the law office where she hired Tucker Kent to draw up the papers for her and pressed Call. She couldn't unleash on Coy, but Mr. Kent was about to get a piece of her mind.

"Good morning," a pleasant feminine voice answered. "Thank you for calling the law offices of—"

Becky interrupted her. "I need to speak with Tucker Kent. *Now.*" She emphasized the last word.

The woman must have sensed the anger in her tone because there was no response for a moment. "He's not available at the moment. Can I help you?"

"Yes," she replied. "I would like to speak to Mr. Kent's supervisor."

A few moments later, a man's voice came on the phone. "This is David Russell. How can I help you?"

"I hired Mr. Kent to draw up some divorce papers for me a few weeks ago. I would like to know why he took it upon himself to contact my soon-to-be ex-husband, and urge him to sign the forms as quickly as possible. And why he found it necessary to add his personal opinion regarding the nature of the settlement I offered."

The man was silent for a moment. "Can I get your name?"

"Rebecca Maxwell." Her jaw ached from clenching her teeth. It was too late to fix the situation with Coy, but at least she could do her best to keep something like this from happening to someone else.

She heard a *click* as she was put on hold. A few minutes later, Mr. Russell came back on the line. "Miss Maxwell, I'm very sorry for your trouble. It seems Mr. Kent took it upon himself to contact your ex-husband. I fear that it's my fault."

"Your fault?"

"Yes, you see, we offered the paralegals an incentive for closing out their cases before the end of the month. I'm afraid Mr. Kent was a little too eager for his bonus. I apologize for any inconvenience."

"I appreciate that, but it doesn't help much. Thanks to Mr. Kent's phone call, I've lost all hope of a reconciliation with my husband."

She hung up before he could say anything else. His apologies wouldn't change anything. She looked around the cabin. Now that she'd caught up on all the backed-up appointments in the area, there was really no reason for her to stay here. She might as well pack up and move back to the ranch. At least it would make her parents happy.

She got out her suitcase. What about the horses? She'd made a deal with Coy to help train them. Conflict tore at her. She didn't want to walk away when the horses were so close to being ready. With Coy injured, it was unlikely that he would be at the barn for a day or two at least. Maybe she should stay.

She left her suitcase open on the bed. She would go work with the horses this afternoon and then she would make her decision.

Before going to the barn, she texted Abbie to see how things were going.

I'm good. They're letting me go home this afternoon, but putting me on bed rest.

She let out a sigh of relief. Thank goodness. Going through one miscarriage had been awful. She couldn't imagine trying to deal with a second one.

She closed the door to the cabin and got in her vehicle. When she got to the barn, Caden was there. "Hi," she greeted him.

"Hey." He looked up from the horse he was grooming.

Max, Caden's dog, gazed at her from his spot next to Caden. Becky bent down to pat his head.

"I guess you're going to be helping until Coy's back on his feet?"

"As much as I can," Caden said. "We're going to start moving into our new house this weekend and Luke and I officially open for business on July 1."

"Congratulations." She smiled.

"Thanks." He began to saddle the horse. "If we

continue with the schedule I think these horses will be ready for the Fourth of July."

"I hope so. Coy has a lot riding on this."

She licked her lips and shifted from one leg to the other. "Do you know what happened to Coy?"

"I know he was riding a bull and got hurt." Steel-gray eyes pierced hers. "He told Randon that he needed to work out some frustration. Can you think of any reason why he would feel the need to do something like that?"

Her gaze dropped to the ground. "He got a call from my attorney's office."

"Your attorney? Why do you have an attorney?"

"He's actually a paralegal." She couldn't look him in the eye. "He called to find out why Coy hadn't signed the divorce papers yet."

Caden's mouth dropped open. "Divorce?"

In a rush, her words began to tumble out and she spilled the entire story to him.

"Wow," Caden said. "That's a lot to take in."

"I know," she said. "Don't worry. I'm packing my stuff and will be out of everyone's hair today. I wanted to do one last ride first."

"You can't leave yet." Caden shook his head. "Coy is not going to be in any shape to work with the horses this weekend and everyone else is helping Stacy and me move into the new house. You have to stay. You're the only one who can handle the horses."

"I don't think Coy wants me here."

"It doesn't matter what he wants," Caden said. "He needs you here. Especially this weekend. The trail ride is the weekend after that. You can leave then."

"Fine." She sighed. "I'll stay. Unless he tells me to go."

Coy tossed the television remote onto the table. He couldn't stand watching any more TV. He itched to go outside and check on the horses. Two of the cabins also needed to be cleaned and he couldn't ask Caden to do that for him. The man had enough on his plate between finishing up the new house and getting ready to open his business.

Maybe Millie would be interested? No. That wouldn't work. Millie divided her time between working at the nursing home and helping Stacy out at the store during the busy season. And right now, it was busier than ever.

Maybe Luke's wife, Emily? No. That wouldn't work, either. She did the bookkeeping for her grandfather's hardware store and was probably helping to get things ready for Luke and Caden's new business. Besides, she and Luke had a toddler who kept them both pretty busy.

He sighed. Once the trail rides took off, he planned to hire someone to clean the cabins for him so he could concentrate more on the horses, but he wasn't ready for the added expense yet. And every day he had to stay off his feet was another wasted day for the horses. The trail ride was ten days away.

There was a soft knock on the door. "Come in."

The door opened and an older woman popped her head inside. "I brought you some lunch."

"Hi, Mrs. Gibson," he greeted Millie's mother. "That smells delicious."

"They are just swamped at the market, so Millie asked me to come by and check in on you. She also told me to stop at the market and get you a sandwich, but I thought you would appreciate a home-cooked meal."

He shifted so that he was sitting more upright and took the plate of food from Mrs. Gibson.

"What can I do to help?" She scanned the room. "Here, let me fold that laundry for you."

Coy waved her off. "No, that's okay." He wasn't comfortable with Millie's mom folding his underwear.

She smiled. "Will you at least let me wash the dishes in the sink for you?"

"I appreciate it," he said, "but you don't have to."

"Nonsense. I need something to do and you need help."

A light bulb went off in his head. "Mrs. Gibson," he began, "would you be interested in working for me? Or know of someone who might be?"

Her eyebrows rose. "What kind of work?"

"As soon as the trail rides get started, I'm not

going to have as much time as I did before, so I could really use someone to clean the cabins for me when the guests leave."

Her hand covered her mouth and she looked as if she was about to cry. Coy's heart raced. What did he say to upset her?

She moved over to him and threw her arms around his shoulders. "Thank you!"

He'd never expected a job offer to elicit that kind of reaction.

"Ever since Darrel went into the nursing home, I've felt kind of useless. All the kids are grown and gone. Well, except for Millie. But Millie's rarely home anymore." She patted Coy's cheek. "I'm going stir-crazy sitting in that big empty house all by myself."

His heart went out to her. Her husband had been suffering from Alzheimer's for years. After a scary incident where Darrel wandered away from the house and got lost, the Gibson family made the painful decision to put him in a nursing home. Millie immediately got a job at the same home so she could look in on him. Mrs. Gibson visited him as often as she could, but she couldn't spend every day there.

"I can't pay you much to start with," he said.

"Don't you worry about that," she said and then laughed. "I'm so bored I'd do it for free."

Coy shook his head. "I can't let you do that."

"Let's get started." Her voice was brighter than it had been. "Which cabins need cleaned?"

He pointed at his laptop on the kitchen table. "If you can hand me that, I'll make sure I give you the right cabins."

He opened the laptop and navigated to the management website. His eyes searched for Becky's cabin. It was still showing as occupied. Was she still here? Or had she just not checked out yet?

"It looks like Cabins Two and Four are vacant as of this morning. Cabin Two is the priority because it's already rented out for this afternoon."

"I'll do that one first," she said. "Where do I find the cleaning stuff?"

"Every cabin should be stocked," he told her. "The cleaning supplies are under the kitchen cabinet and there is a broom and mop in the closet."

"Got it." She was practically bouncing with energy. "Do I need keys?"

"Oh, yes." Coy pointed at his crumpled jeans lying on the floor. "There is a master key in my front pocket. It should open every cabin."

Mrs. Gibson retrieved the keys. "This one?"

"Yes."

"Enjoy your meal. I'll be back to check on you when I'm done."

With that, the woman disappeared through the doorway. Coy leaned against the sofa. He couldn't believe what had just happened. He needed to be sure to thank Millie for sending her mother over. She had been an answer to a prayer.

His gaze drifted back to the open computer screen and focused on Becky's cabin. What was he going to do about her?

## *CHAPTER TWENTY*

BECKY WAS PUTTING the last horse in the corral when Stacy came storming into the barn.

Stacy embraced her in a tight hug. Well, at least as much of a hug as an almost-eight-months pregnant woman could manage. "Thank you for taking care of my sister."

"You're welcome," Becky said. "How is she today?"

"She's good," Stacy said. "She's worried about Coy's barbecue. She was supposed to cater it, but I told her that between you, me, Emily and Millie, we would take care of things."

Becky kept her face smooth. She hadn't planned on staying that long, but she wasn't going to say anything until she was sure.

"You've got some explaining to do." Stacy put her hands on her hips and gave her a hard look. "You and Coy are married?"

Caught by surprise, she simply nodded and braced herself for her friend's ire.

Stacy wrapped her arms around Becky in another hug. "I'm so sorry. Why didn't you tell me about the baby?"

"I don't know." Becky hugged her back. "I guess I was embarrassed that I allowed myself to get into the situation."

"That's why you got white as a sheet when I joked about getting pregnant." Stacy rubbed the tops of Becky's arms.

Becky shrugged. "I wanted so badly to tell you, but again, I was ashamed and embarrassed. Here I was, the one who wanted to get married in the first place, asking for a divorce."

"Why? Do you still want it?"

"I thought he only married me because of the baby and he would end up resenting me." She tightened her ponytail. "And no, I don't think I do. But it doesn't matter now. He does."

"Do you really believe that?"

Her phone chimed and she looked at the screen.

Will you be staying in the cabin?

"Yes," she told Stacy and showed her the screen. She responded to Coy's message.

I'll be out by five.

"He only asked if you were staying, he didn't ask you to leave." Stacy gave her a hopeful look.

"I'm not leaving completely," she said. "I promised to help get the horses ready for the trail ride and I will. I just won't be staying at the cabin."

Stacy took both of Becky's hands in hers and squeezed them. "You're going to stick around? You promise?"

"I promise." She gave Stacy a quick hug and fled from the barn before she could see the tears that threatened to spill from her eyes.

When she got to the cabin, the open suitcase on her bed mocked her. She packed the rest of her things and hauled the suitcase to her truck. Her heart got heavier with every step. She'd come to Arizona to get Coy to sign divorce papers, so why was she so upset? It was for the best. She needed to focus on her career, anyway.

She told herself that as she drove out of Coronado, down the mountain and into the desert of New Mexico. She was still telling herself that when she pulled into her parents' ranch.

"Becky!" Autumn opened the door for her before she got to the house. "Why didn't you tell us you were coming?"

"It was a last-minute decision." She carried her suitcase into the house and trudged up the stairs to her room.

She set the suitcase on the bed and turned to see her mother standing in the doorway.

"What happened?" Autumn's face was full of concern. She moved across the room to take Becky in her arms. "Don't tell me 'nothing' because it's written all over your face."

"Oh, Mom," Becky sniffed, forcing down the lump in her throat.

They sat on the end of the bed and Becky let the tears go. She told her mother about the impromptu phone call from the paralegal and Coy's jealousy over Brady.

Autumn brushed strands of hair from Becky's face. "You really love him, don't you?"

She nodded. "What do I do?"

"He's angry right now, and men don't think too well when they're angry." Her mother shrugged. "Give him time. Let him know that you're not going anywhere, so even if he signs the papers, he's still going to have to see you every day."

Becky wiped a tear from her eye. "That's not at all what I expected you to say."

"What did you expect?" Autumn cocked her head to the side.

She rubbed at the ache in her chest. "I really thought you would tell me to get out."

"Why?"

"Because you didn't," Becky whispered. "I know you only stayed with Dad because of me."

"Oh, honey." Autumn covered her gasp with one hand. "I stayed because I loved your father, not out of obligation to you."

"Then, why did we live in Coronado most of the time, instead of on the ranch?" Becky asked.

"Why don't I have one memory of the two of you being happy together?"

Autumn's face fell. "I thought we hid all of our fights from you."

"It wasn't the fighting that I remember most. It was the cold shoulders. And how you were a million miles apart, even when you were in the same room."

"Your father and I are two very stubborn people," her mother said. "I was young and naive when we got married. I thought I could force him to do what I wanted by withholding the thing he loved most in the world."

"Me?" She had been five the first time they left the ranch and moved to Coronado.

Autumn looked down at her hands, clasped together in her lap. "I'm not proud of how I acted then. I resented all the time he spent on the ranch. I thought because he had ranch hands, he should be able to spend all day with me. I had no idea how hard he had to work to keep the ranch from going under."

"He didn't try to talk you into coming back?"

"Only every day." Autumn smiled. "He never gave up on us, even when I was acting like a spoiled brat."

"But we continued to stay in Coronado?"

"Coronado Elementary School was much better than the school by the ranch. Your father and I decided to keep you there until you were in middle school, but by then, you had made so many friends we couldn't bear to take you away from them. Every summer I would bring you home, planning to stay, but by the end of the summer, you would get so excited about going back to school and seeing your friends, that we couldn't ask you to switch schools."

"So you don't regret staying?"

"No." Her voice was strong and confident. "I know we had a rocky marriage for several years, but it made us into stronger people. A stronger couple. I love him more now than I did thirty years ago."

Becky was glad to hear that her mother was happy. For years she thought she was the only thing keeping them together.

"Do me a favor," Autumn said. "Don't compare you and Coy to me and your father. Or to Coy's parents. Or anyone else. You have to make the right decision for you."

"Thanks, Mom." Becky's heart felt slightly lighter. "I promised Coy that I would help get his horses ready for a trail ride on the Fourth of July, so I'll be late coming home every night. Maybe if he sees that I'm not giving up on the horses, he'll know I'm not ready to give up on him."

COY STARED AT the computer screen. She'd checked out. Her cabin was showing as vacant. A part of him had hoped that she would be stubborn and refuse to leave.

A knock on the door of his cabin caused his heart to skip a beat. Maybe it was Becky. "Come in," he shouted.

The door opened and his dad poked his head in. "Hey."

"Hey, Dad." He motioned for him to come in. "What's up?"

Frank held up a large pizza box. "I heard you were laid up, so I brought supper."

"Thanks." He closed his laptop and set it on the coffee table.

Frank sat next to Coy on the sofa and placed the pizza next to the laptop. He handed Coy a slice. "Stacy said there were some things you needed to tell me."

Guilt twisted his gut. "You better grab a beer, too. It's a long story."

His dad took two beers from the refrigerator and sat back down.

Coy started at the beginning and told him everything.

When he was finished, Frank shook his head. "You two have been married all this time?"

"I'm really sorry I didn't tell you before." He ran one hand through his hair.

Frank stroked his bushy mustache with one finger. "Do you want your marriage to work?"

"Of course I do," Coy said. "But money is obviously more important to her than I thought."

"Are you sure about that?" Frank frowned. "She's never been obsessed with money."

"That's what I thought, too. But when her lawyer's office called, he was pretty convinced I needed money. And she pushed awfully hard for me to talk to her father about a loan for the campground."

"Do you really think it's the money she's worried about? Or the chance to help you fulfill your dream?"

Coy frowned. Could his father be right? She had put her school on hold to help him chase a championship buckle. She'd put a lot of things on hold to help him succeed. Was she using money as a substitute for her time?

## *CHAPTER TWENTY-ONE*

Becky glanced toward the office as she led the bay gelding into the barn. The light was on. Did that mean Coy was here? She hadn't seen him since she'd moved out of the cabin.

He'd obviously been at the barn in the mornings, but he was always gone by the time she got there after work. Caden said it was because he needed to stay off his feet if he wanted to be able to lead the trail ride. She couldn't help but wonder if it was a convenient excuse to avoid her.

She gave the horse one last sugar cube before putting him in his stall and walking to the office. Her hands were shaking as she pushed the door open.

Coy glanced up at her from the desk. "Hi."

"Hi," she said. "How's the knee?"

"I've had worse." He shrugged. "Caden says you've been here every day, working with the horses."

She nodded. "I told you I would."

He gave her a level stare. "Why?"

"We made a deal." Becky picked up the notebook sitting on the edge of his desk and flipped it open to the last page. She made a couple of notes about the horse she'd just ridden. "The horses are looking good. I think they'll be ready for the trail ride."

Coy's mouth pressed into a thin, hard line. "I told you I would sign the papers as soon as you took the settlement clause out," he said. "You didn't have to help out all week."

"I wanted to." She shifted nervously.

As long as she'd known him, his emotions had always been written all over his face. She was the one who kept things bottled in. Now she couldn't read him at all.

She cleared her throat. "My dad is really looking forward to talking to you tomorrow. Mom told me to tell you she's making pulled pork. She knows it's your favorite."

Babbling. She was babbling. She never did that!

His expression remained stoic. "Give your mother my apologies and let your father know that I need to cancel our meeting."

"Why?"

"I changed my mind."

Her mind began to race. Had he found another investor? Had he found another way to make money? "Why?"

"I can't take money from your dad," he said.

Why was he being so stubborn? He needed

money for the campground, so why wouldn't he take it? "You mean you won't."

"All right." He nodded. "I won't. Succeed or fail, I have to do it on my own."

"Have you been doing this all on your own?" She pointed at the board on the wall, covered in the names of the people who had been helping him out by working with the horses. "Caden. Noah. Luke. Millie. Randon. Emily. It seems like you're willing to accept help from everyone but me."

His eyes narrowed. "Your name is on that wall, too. A lot."

"The point is, people are willing to help because they believe in you. They believe in Whispering Pines. My dad is willing to give you the boost you need. Why can't you accept it?"

Coy stood up. "Because if I did, I'd always know that the only reason he did it is because he doesn't want the man married to his little girl to fail. Not because he believes in me."

"That's not fair," she said. "He's always believed in you. Most of the time, I thought he liked you more than he did me."

"Then maybe it's you who doesn't believe in me." He limped past her and out of the barn.

Becky stared after him for a few minutes. A deep pain echoed in her chest, as the cracked pieces of her heart shattered.

In that moment, she knew she couldn't stay.

There was no way she could work with Dr. Evans and risk seeing Coy. Her heart couldn't take it.

Numbness filled her body and she scrolled through the contacts of her phone as she walked to her truck. She found the number she wanted and hit Call.

A moment later the secretary at the Abilene Animal Clinic answered.

"Hi, this is Rebecca Maxwell. I'd like to talk to Dr. Reynolds, please."

COY CURSED TO himself on the entire drive to the Bear's Den. Why had he said those things? Why didn't he tell her that he'd presented his business plan to the bank and they were pleased with his proposal?

When she walked into the office, he thought his heart might leap right out of his chest. He was excited to tell her his news, but then she started talking about him meeting with her dad and he couldn't help himself.

He parked in front of the café and went inside.

Maggie grinned when he came in. "Hi, Coy. Here's the menu I prepared for you. Don't worry, Abbie already approved it."

He took the clipboard she handed to him and looked it over. Caden and his brothers were cooking the meat for the barbecue, but Abbie had been in charge of all the side dishes and the desserts. Being on bed rest, she obviously couldn't cater the meal. Fortunately, Maggie had volunteered to take over.

The price was much more reasonable than he'd expected. When his gaze stopped at the bottom of the sheet, he knew why. "What's this discount for?"

"That is the discount I'm giving you because you're going to give Jacob riding lessons," Maggie said. "He might want to take some of your rodeo classes, too."

Coy's chest swelled a little. "It would be my honor to give Jacob any type of lessons he wants, with your permission, of course. But you don't need to give me a discount for that. I'd do it for free."

"I know." Maggie's dark eyes softened. "But the discount stands."

He pulled his checkbook out of his back pocket and wrote a check for the amount on the sheet.

Maggie handed him a receipt. "I'll have everything at the campground Saturday morning."

"Thank you," he said and headed for the door.

Just as he was getting into his truck, his phone rang. He glanced at the screen and frowned. It was a Texas number.

"Hello," he answered.

"Mr. Tedford?" The voice was way too familiar.

"I told you not to call me again," he said. "I'm not signing the papers."

"I called to apologize," Mr. Kent said. "I overstepped my bounds."

"Okay. Thanks for calling." He was about to disconnect the call, but another voice on the line stopped him.

"Mr. Tedford, this is David Russell. I'm Mr. Kent's supervisor."

Coy let out a heavy sigh. Kent was bringing out the big dog. "Like I told Mr. Kent, I'm not signing."

"I understand. I just wanted to clear up a few things. Namely, that some of the comments he attributed to Miss Maxwell were incorrect."

"What do you mean?"

"I lied." Mr. Kent's voice was soft. "I was trying to close the case so I could qualify for a bonus and I just said those things so that you'd sign the papers. Your ex-wife never mentioned your money, or lack thereof, to me or anyone else. She said she wanted to offer you a settlement because she wanted to make sure you were able to continue following your passion."

His pulse thundered in his ears. "I see. Well, thank you for clearing that up."

His hands were shaking as he disconnected the call. Becky hadn't told the lawyer he needed money. He started the truck's engine and headed back to the campground.

# *CHAPTER TWENTY-TWO*

"Becky?" He rushed into the barn as fast as his knee would allow. "Becky?"

There was no answer. In his hurry to get inside, he hadn't noticed if her truck was there or not. He hobbled back outside. Not another vehicle in sight.

He picked up his phone and tried to call Becky, but she didn't answer. He called Stacy. "Hey, I just wanted to let you know that I'm driving to the Maxwell Ranch."

"This late?" Stacy asked. "Why?"

"I have to convince that stubborn wife of mine to take me back."

"Good luck with that," she said. "First, you have to convince her that the baby wasn't the only reason you married her."

"Wait. What?" Coy frowned. "That's ridiculous. I always wanted to marry her."

"She doesn't know that. She thinks you were going to end up resenting her."

That made sense. But why didn't she tell him that? For the entire two-hour drive, he rehearsed the things he wanted to say to her. When he finally arrived and saw Becky's truck parked in front of the large ranch house, he let out a sigh of relief. Then he knocked on the front door and waited.

"Coy?" Autumn opened the door. "What's wrong?"

"I need to speak to Becky. It's very important."

"Of course." She opened the door. "I'll get her."

He paced the large entryway until Becky appeared.

"Coy? What are you doing here?"

"We have to talk," he said. Taking her hand, he pulled her through the large French doors that opened up into the den.

Once they were alone, he faced her. "Do you really think I only married you because you were pregnant? Is that why you were so upset after the wedding?"

"Yes." Her chin lifted in defiance. "I wanted to marry someone who *wanted* to marry me. You never did. You just did because you had to."

The tone in her voice set his teeth on edge. "Then you don't know me, either. I wouldn't have married you if I didn't want to."

"Right." Sarcasm laced her reply. "You were so anxious to get me down the aisle that you never mentioned it. And every time I did, you changed the subject faster than those bulls you loved to ride.

"And you know what the worst part was?" Her

voice cracked. "When we stood in front of the justice of the peace, I was so scared you were going to resent me for making you get married, but you acted like it was your idea all along. Like you were the one who'd been trying to convince me to get married for the last ten years."

"I was happy and it *was* my idea all along," Coy said. "I finally had a good reason to go against your dad's wishes."

Her mouth dropped open. "What are you talking about?"

His gaze flew to her hand. "Where is your ring?"

She reached under the collar of her shirt and pulled out the gold chain she wore around her neck. A diamond ring hung on it.

Coy picked up the chain and let it drape across his fingers with the ring on his palm. "I bought this ring with the first money I ever made riding bulls."

He could feel her heart beating beneath his hand. Her pupils dilated at his nearness.

She swallowed. "I don't understand."

"You always said it was important that I ask your father for permission to marry you. So I did." Being so close to her made him want to pull her into his arms and never let her go. He dropped the chain and stepped back. "He offered to pay for my expenses if I broke up with you."

Becky gasped. "Why would he do that?"

"Ask him."

Becky opened the door and stepped into the entryway. "Dad!"

A few seconds later, Levi appeared from the kitchen. "Hi, Coy. How are you?"

She crossed her arms and gave him a hard stare. "Did you offer to sponsor Coy's bull riding in exchange for him breaking up with me?"

"No." Levi shook his head.

Coy's mouth gaped. "Yes, sir. You said—"

"I said I'd sponsor you if you went on the circuit alone. *Alone.* I never said you had to break up."

"How else was I supposed to take it?" Coy's voice was defensive.

Her father laughed. "As I recall, you got offended and took off pretty quick. You never let me explain that I thought you'd ride better if she wasn't there to distract you. Besides, I needed her home," he said. "How else was she going to learn to run the ranch?"

Becky's gaze shifted from her father to Coy and back again. "So you weren't trying to force us into breaking up."

"No." Levi turned to face Coy. "That night, you asked for permission to marry my daughter. I never gave it to you, but not because I didn't want her to marry you. I wanted you to get the rodeo out of your system so you wouldn't have any regrets about putting her first."

Coy's face paled. "And now?"

"I'd still be proud to have you as a son-in-law."

Becky's heart felt as if it were about to burst as she watched the doubt melt from Coy's face.

"Thank you, sir." He shook Levi's hand. "If she'll still have me, I'd like the opportunity to show her that I'll always put her first."

He turned to look at Becky and took her hand. "I'm sorry. I've been prideful. And selfish. And…"

Becky stopped his words with a kiss. His arms wrapped around her and she drank him in.

When the kiss ended, Coy was as breathless as she was. "Does this mean you'll give me another chance?"

"Becky," Autumn called from the next room. "Dr. Reynolds is on the phone. He needs to know what date you want to start work so he can get your contract to you tonight."

"Contract?" Both Levi and Coy spoke in unison.

Coy frowned. "I thought you were going to work for Dr. Evans?"

Becky took a deep breath. "Dr. Reynolds made me an offer that's hard to refuse."

"Is Dr. Reynolds with the clinic in Abilene that's been calling for you every day for the last two weeks?" Levi asked.

"Yes."

Coy let go of her and stepped away. "Is that what you want? To go to Abilene?"

Her stomach quivered. Less than a minute after they'd reconciled, and he was ready to walk away. She lifted her chin. "What if it is?"

Coy's brow furrowed. "It'll be a while before I can move to Texas. I have to find someone to take over Whispering Pines. I have to cancel some camps and—"

Becky stopped him. "You mean, if I want to take the job, you'll go with me? You'd give up the campground?"

His blue eyes warmed. "The campground means nothing without you. Where you go, I go."

A laugh escaped from her throat and she threw her arms around him. "Then take me to Whispering Pines. Take me home."

Coy picked her up and twirled her around. "I do have one request."

"What's that?"

His fingers reached for the chain holding her ring. "I want to get married again. In front of all our family and friends. I want the whole world to know it."

She tilted her head back and laughed again. "Do you think it's too late to turn the Fourth of July barbecue into a wedding dinner?"

"I think that's a great idea."

He kissed her again and Becky swore she could already see fireworks going off.

## CHAPTER TWENTY-THREE

BECKY STOOD IN front of the mirror in Coy's cabin and checked her hair for the tenth time. So far the day had been perfect. Even after six trail rides, the horses had behaved. The campground now held more family and friends than campground guests, but she was sure there would be enough food for all of them.

The sun had just set and the sky was still streaked with pink and orange clouds.

Her mother wrapped her arms around her from behind. "Even after leading trail rides all day, you're still the most beautiful bride I've ever seen."

Becky glanced down. After the last trail ride, she'd only had time for a quick shower before changing from her jeans to a white denim skirt. In honor of Independence Day, her blouse was red, white and blue, and she even wore bright red boots to complete her patriotic wedding ensemble.

Stacy poked her head into the cabin. "We're ready. If you walk down the aisle right now, I have it on good authority that the fireworks will begin with your first kiss."

Levi laughed. "I guess having the county sheriff as your father-in-law might have helped with the timing."

Becky laughed, too.

"Are you ready?" Levi offered her his arm.

Tears filled her eyes. "I've never been more ready."

Khatia and Marina led the way, sprinkling red, white and blue confetti instead of flower petals, which had been impossible to find on such short notice.

She squeezed her father's arm as he led her through the common area of the campground, which was covered with twinkling lights and crowded with people. She had no idea how many people were there. She didn't care. She just wanted to reach the handsome bull rider standing at the end of the path who was watching her with the same level of joy as she felt.

As soon as they stopped in front of the pastor, Coy pulled her into his arms and kissed her.

The crowd laughed and the pastor cleared his throat. "You're supposed to wait for me to say 'You may now kiss the bride,'" he whispered.

"Sorry." Coy didn't look at all sorry, but he stepped back far enough for Levi to retake his place.

Twenty minutes later, the vows were said and the

pastor pronounced them man and wife. Again. Just as Coy's lips covered hers, fireworks filled the sky and she knew she had everything she ever wanted.

* * * * *

*If you loved this book,
check out the previous books
in LeAnne Bristow's
Coronado, Arizona miniseries:*

His Hometown Redemption
Her Hometown Cowboy
Her Hometown Secret
Her Hometown Soldier's Return

*Available now at Harlequin.com!*

# Harlequin Reader Service

# Enjoyed your book?

Try the perfect subscription for Romance readers and get more great books like this delivered right to your door.

See why over 10+ million readers have tried Harlequin Reader Service.

**Start with a Free Welcome Collection with free books and a gift—valued over $20.**

Choose any series in print or ebook.
See website for details and order today:

# TryReaderService.com/subscriptions